Ma'am Jones of the Pecos

BARBARA JONES, *known to family and friends as "Ma'am." Mother of ten children in the turbulent days of Lincoln County, Ma'am epitomized the diverse and demanding roles played by the pioneer woman on the New Mexican frontier. Barbara was mother, homemaker, nurse, storekeeper, and teacher. She could handle a cookfire, a needle, a bandage, a rifle, or a square dance with equal competence.*

Ma'am Jones
of the Pecos

by EVE BALL

THE UNIVERSITY OF ARIZONA PRESS

Tucson, Arizona

About the Author

EVE BALL has delved deep into Southwestern history for more than three decades of close friendship and communication with authentic actors in the pioneer drama of New Mexico. Her good neighbors in the Ruidoso highlands area of New Mexico have been not only Anglo-and Spanish-American old-timers, but also elder Chiricahua and Warm Springs Apaches, at home on the Mescalero Reservation. Descendant of Tennessee-Kentucky plantation owners who migrated west, Mrs. Ball earned a master's degree at the University of Kansas and taught school on the plains for several years before settling in the Ruidoso. She is also the author of the highly acclaimed *In the Days of Victorio: Recollections of a Warm Springs Apache* (UA Press, 1970), and the editor of the colorful Lily Klasner autobiography *My Girlhood Among Outlaws* (UA Press, 1972).

Fourth printing 2003
Third printing 1980
Second printing 1973
First printing 1969

THE UNIVERSITY OF ARIZONA PRESS

I.S.B.N.–0–8165–0404–0 (p)
L.C. No. 68–9336

Foreword

To every American boy who has read books and magazine stories about the old frontier, or watched "Westerns" on the screen, Wild Bill Hickok, Kit Carson, Wyatt Earp, and a few others are familiar names. But there were many other people, unheralded and unsung, whose stories can perhaps give us a truer picture of life — and death — as it really was in those early days.

Life to them was mostly hardship and hard work. Not that their existence was all drab and uneventful — far from it. There was always the danger of attack by Indians who were not to be deprived of their ancestral lands without resistance and retaliation. Too, the new country offered a haven for fugitives from other parts — rustlers, killers, and others sought by the law — and these posed a constant threat to peace and safety.

The parts played by men who enforced the law, and those who broke it, offer a strange phenomenon — one man often played both roles. The section of New Mexico where Heiskell Jones and his family settled offers more than one example. After Henry Brown left Lincoln County, he was presented with a gold-mounted rifle in recognition of his efficiency in law enforcement as city marshal of Caldwell, Kansas — before it developed that he had taken up bank robbery as a sideline.

Although the Selman gang's record of rape, robbery, and cold-blooded murder in Lincoln County furnishes one of the most shocking pages in the history of New Mexico crime, John Selman went on to be elected as a law-enforcement officer at El Paso, Texas.

In those days of factional conflicts, the line of distinction was quite fuzzy between enforcers of the law and the breakers thereof. Commissions as special constables or deputy sheriffs were handed out rather freely to those in political favor, and the man who happened to be wearing a badge, even if no wages went with that badge, entered an encounter as an officer, while his opponent was automatically on the other side of the law. This was an important factor in those times when conflicts were settled by personal encounter more often than in the courts, and when loyalty to friends or relatives drew more than one peace-loving man into acts of violence.

The lives of Heiskell Jones, his wonderful wife, their nine sons and one daughter, will be better understood if one recognizes the standards of their time and place and appreciates the conditions that faced them. The Joneses were surrounded by violence and had their share in some of it. But there were other aspects of their lives that were even more compelling in the story of this remarkable family.

ROBERT N. MULLIN

Contents

Contents (Cont.)

ILLUSTRATIONS

Preface

The wild and perilous days of the old Territory of New Mexico are still close and deeply personal to many residents of the modern state of New Mexico. Even after World War II there were people around who had lived through the turbulent times of old Lincoln County. The Joneses, for instance, had been the first Anglo family to establish a permanent home in the Pecos Valley, and although Heiskell and Barbara were long dead, five of their nine sons still lived when I started work on this volume. They were elderly men who vividly remembered having experienced or witnessed some of the tragic events of the Lincoln County War.

Lincoln County in the nineteenth century made up almost one-fourth of the Territory. Despite the fact that its history has often appeared as a long stretch of violence highlighted by the names of famous outlaws, a large portion of its five-thousand "wanted" men were fugitives from somewhere else. Like most of the frontier West, Lincoln County was settled and in large measure tamed by decent, honest folk who handed down not only land, cattle, and rugged pioneer qualities, but traditions of community and cooperation to their descendents.

After years of living among these people and this heritage, I felt strongly that the true history of Lincoln County should be told. And what could be a better way to tell it than through the personal and very human saga of a single pioneer family? Of course my thoughts turned first to the Joneses.

When I began gathering up the threads of Lincoln County history, two of the Jones "boys" — Sam and Bill — still lived on ranches in Rocky Arroyo. A third, Frank, had a home at McKittrick Spring, a few miles southwest of Carlsbad, and Nib Jones lived at Globe, Arizona. Tom, said to be the first Anglo white child born in Old Lincoln County, was still living, and was at Hemet, California.

Sam Jones received me on the *portal* of his large, comfortable ranch house on Rocky Arroyo. He was short, wiry, and hospitable. He was also plainly curious as to why I was there. I lost no time in telling him. He assured me I was victim of a joker who knew the Jones boys never "talked" and had no intention of doing so. But I was welcome and must stay for dinner. His daughter, Opal Clark, was much like Ma'am Jones, his mother, had been. They always expected people to drop in, and it had been nothing for Ma'am to feed twenty or more unexpected travelers.

But a book about his family? No, Sammy thought not. Why should anyone want to write their history? Did I think they had been outlaws? On the contrary, I said, I had heard his mother spoken of as "the angel of the Pecos." That wasn't too far off, Sammy admitted. In an era when there were no doctors, Ma'am had cared for the ill and wounded, nursed the sick, and helped bury the dead. She fed all who came to her home. And of course, like other pioneer women, she had done all this without the basic conveniences that women of today take for granted.

Sam Jones leaned back in his rocking chair, and his keen blue eyes seemed to be looking into the past.

"Young folks today have it so easy. They don't know nothin' about what it took to make this country what it is today."

"And will they ever," I asked, "unless somebody like you tells them?"

"I reckon not," he conceded. "Take this highway now. It's supposed to be a great engineerin' feat. Shucks! They just followed our old wagon trail up Rocky Arroyo. They wasn't any other place to put a road."

"How long you goin' to be here?" was Sam's next question.

"I'm going back to Carlsbad this evening, and if you want some time to think it over I could drive back in the morning."

"I'm ridin' fence in the morning'," he said. "Ever set a hoss?"

"Several," I admitted.

"Savvy cow talk?"

"You're the judge."

He chuckled. "Think maybe Opal can fix you up with some Levi's," he said. "No sense in driving all day. Waste a lot of time. An' it's downright lonesome on Rocky, now that so many are gone. You're here now; might as well stay."

•　•　•

Gathering the story of the Joneses from rocking chair or saddle was pleasant indeed. Sam took me to see his older brother Bill who lived up the arroyo and was in his nineties. I visited Frank and his wife at McKittrick Spring and drove to Arizona to talk to Nib at Globe. Each brother told his own version of his youth on the Pecos. I took these stories in shorthand and typed them up for correction by the narrators.

But the human memory is limited in its accuracy, and literally years of research followed for verification. I was fortunate in having the aid and advice of Maurice Garland Fulton of Roswell, whose detailed, daily record of the Lincoln County war resulted in a history written over a thirty-year period. Not only were histories and archives searched, but facts were checked with many individuals who had been associated with the Jones family. Such varied researches of course produced a wealth of material from which footnotes and bibliography could be made, but this documentation — now readily available to the historian, does not belong in the book with the story of Ma'am and her boys.

It turned out that for seventy years the Jones boys had refused to "talk," in part because of the loyalty among old ranch families that makes them hold back stories that might reflect upon their neighbors — a loyalty extending to the third and fourth generations. In spite of this restraint, however, so much talk — and some writing — had distorted facts sufficiently that a chance to straighten out the record came to seem desirable to the Jones brothers themselves. For even facts themselves, without interpretation, can become an unjust record without somebody — like Sam or Bill — around to point out the motivations behind the deeds and actions in the frontier drama.

Besides the core contributions of the informants, I wish to acknowledge the help of Robert N. Mullin, who completed the Fulton history on the Lincoln County War and wrote the foreword for this book. From the depth of his knowledge of Southwestern history he offered many valuable suggestions.

Sydney Coe Bonnell, daughter of Frank Coe, read the manuscript and offered constructive criticism. The record benefited also from a hundred or so venerable New Mexicans — Anglo, Spanish, and Apache — who gave invaluable information.

I am grateful to two of the Jones daughters — Mrs. Opal Clark and Mrs. Nita Clark — for their reminiscences. Other helpful sources included Scout Big Mouth and his son Percy, Mescaleros; Paul Blazer, grandson of Dr. Blazer of Blazer's Mill; Fred Griffin, early settler who lived near the Mescalero Apache Reservation; Mrs. Mell Boyd Williams; Mrs. Belle Davenport, daughter of Lib Rainbolt; Frank Wycoff, nephew of Lib Rainbolt; Judge W. C. Crain, of Sweetwater, Texas; Mrs. Davidson and Mrs. Church, daughters of John Bolton; Willie Magoosh, son of Chief Magoosh; Bessie Big Rope, Mescalero Apache; Carisso Gallarito, known as Crook Neck, Mescalero; Solon Sombrero, grandson of Chief Natzili, Mescalero; Ramon Maes, Spanish-American.

Others include Anne Coe Titsworth, daughter of Frank Coe; Bert Bonnell, son-in-law of Frank Coe; Si Hogg, early settler on the Peñasco; Almer Blazer, son of Dr. Blazer; Frank Mayhill, early settler south of the Reservation; William Johnson, grandson of Hugh Beckwith; Fannie Slaughter and her sister, Sallie Slaughter, daughters of Charlie Slaughter; Mrs. Joe Welch, Sr., and her brother, Bill Ward.

Included also are Mrs. Nancy Dunaway, of Old Seven Rivers; Sixto Sedillo, of San Patricio; Judge Edward (Ned Shattuck), Carlsbad; W. P. Wilburn, grandson of W. P. B. Wilburn; Mrs. R. D. Champion, daughter of Lewis Netherlin; Joe Welch, nephew of Bill Ward; Bernard Clark, Farnham, Surrey, England (letter); Cliff McKinney, son of Deputy Sheriff Tip McKinney; Harty, Mrs. Herschel; Williams, Nick, Frank Stetson; Cicero Stewart, former sheriff of Eddy County; Dee Harkey, U.S. Marshall; Mrs. Mamie Perry, daughter of George Coe.

Others too numerous to list corroborated reports. I had access also, through Mr. Fulton's courtesy, to the letters of John Tunstall years before they appeared in print; and William Johnson made letters and records of his family available, as did a number of other individuals.

Finally I wish to thank the University of Arizona Press for applying its publishing skill to round out the manuscript and bring it into being as a book.

EVE BALL

Pecos Valley Talk

Characteristic Terms of the Region

Alcalde (Spanish) — Magistrate or chief official of a village
"Augurin'" — Arguing
Casita (Spanish) — Little house
Chosa (Spanish) — Crude hut
Criada (Spanish) — Domestic servant
Gouyen (Apache) — Wise woman
Indah (Apache) — White man
Nantan (Apache) — Chief or officer
Ow (Apache) — Yes
"Pecosed" — Drowned in the Pecos River
Pilgrim — Traveler on the frontier
"Reppin'" — Representing, as a salesman for a firm
Ristra (Spanish) — A string of chiles
Tsach (Apache) — Cradle
Ussen (Apache) — God
Vegas (Spanish) — Meadows
Vigas (Spanish) — Roof beams

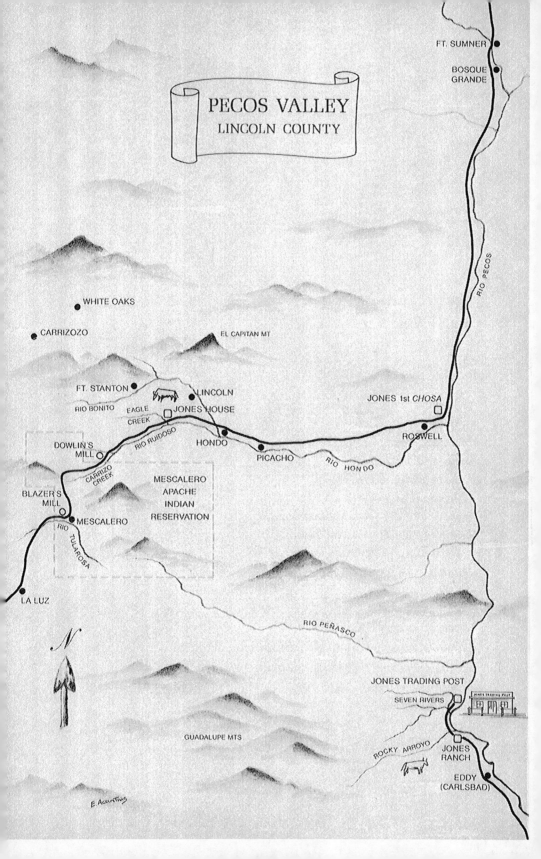

PECOS VALLEY
LINCOLN COUNTY

FT. SUMNER

BOSQUE GRANDE

RIO PECOS

WHITE OAKS

CARRIZOZO

EL CAPITAN MT

FT. STANTON

LINCOLN

JONES 1st *CHOSA*

RIO BONITO

EAGLE CREEK

JONES HOUSE

DOWLIN'S MILL

RIO RUIDOSO

HONDO

PICACHO

RIO HONDO

ROSWELL

CARRIZO CREEK

MESCALERO APACHE INDIAN RESERVATION

BLAZER'S MILL

MESCALERO

RIO TULAROSA

LA LUZ

RIO PEÑASCO

N

JONES TRADING POST

SEVEN RIVERS

JONES TRADING POST

GUADALUPE MTS

ROCKY ARROYO

JONES RANCH

EDDY (CARLSBAD)

E. Acurstius

The Pecos   1

"Seventy years ago," said Sam Jones, "we wasn't writin' no books.
We was tryin' to stay alive and keep our cattle." His shrewd eyes
twinkled as he added, "And like everybody else, maybe git a few
more. If a man couldn't pertect his family, his critters, and hisself,
he had no business in Old Lincoln County."

Sammie settled back on the *portal* of his home in Rocky Arroyo
with the leisurely manner of a man with a story to tell.

"Some folks criticizes the people who lived then and what they
did; but I ain't sure that folks is any better now. In the seventies it
was a matter of who was fastest on the draw. Nowadays it's who has
the money to hire the smartest lawyer. And lawyers is like race hosses.
If you want to win, you got to put yore money on the fastest hoss.

"Young people these days," he continued, "think this country came
with paved roads and that the good Lord built the bridges over the
rivers. Folks nowadays have no idee of the hard work it took to make
this Pecos Valley a place to live. Think it was all done with six-
shooters. Well, it wasn't, not by a long shot . . . ."

"Pecos water!" grumbled Ash Upson, as he dipped a bucket into
the river. "No wonder the Mescalero Apaches ran away from the Bosque

3

Redondo. They hadn't had a decent drink of water since they were driven from the Río Bonito in '63."

Heiskell Jones emptied a huge gourd dipper without removing it from his lips. He took a long, deep breath and said, "It's hard to down it without takin' a breath, but if you can, it don't taste so bad. The further south we go the worse it gets. I don't blame the children for fussin' about it."

"We're getting close to the Hondo now; might make it tomorrow," Ash said. "It's good water; but in this country any water is good."

"Don't know what we'd have done, Ash, if we hadn't picked you up as we pulled out of Denver. Makes a sight of difference havin' somebody along that's been over the country before. I wouldn't have followed the Pecos if you hadn't told us. Like as not we'd all have been dead by this time."

The two men toiled up the sandy bank to the camp. There a neatly dressed young woman was making preparations for the evening meal. She lifted a dark-eyed baby from the wagon and held the dipper to its lips.

"I wanna drink," said a small boy at his mother's feet.

"As soon as Minnie's finished."

The boy tasted, made a wry face, but drank. Barbara Jones suspended the bucket from a hook on the side of the wagon.

"Think we can make out all right here, Miss Barbara?"

"We've managed with much worse, Heiskell. Jim's picking up wood. It is good to have it after using buffalo chips."

"And where's John?"

"Watering the cattle and horses."

"Not many women have your grit, Mrs. Jones," said Ash Upson. "And there's plenty of men who find this country too much for them. A year ago I saw several wagons leaving."

"Those people may not have needed a home as badly as we do."

While her husband cut slices from the haunch of an antelope, Barbara deftly mixed biscuit dough in an oval wooden bowl. A half-grown boy brought wood and built a fire.

"As soon as John comes you boys take Billy down to the river and bathe. Don't go far."

"Yes, Ma'am."

She placed some fat in the Dutch oven and set it near the fire. When it was heated she pinched bits of dough from the mass and nestled them snugly into the cooking utensil. Heiskell strung slices of meat onto a green stick and put it over the coals. Then the men joined the boys in the water. Barbara bathed the baby. Then she stood and took the pins from her long black braids. She combed her hair and wound the braids again about her head. The coronet accentuated the stately grace of her slender body.

"Time to put the coffee on?" inquired her eldest, as he appeared over the bank.

"We can't have coffee at night any more — just for breakfast, John. Our supply is low. Take care of Minnie while I start more meat. Everybody'll be hungry."

"Let me put some coals on the lid of the oven first."

Little Minnie put her chubby arms around her brother's neck and laughed.

"My!" Barbara commented, "You're getting tall, John, almost as tall as I. And you're not even twelve yet."

"I'm almost a man, Mother."

Ash Upson struggled up the bank and stood watching. "I declare, Miss Barbara, you're the neatest person I ever saw. We've been weeks on the road in all this wind and sand, and you look as though you'd stepped out of a bandbox. How do you manage to keep yourself and these children so clean?"

"With the river handy why shouldn't we be clean? Cleanliness comes natural to the Dutch. They say it's next to godliness. Sometimes I'm afraid we put it first. When we decide on a place to live, good water is going to be the first consideration."

"Good soil's mighty important," said her husband.

"We'll look for both."

Eating their supper they faced a brilliant sky. Silhouetted against it was a distant peak, dominating the range.

"That's Sierra Blanca," said Ash. "The White Mountain is the highest in this country, higher than the Capitán north of it; it's further away and looks lower. Between the two is a beautiful valley and a river fed by snows. The Río Bonito flows east till it's joined by another stream from Old Blanca, called the Río Ruidoso, or Noisy River. Together they form the Hondo, which runs east to the Pecos. That's the one I'm hoping to reach soon — the Hondo. When we do we'll have good drinking water."

"Then I hope we make it soon," said Jim. "This old Pecos water —"

"Is water," finished his mother. "It has saved our lives and we're thankful for it."

"Will we get there tomorrow?"

"We ought to let the cattle rest tomorrow. Ol' Pied's feet are awful sore. We should 'a shod her like we did the oxen. Them oxen have sure held out. When we hit the Pecos I can put them right to plowin'," Heiskell said.

"It's too late to plow, ain't it Pa?"

"We'll chance it. I'm goin' to plant some corn and vegetables. We've hauled seed all the way from Virginia so we could have vegetables."

"Virginia?" asked Ash Upson.

"Yes — first to Iowa, then to Denver."

"The Apaches live on game," said John.

"But you like biscuit," his mother reminded him.

Ash Upson drew a worn map from his bedroll and spread it on the sand near the fire. He put his finger on a spot between the mountain ranges. "Pretty little town right here — La Placita [later Lincoln]. The people are Mexican and friendly. You might be wise to go where you'll have neighbors."

"We certainly want neighbors, but wouldn't those people have taken up all the best land? They've been there a long time."

"Several years. Came in from the valley of the Río Bravo [Río Grande] when there was a flood. But there's still plenty of good land to be had. Near them there's less danger from Apaches. The Mexicans have built a sort of fort they call El Torreón — The Tower. They keep water, food, wood, arms, and ammunition in it for protection against the Indians."

Barbara Jones interrupted. "When we left Denver we worried about the Comanches, and we haven't seen an Indian except those miserable prisoners at Fort Sumner. Since then I've been far more disturbed about sickness than Indian attacks. At the Bosque Redondo the Navajos were dying like flies from smallpox. The soldiers were making them throw their corpses into the river. That's why the Apaches ran away."

"It's a terrible place," agreed Ash. "Neither the Apaches nor the Navajos should ever have been put there. It's all Carleton's doings. When he got to New Mexico with his California Column and found no Confederates left in the Territory, he trumped up a lot of stories of Apache atrocities to keep his job. It's terrible what men will do for money."

"Aren't the Indians depredatin'?" asked Heiskell.

"Nothing to speak of; anyway, not if they're let alone. Carleton started egging them on, and they retaliated. The amazing part of it is that Kit Carson aided him. I'd have thought better of Kit, for he really knows Indians."

"It hasn't been long since the Mescaleros skipped out," said Heiskell. "Fellow in the tradin' post at Sumner told me to look out for them. They're supposed to have come back to the White Mountain because that's always been their stompin' ground."

"Can't blame them for lighting out. There wasn't food enough for them before thousands of the Navajos were brought there. Neither

Navajos nor Apaches want to farm. They're hunters. They both raise a little corn and beans, but they want meat. When the Mescaleros were free they raided in Mexico and drove off cattle and horses, mostly horses. They like mule meat, too."

"Didn't the government feed them?"

"Promised to if they went on a reservation, and does furnish a little food, but it expects them to raise what they eat."

"Why don't the soldiers turn them loose?"

"They destroyed practically everything the Navajos had. They trapped them in the Canyon de Chelly, killed their sheep, burned their corn and beans, and chopped down their peach trees. Then they drove them like cattle to that God-forsaken place at Fort Sumner. All along the way soldiers attacked the women. That trip was one of the most disgraceful things the government ever perpetrated."

"Sumner beat anything I ever saw," said Heiskell. "Humans was penned like animals, starvin' to death, and dyin' of diseases they got from the soldiers. If ever them Navajos get loose, all hell's goin' to be poppin' or I miss my guess."

"Reckon they'd head this way?" asked Heiskell.

"No," replied Upson, "they'll go back to their own country. It's a desert, but theirs. What water they have is good. Besides, they believe that if they ever cross two rivers something terrible will happen to them. And goin' to Fort Sumner they did cross two — the Río Bravo and the Puerco. Looks like there might be something to their ideas — conditions at the Bosque."

"Indians are modest. But no woman ever left the line of march from the Navajo country without being victimized. It's my opinion that the white people will pay for these things some time," Ash declared.

"Did the government want the Navajo land for settlers?" Heiskell asked.

"No. White people wouldn't live there. There's plenty of good land other places. Take this Mescalero country now, fertile little valleys, good water, timber, rich soil, game. The Mexicans took notice of that years before floods drove them from the Río Bravo [the Río Grande]."

"And we'll be in Apache country?" said Barbara slowly.

"Yes," Ash replied.

"It's their land; it has been from the first. They've been cruelly treated by white people. They'll think we are like those who have abused them."

"Not too late to turn back, Miss Barbara."

"In sight of the promised land? After putting our hands to the plow?"

"We can't turn back. We were warned against Kiowas and Comanches, and haven't even seen one. The Apaches may not come near us either," Heiskell stated.

"Not if we stay here on the Pecos," Barbara replied.

"That won't help. The Mescaleros often come to the Río Pecos to hunt. They cross it and go to the Llano Estacado when the buffalo herds come south. Way over yonder — see that shadowy bluff? That's where the Llano begins. The Apaches will be your neighbors, I'm afraid," explained Ash Upson.

"Couldn't we make friends of them? My mother always said that if one takes a good neighbor with him he'll never lack for good neighbors. Isn't that true of Indians, too? And from what I've heard of the California Column, don't you think we'd be as well off with Apaches as with some of those soldiers?" asked Barbara.

"It's for you to decide," said Ash. "I want to go on to the Río Bravo and then north to Albuquerque. I've the idea of starting a newspaper there. But I'll have to work till I get some money."

"When you goin' to get married and settle down, Ash?" asked Heiskell. "You must be all of forty."

"Thirty-seven, and I've heard the owl hoot. A man can't settle down till he's got a start."

"You mean he can't get a start till he settles down," said Barbara.

The last rays of the sun struck his cheek, upon which a jagged scar gleamed vividly. Barbara wondered how Mr. Upson received that wound, but she restrained her curiosity.

"Is there a newspaper at La Placita, Mr. Upson?"

"No. Few people there can speak English."

"Wouldn't you want to farm? Heiskell wants nothing else; he thinks it's the best life there is. It would be good to have you for a neighbor."

"I'm a rolling stone, Miss Barbara. It's said that they gather no moss. But they sometimes acquire polish."

"One can have both. First, we need the farm."

"You'll get it, Miss Barbara. Did I ever break a promise to you?" asked her husband.

"No, Heiskell. But you've refused to make several I've asked of you."

"If a man is any man at all, he keeps his word. He can't have any self-respect unless he does. If that's gone he's a pretty sorry. So I just don't make a promise unless I'm sure it'll be kept. All we've got to do now is select land for that farm. Then we'll be New Mexicans."

"Which side was New Mexico for in the War Between the States?" asked John. "Did it fight for Virginia?"

"How about it, Ash?" Heiskell questioned.

"There were some Confederates in here for awhile. Parts of Fort Stanton, over beyond Placita, were burned. But they had left before Carleton got here from California. Many of the people in the Territory are Northern sympathizers. There's even talk of naming the whole southeast quarter of New Mexico after Lincoln."

"Minnie's asleep, John. Put her in the wagon. And get out the blankets for you and Jim."

"Uh, huh."

"Answer your mother politely," ordered Heiskell.

"Since we left Virginia we've been getting careless about our manners," Barbara commented. "Just as soon as we get settled I'm going to get The Book out and hold Sunday School regularly. And I'm going to have the boys make their manners as they did in Virginia. They're going to stand when a lady enters, and they're going to call all grown people Mr. and Mrs."

Jim groaned.

"I'm partly to blame," said Heiskell, "I've been calling Mr. Upson by his given name."

"It's different between men," said Barbara. "But the boys mustn't do it."

Weary though she was, Barbara lay awake. When Mr. Upson's deep breathing indicated that he slept, Barbara asked Heiskell to explain things she had long pondered. Why would a man of Mr. Upson's obvious education have come to this wild country? Why had he left Denver walking? And how did he get the scar?

"Don't know. That's his business."

"You don't think he was run out of Denver?"

"We left Virginia without being run out. Denver, too."

"Of course. But I sometimes wonder if you feel right about leaving Virginia."

"I'm still all mixed up. When Virginia split up over the war that we all knew was coming, I just couldn't take up arms against the South. And we couldn't stay in Braxton County in West Virginia if I refused to go into the Union Army. Besides, hadn't I promised you I'd never fight? Is an army fight any different than a man to man one?"

"You made the right decision, and you shouldn't worry about it."

"I dragged you and the children to Iowa — too cold a place for humans. And Denver's just as bad."

"It wasn't the cold in Denver I minded; it was the killings."

"They can happen anywhere — maybe down here."

"There will be none here if we're the only family."

"We won't be very long. Others will come."

"Besides, nobody has to fight. Virginia outlawed dueling."

"This is a new country. I've given my word against fighting, but if we're ever attacked I'll have to do it to protect you and the children."

"You've always been a good citizen, Heiskell. For the sake of the boys —"

"A dead citizen's no good to anybody."

"Don't talk that way. What would the boys think?"

"We have to face facts. I can't be with you all the time. The boys must learn to take care of you and Minnie when I'm away."

"Do you want them to practice shooting?"

"Yes; and you, too. They're pretty fair shots already."

"I'll never lift a gun against a human being."

"That's somethin' everybody has to decide for himself. If it comes to my life or his, I'm going to shoot. And I hope you'll come to see things that way, too. If not, we have no business in this country."

"We're here, and we're here to stay. There's opportunity —"

"That's what Ash says. Supplies from Santa Fe and Las Vegas have to be hauled to the fort near La Placita. We might raise green stuff to sell."

"We'll do well to raise enough for ourselves this summer."

"I reckon so. But there'll be other years."

"And tomorrow's a good day to think of that, and to impress it upon the boys."

"Tain't Sunday, is it?"

"No. It's the Fourth of July."

"The Fourth of July, 1866. We'll write it in The Book so we'll never forget what day we came."

The Hondo

2

The Jones family camped on the Hondo, about six miles from its confluence with the Pecos. They found it disappointing in size but amply rewarding in its abundance of clear, cool water.

"I've never tasted anything better than this water," declared Ash Upson.

"Not even whiskey?" queried Heiskell.

"Not even whiskey; and I'll confess that I like it far too well. Right now I wouldn't exchange a dipper of this water for all the liquor in the Territory."

"Then it's a good time for both of you to take a stand and swear off drinking," said Barbara.

"I've done so, many times," admitted Ash.

"I haven't," said Heiskell. "I knew I couldn't keep such a promise, and I figger a man's word ought to be good."

Barbara decided it was time to change the subject. "We're fortunate. We've reached the promised land — and without sickness or mishap. After weeks in the wilderness we've much for which to be thankful."

"Why not stay here?" asked Ash. "There's good soil, good water and plenty of it, and enough wood along the river to build a *chosa*. You won't have to cut trees, just use driftwood."

11

Under Ash's direction the Jones family began excavating a ditch to outline the house. They dug it about two feet in depth and a little less in width. On either side within this trench they placed upright logs and poles to form walls; then they filled the intervening space with loose soil. Across the top of the walls they laid long cottonwood poles, and at right angles to them, boughs. Upon the top they heaped earth to the depth of a foot and tamped it. Rains, Ash warned them, inevitably caused leaks, but the roof could be easily repaired. Anyway there were not apt to be any rains before late autumn.

Slits were cut in the walls to admit light, but they had no door other than a blanket hung over the opening. Heiskell promised to construct a fireplace but thought it more urgent to plow a plot and plant a garden. Though warned that nothing would grow without irrigation, he thought they could make a sled of poles and haul water in the two barrels. Ash shook his head and advised them to reserve enough garden seed for another planting. They might decide to go on to La Placita, or to Picacho. Even there they'd raise nothing without digging a ditch to run water to their field.

While they worked Ash Upson entertained the family with stories. Though the Joneses asked few questions, they decided that this could not be his first trip to the area, because of his knowledge of the country. There were no tributaries, he told them, from the east. The Staked Plains were high and dry. At times the rain filled shallow depressions, but usually they dried up quickly. Consequently the Llano was a barrier to migration from the east. Undoubtedly a time would come when there would be a settlement where they had stopped, for already there was some travel north and south along the Pecos. Just wait until people began coming in from the east.

Barbara Jones craved knowledge both for herself and her children. She'd taught those old enough to learn to read from the big Bible. She kept it in the trunk. It was her only book and contained the records of births, marriages, and deaths. She wanted her family to know its contents, but she wished also for them to learn things it did not contain, such as ciphering, geography, and history — especially that of their own country. She wanted her children, above all else, to be good citizens, and she believed The Book did teach that. She wanted them to know how to be healthy, too. And could people living almost entirely on meat be strong and well? Ash reminded her that many primitive peoples live on meat. The Kiowas and Comanches depended upon the buffalo not only for food but for clothing and shelter as well. And they were surely strong and vigorous.

"But there are no buffalo here," Heiskell said.

"Not now," agreed Ash. But he assured them that in the fall, vast herds, now far to the north, would migrate with the coming of the cold. They kept to the Llano, going from one watering place to the next. Almost due east, possibly thirty-five miles, there were lakes where the herd stopped. To the south was more living water at Monument Spring. The army had erected a pile of white stones on a hill near the spring as a guide to those crossing the plains. And still further south was the great Comanche Spring [Fort Stockton] well known to both buffalo and Indians.

Following the herd came the nomadic tribes of the Middle West. Intercepting the herd from the White Mountains, the Apaches hunted to obtain a year's supply of meat and hides. They jerked the meat where it was killed, and the women scraped the flesh from the skins in preparation for tanning them.

Ash warned Heiskell that if he attempted to kill one of the huge animals he should be very careful to avoid a conflict with the Apaches. As cold weather came the Joneses were to watch for an enormous dust cloud in the northeast caused by the moving herd. They could ride toward Four Lakes, kill one or two buffalo, and leave with meat and hides as quickly as they could if they hoped to avoid an ambush, for the Apaches laid claim to all that part of the country.

*   *   *

In September a troop of cavalry stopped at the Jones *chosa*. It was escorting freight wagons laden with supplies for Fort Stanton. Heiskell invited the troops to spend the night. He could give them meat but was out of flour. The sergeant then ordered a trooper to bring a barrel of flour from the wagon. When he saw the delight with which it was received, he sent for coffee and sugar. Heiskell went to his trunk and counted his meager hoard of coins. These he offered in exchange for ammunition. The sergeant shook his head; he was not permitted to sell government supplies but would give them a few rounds of ammunition. And he advised the Joneses to leave the Pecos, go nearer the fort, and stop at one of the Mexican settlements near Stanton. Didn't they know they might be attacked by Apaches and killed any time?

As Ash Upson had predicted, watering a garden from barrels did not prove feasible. Heiskell decided to make the advised change in location but yielded to the entreaties of the boys to postpone going until after the buffalo run. The boys climbed daily to the roof to look for the tell-tale dust cloud that would signify the coming of the herd.

Not until the dust cloud was sighted did Heiskell break the news to Jim that he was to stay with his mother and the younger children. John was the better shot, and they could not waste ammunition. Barbara knew how great was her younger son's disappointment, and she explained how important an assignment he had in being the protector of the family.

Though she told herself there was nothing to fear, she slept little. Now that the heavy door had been made and hung with thick pieces of leather, it could be bolted on the inside with a very heavy board dropped into notches on either side of the door.

Toward morning Barbara was awakened by the scream of a horse. She and Jim hastily dressed, took the rifle, and left the house in time to see a dark shadow steal from a fallen filly and fade into the darkness. Investigation of the filly showed that it had been hamstrung and would never walk again. After Jim had fired a merciful shot, Barbara placed the rifle within their reach, and Jim built a fire near the animal. Together they skinned it. When they had finished and placed the hide on top of the *chosa,* dawn was breaking. The attacker, Barbara told Jim, must have been one of the dreaded lobos of which Mr. Upson had told them.

The next day Jim saw moving specks to the east, and two hours later the returning hunters rode up the Hondo. The pack horses were carrying the meat and skins of two buffalo. Heiskell announced proudly that John had killed both. Both parents understood Jim's reaction, and they were determined to give him a chance to hunt. Excellent though John's marksmanship was, he cared little about hunting. But Jim loved it and deserved his reward, which was to come later.

•   •   •

A month or so later, John saw buzzards circling something on the Hondo, and Barbara left the younger children with Jim while she and John went to investigate. As the birds did not alight, whatever they were watching must still be alive. It proved to be a young Apache, lying at the river's edge, knife in hand. When Barbara bent over him she extended her hand and he laid his knife in it. She placed it beside him and began an examination of his injuries. Both bones in the lower part of one leg were broken. She left John with the Indian while she went to the house for bandages. When she returned, John had cut saplings for splints.

"Have you ever set a bone, Mother?"

"No, but this must be done."

"What if he won't let you?"

"I think he will. Anyway, we must try."

When they approached the Apache he pointed to tracks beside him and said, *"Caballo!"* Then, *"Río!"*

"Río! That's water," said John. "That's what Ash Upson called it."

He dipped some from the stream in his hat and gave it to the young man. The Apache drank eagerly but continued to point to the tracks and the river. Perhaps he was asking John to go up the river after his horse. If he had lain there two or three days, as he appeared to have done, the horse would have gone back home. It would be useless to attempt to follow it.

Barbara held the splints and bandages before the young man and pointed to his broken leg. He nodded. Then John, at Barbara's command, held the Apache's foot and pulled as hard as he could, holding the leg straight, while she applied bandages and splints. The Indian braced his elbows in the sand and pushed back with all his might. Barbara deftly wound the bandages about the break, applied the splints, and firmly bound them with more of the wrappings. When she had finished she saw that the Apache's face was wet, though he hadn't made a sound. To her surprise, her face, too, was covered with beads of perspiration.

With John's help she got the young man to his feet, and they lifted him face down, across the saddle. John led the horse and she walked beside him to the *chosa*. They took him inside and laid him in front of the fire. Barbara got an old flannel gown and a blanket. Then she heated some water and told John to bathe him. The Apache surrendered his moccasins but firmly resisted John's attempt to remove his breech clout. He seemed to like the bathing. When it was finished, he laid his hand on his chest and said, " 'Migo."

When Barbara returned the Indian repeated the gesture and the word. They concluded that he was giving his name and called him by that word.

Barbara gave him a cup of hot broth and he drank it greedily. He extended the cup for more but made no reaction when she shook her head. After a few minutes she gave him a second cup, and later a third.

Heiskell came in at dark and was disturbed at the presence of the uninvited guest. He'd go back and set the whole tribe on the Joneses. If this hadn't happened the Apaches wouldn't have known of the Jones family's being there.

Barbara said quietly that if Mr. Upson knew Indians, they'd known it all the time. And if she knew people, the Indians were people and would appreciate the help given to one who might have died if not rescued.

Heiskell grunted and admitted that she might be right.

Next morning Heiskell made a rude crutch of a forked limb, and 'Migo raised himself to a little bench and later to a standing position. He quickly acquired the ability to walk with his crutch and immediately went outside the *chosa*. There a stump served as a seat, and he insisted on sleeping by it.

He had the children bring him bits of stone and pieces of saplings from the river. By gestures he made them understand his wants. The boys watched him fashion a bow and shafts for arrows. They watched him chip bits of stone from a piece from which he made points. From the back of a newly killed antelope he stripped long pieces of tendon. These he chewed until they were transparent, and with them he bound together the two pieces of the bow and fixed the points to his shafts. To the boys' surprise, the tendon adhered as though applied with glue.

Heiskell still had misgivings about the young man's presence and warned John that some morning 'Migo would be gone. It turned out as his father prophesied. John's horse, too, was gone. But 'Migo had not taken saddle or bridle. He'd ridden away bareback. Heiskell was indignant, even when John told him he'd given the horse to 'Migo.

Less than a week later the horse returned, with bow and arrows tied to its mane.

Cattle

3

As spring advanced, the Jones family watched for the return of the buffalo herds from the south. When a queer-looking cloud was seen down the Pecos, the family prepared for a hunt, and they rode down the river.

"There's too much dust for stragglers, and it's too close to the river for buffalo. Ash says the main herd always stays up on the Llano."

"Couldn't be Indians, could it?"

"Don't think so. Too much dust."

The cloud wavered along the river. A whitish patch emerged from it. A mottled mass followed and oozed forward like a spotted serpent. Detached dots gradually assumed form.

"It's a wagon, Pa, and there's men, horseback. And cattle!"

"Believe you're right, John. But why would anybody move cattle?"

"Don't know. But it's cattle, all right."

An hour's ride brought Heiskell and the boys within shouting distance of a man who rode ahead of the herd.

"Howdy! Wasn't expectin' to see folks here. Thought at fust you was Indians," said the man.

"We wondered about you, too," replied Heiskell.

The trail boss wheeled from his course and joined them.

17

"What in 'tarnation you doin' in this God-forsaken place?"

Heiskell Jones explained that they lived up the river, on a little tributary; that it was not a bad country, but a very good one. He told with pride of their *chosa* and of the good crop they'd raised. And he invited the stranger to visit his family.

"You don't mean to say you brought your wife out here?"

"Yes, and she likes it. We're aimin' to stay here and farm."

Heiskell hastened to add that they planned to sell their crops to the soldiers at Fort Stanton, providing they had a surplus. This first year they did not, but everybody liked vegetables, and a man could always sell roasting ears, now couldn't he? Of course, they'd have to move closer to the fort.

The stranger nodded.

Then Heiskell told of his need for ammunition and the refusal of the cavalry officer to sell him any.

"They're forbidden to sell it," the stranger explained.

"For that matter, we couldn't have bought it, anyway; we'd have had to trade something for it. I was hopin' we could manage to give you something in exchange — that is, if you got plenty so you can spare some."

"Might fix you up. We brought a-plenty. And when we get to Fort Sumner we can get more."

When they had eaten, the stranger counted out ammunition for both six-shooter and rifles. "Now, you take a hunk of that beef and a sack of coffee. We got a-plenty."

Heiskell looked longingly at the coffee but shook his head. Then he said, "I don't have any money."

"Money! What's that?" asked his host. "Seems like I've heard of it, but I don't want any."

"Well, if you'll come by the *chosa* and spend the night with us . . ." replied Heiskell.

"Cain't I reckon. Got a fambly of my own to look after."

"Family?" asked Heiskell.

"The herd and the men. My name's Bostick, Tom Bostick. Trail boss for Bill Cloud. There's a raft of us Bosticks. I'm delivering steers to Fort Sumner for the government. Cloud's got a contract to supply beef for the soldiers — Indians, too. The soldiers ration it to them."

Heiskell nodded. "Bout time; they're starvin' by the hundreds. They get diseases from the soldiers — smallpox and such."

"Those soldiers! Of all· the no 'count outfits I ever saw in all my born days, they're the worst," replied Bostick.

"Sure enough?" asked Heiskell.

Bostick continued, "The government insisted on sending a military escort for the cattle." And he added that the first troop was composed of Irish who were fairly competent when sober and who made little trouble after their supply of liquor was exhausted. Of course there was no place at which it could be replenished.

At Fort Concho they were outfitted with a corporal and squad of an entirely different kind. If they had been attacked by Indians, it was the military who would have needed protection. They were, Bostick said, the most worthless men he'd ever encountered.

When asked if he were still encumbered with them, Tom Bostick explained that when he reached the Horsehead Crossing on the Pecos he had sent them back.

"Where's the Horsehead?" asked Heiskell.

"South of the Texas Line two or three days' ride."

Heiskell inquired why Bostick preferred coming up the river on the west side and learned that all "pilgrims" did so in order to get good water. There were many little tributaries of the Pecos from the mountains, but none from the Llano Estacado. Hadn't Heiskell Jones crossed the river at Fort Sumner?

He nodded and asked if this were the first herd to be driven up the Pecos.

"I think not. John Chisum is trying to get the contracts to supply the army — Indians, too — with beef."

Tom Bostick had started with 1160 head but estimated the herd now contained about 2500 animals. Cattle, he explained, voluntarily join those being driven through, and it is sometimes difficult to get rid of them. In Jack and Young counties in Texas many settlers had been intimidated by Indians and had left, abandoning their cattle. As Bostick's herd came through, the other animals joined it. Some were turned back, but still there were far too many.

Were they of any value? Well, until recently they had not been, but with the need of food for the military and Indians, they might be. However, he had far too many drags, and Heiskell was welcome to take as many as he pleased. There was good grass on the river and they'd supply him with beef.

When John pleaded with his father to take a few, he received permission to do so.

•   •   •

When the herd passed, the boys tried desperately to cut and drive several head too weak to keep up with the main body. Heiskell thought it nonsense, but he did not forbid it. They moved slowly with their cows and arrived at the *chosa* with several.

Twice more that season herds moved north up the Pecos. One herd was the property of Colonel Goodnight and Oliver Loving. Owners of the other herd identified themselves as the Rainbolts. They promised to stop as they returned from Fort Sumner and bring ammunition to the Jones family. And they kept that promise.

"We're ridin' up the Hondo a piece," they announced, "to look for a place to live and run cattle. Figger on bringin' a bunch here so we won't have to drive so far. No sense comin' such a fur piece acrost Texas when they's plenty of good range here. Just look at that gramma grass — belly deep to a hoss."

Heiskell looked over the motley bunch of long-horned, scrawny cows in the corral. "Always heard they could kill one and pack all its meat in its horns," he told the boys. "Danged if I don't believe it. I'd rather have Ol' Pied and her heifer than all the longhorns on the trails. We've done without milk ourselves to keep some of them pesky calves alive; and the whole passel of cows wouldn't give as much as Ol' Pied, even if anybody could milk 'em. Why do you want to fool with 'em?"

"I just like 'em, Pa. I'm not ever goin' to farm; I'm goin' to run cattle."

"Me too," said Jim.

"Got to set up nights with the blame things or else build corrals. Either's a plumb nuisance. Besides, they'll eat up our crops."

"I'll herd 'em," said Jim.

"You'll not either one make farmers," grumbled Heiskell.

"Why should they?" asked Barbara. "Especially if they don't like to farm?"

"It seems to me like they's not no real livin' outside of farmin'."

"I feel as you do. But we chose for ourselves, and the boys should do the same. Nobody succeeds at something he dislikes."

"They don't want to do nothin' but hunt and practice with them ropes. Ever since they seen them cowboys they're just hog-wild about ropin'."

"I know. But they mind us, they never do anything bad, and they never refuse to do anything we tell them to do."

"They better not!"

"Do you think it would be all right for them to be away over night?"

"You don't mean — ?"

"Yes, and soon — perhaps tonight. Jim earned it long ago!"

The boys set off gleefully, with permission to be away three days. When they rode in later with game, no one came out to greet them. They hurried into the *chosa* to find their mother in bed.

"You sick, Mother?"

"Not now, John. You have a baby brother."

The boys approached her self-consciously.

"Awful little, ain't he?"

"He's a big baby, a fine big boy. And his name's Thomas Edwin — Tom for short."

"Can't even walk," said Jim.

"Of course not."

"Funny," commented John, "a baby antelope a day old can outrun a horse. I tried to rope one." He cautiously touched the baby's hand, and its tiny fingers closed on his and clung.

"Let's keep him, Mother; I like him."

"I've already put him in The Book with the rest — and his birthday, April 27, 1867. He's the first white child born in the whole county."

•   •   •

Twice that winter Heiskell Jones made trips up the Hondo, once for supplies at Lincoln and once to select a site for a home. Near the village of Picacho he found a broad, level meadow on the river. It would, he knew, be a good place to raise corn, and the surrounding hills would afford range for cattle. Since the boys were so insistent upon keeping the cattle, he could not overlook pastures. There was a spring near which he'd build.

Heiskell went to the village and talked with the *alcalde* — the mayor. He was very courteously received and was delighted to find that the mayor understood and spoke English. The mayor assured Heiskell that he was welcome. There was plenty of land available, and no one else wanted the piece that Heiskell had chosen. And he added that he and other neighbors would help the Jones family with the building of a *chosa*. When Heiskell explained the lack of money, the mayor minimized that by saying that nobody had money, but that all who came had friends glad and willing to help a newcomer establish a home.

For the first time Heiskell Jones learned the meaning of the word *amigo* — friend. So, the Indian had not been giving his name but was describing the status of their relationship. The mayor and Heiskell were *amigos*. All Heiskell need do was select his building site, and the community would make a fiesta of the task of building. But first they must prepare the adobes. They would start immediately.

It was, Heiskell said later, a much better home than they had built on the Hondo. He and Jim planned to take a load of their possessions to Picacho and start work on the house. When it was completed they would return for the family and the cattle. John was to stay with his mother and the small children.

When Heiskell and Jim returned, Barbara was ready for moving. The door had yet to be taken down, but the vegetables had been harvested and all clothing and bedding washed. Heiskell explained that because of the terrible hills that must be climbed, he wished to start very early. They would have to spend one night in camp. He wished to reach the foot of Dead Man's Hill the first evening, for taking a wagon over it would be difficult. It would be like driving up steps, broad irregular steps.

When the Joneses arrived at their new home, a fire had already been laid. Upon a crude table was a generous supply of food. With tears in her eyes Barbara asked to whom they were indebted, and Heiskell replied that their new neighbors, their *amigos*, had provided for the arrival. Mrs. Romero, Mrs. Chávez, in fact every woman at Picacho had no doubt contributed. Tomorrow they would come to welcome her.

"I'll be a good neighbor," Barbara promised.

"Got a surprise, Miss Barbara. Just look here." Heiskell lifted a cowhide and proudly displayed a second room.

"Oh, Heiskell, we're rich! I never hoped for as good a house. We do appreciate all the things you do for us."

"It'll be handy, all right, and the boys can have good beds."

"If you're away we'll have neighbors close. I do hope we can find some way to repay them."

The family settled comfortably into their new quarters and planted a garden. The Mexicans contributed seed of chilis, pinto beans, and peaches. They told Barbara, "Chilis are good; they are good for *señores* and good for *niños*."

Heiskell learned that cowhides were exchangeable in Lincoln for twenty-five cents' worth of merchandise, and he began to revise his opinion of cattle.

Old Pied's second heifer was the source of much happiness. She was a good cow, and though the calf was half rangestock, it might make a good milk cow. If the boys didn't so dislike milking! But they had to do it, for Heiskell worked in the field as long as he could see, and he would not permit Barbara to do the outside work except in emergencies.

"I don't hold with forcing children to mind, but if they won't do it without punishment, I'm going to whip them."

"There always comes a time when they're too big to be handled physically. Then what's to be done?"

"You have funny ideas of raising children, Miss Barbara."

"Hasn't it worked well so far?"

"Yes, it has. But John's only thirteen. Just wait three years. If that boy ever takes the bit in his teeth . . . Still, I'm leavin' the management of the children to you, for everything but the milkin'. That they've got to do."

"If we don't consider the boys' wishes in some matters, how can we expect them to defer to ours when they're grown?"

"Don't know. We'll do the best we can and hope it will be for the best."

"We're very fortunate," said Barbara. "What more could anyone ask of life?"

"For one thing, some lumber. There's a mill over on the Tularosa; belongs to a Dr. Blazer, a dentist. Now if he grinds corn — "

"Mrs. Chávez grinds hers with two stones, a metate and a mano. She makes delicious meal and is going to teach me how."

"Is that what she uses in her tortillas?"

"Yes, and aren't they good?"

"But I don't want you grinding corn by hand."

"It's not much different than grating corn by hand. I've always done that."

"And those corn cakes you make are the best I ever ate."

"Right now I'm far more concerned about clothes than food. We're wearing out everything we brought with us, or outgrowing it. The boys are growing up, but John isn't big enough to wear your old clothes. And his are so nearly gone that I simply have to make more. They won't do for Jim, for they're in tatters. What are we to do?"

"What do you think?"

"Make over all we can for Bill and Minnie. Tom's using the older boys' baby clothes. I've a notion to try my hand at making buckskin shirts and leggings for you and the older boys. I could use your worn out things for patterns."

"We'd better get at it before time to plow."

The entire family set to work. They obtained tanned buckskin from neighbors. Barbara cut out the garments. Heiskell and the boys punched holes for the needle. Recalling 'Migo's method, Barbara used sinew instead of cotton thread. Small pieces of skin were used for making moccasins.

"Of course John will get the first new clothes," complained Jim.

"Only because he needs them worse than you do. His old ones are simply gone. Yours will be made next."

"How about Billy?"

"I've been thinking a lot. He outgrows things so fast that it wouldn't pay to make up buckskin for him. I think I'll dress him as the Mexicans do their little boys — in a long shirt down to his knees, and high moccasins. That's all they wear, and they get along nicely."

"And you, Mother?"

"For a while I can manage. I'll make over the worst-worn things for Minnie. But we'll have to manage for some cloth before very long. It may be buckskin for me, too."

"Like a squaw, Mother?"

"We won't say that word. The Indian women don't like it. There were two here yesterday. The younger wore a fringed buckskin dress, and it was beautiful. It was neatly made and trimmed in beads and little metal jingles.

"And there's another thing: we simply have to have more beds. Nobody has geese or ducks, so we'll make wool mattresses. I can get wool from Mrs. Romero, but we'll have to buy cloth for ticks. Heiskell, the first time you go to Lincoln, please look for some. I'm making a list of things we can't get along without, and I've another list of things less important."

•   •   •

It was a busy year. In addition to the routine of cooking, washing, sewing, and mending, Barbara dried beans and peaches, made soap, carded and spun wool, and knitted stockings. No member of the family was idle. Even Minnie ran errands and stood on a bench to wash dishes. It did not occur to the boys that any task was women's work. All benefitted by what was done, and all participated. While Barbara knitted by firelight, Heiskell mended harness or shoes. One of the boys lay on the floor with the huge Bible spread on a skin and read aloud, spelling the unfamiliar words. Bill joined his brothers beside The Book and sometimes surprised them with his knowledge of the legends below the illustrations. Though no attempt was made to teach him, he began reading. Barbara thought he had memorized the story of Goliath, and tested him. He recognized many isolated words. And they let him attempt to read familiar stories.

"What's this writing, Mother?"

"It's our record. I told you the names of your Grandfather and Grandmother Culp. Here are the dates of their births, marriages, and deaths. This is the list of your birthdays. You are all here: John, you and Jim were born in Virginia; Bill and Minnie in Denver; and little Tom is a New Mexican."

"Were you afraid to leave Virginia, Mother?"

"Your mother's Black Dutch and not afraid of anything," said Heiskell.

"I'm Black Dutch too, and I'm not afraid either," stated John.

"The rest of you are just as much Black Dutch as John, even if you do look like me," said Heiskell. "And I'm Red Irish."

"Are the Dutch white people?" asked Bill.

"How 'bout it, Miss Barbara?"

"Your father likes to tease me, but I'm proud of my Dutch blood. The Dutch have been a clean, brave, enterprising people. They've been colonizers. They've left their homes to go to new countries and develop them."

• • •

That fall the Jones family had a visitor. He rode up and was invited to get down and spend the night. There were, he said, many herds being driven up the Pecos. Oliver Loving, whose cattle had passed the preceding summer, had been attacked by Indians near the Texas Line and had been wounded by an arrow. He had traveled by night, hidden by day, and reached Fort Sumner in very bad condition. His arm was amputated there, but he died. His body was placed in a coffin, which was in turn put into a very large pine box, with a thick layer of charcoal between the two. It had been hauled in a wagon back to Weatherford, Texas, for burial. "Bill Bostick," the stranger said, "helped take the body back."

"We saw Bill Bostick when he went north with a herd." Heiskell said.

"He told me. Settlers will be coming. I'm up here, myself, looking for a place for cattle. Think I'll bring my family next spring. The name's Rainbolt — Lib Rainbolt. Been to Fort Sumner with a bunch of steers."

"One of your family stopped at our *chosa* down near the Pecos."

"So you're the Jones family. My brother Jim spoke of you. He's holding the wagon on the Pecos till I get back. In fact, he's at your old *chosa*. We may be your neighbors before long. I like this Hondo country."

"We'll be very happy if you come. There's plenty of good land to be had."

"A man by the name of Casey is coming; says he's going to start a grist mill on the Hondo."

"We need a mill."

"Apaches bother you much?"

"Not so far. We seldom see one. The Mexicans live in fear of them, though I don't know why. When they come, we feed them and treat them as we do everybody else. They usually eat and leave. They never spend the night. And they won't talk much, though many of them know Spanish. We just never think of being afraid."

"What if you're left here alone, Mrs. Jones?"

"Oh, I ask them in, feed them, and they leave." Barbara said.

"Mother's Black Dutch and not afraid of nothin'," said John.

Barbara gave him a severe look.

"I'm not afraid, neither," said the boy, "because I'm Black Dutch, too."

"John!"

"Think we'd have trouble with the Mexicans?" asked the visitor.

"I don't see why," Barbara answered. "They're a kind and generous people. We find them very good neighbors. Our children are talking more Spanish than English. It's amazing how they pick it up. The neighbors call Bill "Faustino" — we don't know why — and they like to hear him say their words."

"If you're hesitating because of either Indians or Mexicans, forget it; neither will bother you if you treat them well," said Heiskell.

"And they're friendly?"

"In their way. And it's a very good way."

Roots

4

The following summer passed quickly. The neighbors helped Heiskell fence a small field for corn and build a corral. The Joneses repaid work with work. In cases of illness, they harvested crops and did whatever was needed for the stricken family. Barbara's skill with illness was soon recognized, and she was often summoned to the sick.

She also learned from the Mexicans. She had been skeptical at first as to the value of chili as a food, but she saw people living on mutton, beans, and chili, and thriving on the diet. Since the Mexicans did not eat other vegetables to any great extent, she decided that there must be good food properties in the pepper. And her family learned to like it.

"Vegetables are just fodder. Meat is the food for man," said her eldest.

"And you're a man?"

"I'm fourteen. If that isn't a man, what is?"

"Being a man is not just a matter of age, John. It's how a boy acts that determines when he becomes a man."

"Don't I act like one?"

"Most of the time you do, but not when you're sulky about having to milk."

"Then I won't sulk any more, Mother."

"Now you're talking like a man. I'm proud of my boys."

"Me, too?" asked Minnie.

"You, too, my precious ewe lamb."

"What's a ewe lamb?"

Barbara lifted the child to her lap and kissed her. And she explained.

"It's in The Book," Bill informed his mother. "I saw a picture of a lady carrying a ewe lamb in her arms."

"That's not a lady; that's Jesus."

"Wearing a dress?"

"No, a robe. All men wore robes at that time."

After she had put the small children to bed she said, "John, I've something to tell you. You're to stay with me while your father and Jim make a trip to Lincoln. I know you want to go, and we'd like for you to; you may next time. They'll take the wagon and bring back a load of supplies. I hope you're not too greatly disappointed. I dislike keeping you here, but I need you very badly."

John accepted her decision without protest. He was, Barbara thought, really growing up and justifying his claim to manhood.

"If the corn brings enough, your father will get you a six-shooter. But this isn't a promise; it all depends upon the price of corn."

"I'd stay, anyway, Mother."

"I felt sure of that, John. The gun isn't a bribe, or a reward either. It's just something we want to do for you." John's eyes thanked her.

"Think you'll make out all right?" asked Heiskell, as he and Jim mounted to the seat of the wagon.

"We'll be perfectly all right. You just go on and don't worry about us. We have good neighbors, if we need them."

Before midday Barbara doubted the wisdom of her decision. She baked a big quantity of bread; she put a huge roast over the coals; and after they had eaten their noon meal she churned. Then she paced the floor, knitting in hand. She wished that she had not let John go to the field to stay till sunset. When he returned earlier than she had expected, she sent him to do the milking. Then she set about preparing supper. When John entered the house he found her gasping for breath and bathed in perspiration.

"Let me strain the milk and you go over to Picacho for Mrs. Romero," Barbara said.

"I can't leave you like this, Mother."

"John, you must. There's going to be another baby, and soon."

"I've known that for a long time. And I can take care of you. I'm afraid to leave you."

"Put the big kettle on and fill it with water. Give Minnie and Tom their supper and put them to bed. I've been cooking all day and there's plenty of food to last for three or four days. Then go for Mrs. Romero."

John saddled a horse and started down the river. On a sudden impulse he returned. He found his mother clinging to the door in agony.

August 5, 1869, Samuel Dawson Jones, with John as his mother's only attendant, was born. He registered a husky remonstrance against his discomfort and surroundings.

"Strong little devil! Kicks like a steer!"

"I know," said his mother.

"Listen to him yell. Reg'lar damn Apache!"

"John, such language!"

"You used some yourself, Mother."

"I was praying."

"Did a little myself," her son admitted, sheepishly.

"Don't you tell your father."

"No danger. Now, Mother, take this little kicker and go to sleep."

"Not till I've put him in The Book."

"Can't you do that in the morning?"

"I made some pokeberry ink, special. I can't sleep till I write his name. Bring me The Book."

She wrote the child's name and the date of his birth.

"I had the other children christened, all but Tom. There aren't any preachers out here, and I think the good Lord will understand."

"This boy'd better mind you, Mother. If he don't I'll spank his bottom harder than I did tonight. I know now what Pa meant when he said you are always right. Now, go to sleep."

•   •   •

Heiskell returned enthusiastic about moving. There was a John Bolton in the commissary at Fort Stanton, an Irishman who had been working for the army. He was a civilian in the sutler's department. He told Heiskell the army needed a man to butcher the cattle and distribute the beef to the Indians. The work was too much for one man, and they would give Jim a job too. That meant Heiskell and Jim's being away from home Friday night each week. And it would leave them five days for farming.

Barbara asked why the Indians could not butcher their own beef.

"The government figgers they waste the meat. It don't last no time."

"Probably because they aren't given enough. Who ever heard of an Indian's wasting anything?"

Heiskell replied that the Indians, accustomed to hunting, thought that an animal should be run before being killed. They thought the blood drained better, and that consequently the meat was better. Then, too, with a disinterested person to kill and divide the beef, families would share equitably. The animals were to be killed Friday and the meat distributed Saturday. Those in charge thought the Apaches would have food enough to last a week. They would not, Heiskell said, because when they have food they gorge. Then they starve till they get more.

They were supposed to get other food — flour, beans, sugar, and coffee. But he doubted that they knew how to use such things.

"They eat anything I give them," Barbara said.

Because she realized that her husband felt the job offered him a steady source of income and, therefore, was best for the family, Barbara acquiesced to the move. It would be good to have cash each month and be able to buy some of the things so badly needed. And home, she reflected, is where one can do best. It would be very wrong to let her husband know how badly she disliked having to move again.

The work was to be done at Fort Stanton, but there was no place there for civilians to live. At the mouth of Eagle Creek there was an old adobe, just one large room, but it was in a canyon, sheltered from the wind. There was good water, good soil, and plenty of wood. Mexican families in the vicinity would help build another room. Heiskell and Jim could go immediately to prepare for the moving.

There was good range at Eagle Creek. John might not consider it equal to that on the Hondo, but it was adequate. He might wish to look it over before moving the cattle. But John had other plans. He had decided to remain where he was. The family could go, but his place was with the home and the cattle. If his father preferred the Ruidoso, well, he could have it. John would keep the Hondo place for his own.

Barbara could not help but approve John's decision as she talked it over with him.

"I'm a man now, Mother."

She nodded.

"And it's time for me to get a start. I'll look after all the cattle except your milk cows, and you decide how many I should have for caring for them."

Barbara regretted the necessity for the separation, but she understood the boy's attitude. She could make his clothes, visit him occasionally, and keep in close touch with him. He had good neighbors. And he reminded her that Magoosh 'Migo might visit him occasionally.

There was a growing market for cattle. One could not sell directly to the fort but to the man who had the contract to supply the beef.

Also herds were being driven to Kansas, and steers could be sent with someone going to the terminal of the railroad. Men were driving up the Pecos to Sumner and then northeast to the railroad. Running cattle would eventually be profitable; it was already promising.

Heiskell had reversed his opinion concerning cattle, and the boys were delighted. Jim wished to stay with John, but his father could not do the butchering without help. Heiskell suggested that they buy cattle with the money paid to Jim, and take them to John for grazing. There was not much danger of Apaches stealing them, for they preferred the meat of horses and mules to beef. Deer about Fort Stanton had been ruthlessly killed by the soldiers, just for sport. It had therefore become almost impossible for an Indian to secure venison with bow and arrow. The Apaches were not permitted to have arms and ammunition, though secretly many did have them, and they could no longer leave the vicinity of the fort to hunt buffalo.

Heiskell explained to his wife that the government would not let the Apaches have guns.

"They could kill turkeys."

"They don't eat turkeys — not many don't. 'Migo says it's because turkeys eat snakes, and Apaches have a horror of snakes."

Again Barbara Jones stayed in her old home until the new one was ready for occupancy. Then the family took up its abode on Eagle Creek, and with them went the milk cows, oxen, some of the saddle horses, and the meager store of household equipment. The cattle and the small remuda were kept at Picacho for John.

"Good thing we work oxen," said Heiskell, "for the Apaches don't bother to take them."

"I've gentled a horse for Mother," said John. "She can put the side saddle on him and ride down to see me."

"I'll do that," said Barbara, "just as soon as I get the house in order. I can carry Sammie on a pillow."

"And you can ride over to Fort Stanton with me and Jim some time, Miss Barbara. Be lots more comfortable than riding in a wagon. The trail up Devil's Canyon is rough," Heiskell said.

"You say we'll have neighbors on the Ruidoso?"

"Some fine Mexican families and lots of Indians."

"They won't bother us," said Barbara, stoutly. "We've trusted them and treated them well. The Book says if we treat others as we'd like to be treated, we'll be all right. And you see it works."

"Reckon our six-shooters have anything to do with it?" John asked.

"They may," replied Barbara, honestly. "But I really believe that your friendship with Magoosh has helped more."

"But my being a good shot is part of it," insisted John. "No Apache respects a coward. Magoosh likes you too, Mother, not only because you healed his leg but because he knew you weren't afraid of him."

On the Ruidoso they found the neighbors friendly and hospitable. They dropped in on weekends when Heiskell and Jim rode up Eagle Creek and over the divide to Fort Stanton. They looked in while father and son butchered the beef and prepared it for distribution Saturday morning. The two days' work provided a little cash, and five days at home enabled them to put in a crop and cultivate it. Barbara began to plan carefully for the purchases she could make at La Placita — they were calling it Lincoln now.

As night drew near without either Heiskell or the older boys, she was sometimes apprehensive. But she was determined not to communicate her fears to the children. Bill was the man of the house now that the others were away. As she cooked their supper she sang to create an atmosphere of confidence she did not feel.

Bill dragged the rifle from its pegs and loaded it. At seven a boy should not be handling a gun; yet he had to learn to shoot sometime. Very reluctantly Barbara had acceded to her husband's insistence upon her becoming a good shot. And she knew that the younger boys must learn also.

Jim returned with plans for trapping turkeys. Wild ones abounded in the canyon. They gobbled on the hillside above the house. There was a well-defined trail by which they came to water. Jim studied the terrain until he found what he considered a suitable spot for a trap. He dug a rectangular hole four feet long and constructed a cover of strong boughs with a trap door in the center.

The birds could jump from the bottom of the pit to a shelf upon which corn was scattered. Jim concealed the evidence of his work as well as he could. Up the trail he strewed grains of corn. The turkeys had to pass between a tree and a boulder to reach the water — or make a new path.

For several mornings the boys failed to catch anything, though the corn disappeared. Eventually they were rewarded with three birds. Jim released the old gobbler and dressed the hens.

"I'll make cornbread dressing," his mother promised, "and one turkey is enough for us. Would you like to ride over to the Sedillos and take the other to them?"

From that time on they baited the trap only when they needed meat.

"I don't for the life of me see why they don't get out," said Barbara. "They could, easily. When the greedy things jump up on that shelf they stay there."

Jim replied, "Now if we could just figure out a way to kill deer without wasting bullets!"

"How'll I ever be a good shot without using bullets?" inquired Bill.

"You'll have to use some, but be very saving with them."

•   •   •

Few days passed without someone riding in with a gift of corn, chilis, or meat. Barbara shared her precious stock of garden seed with her neighbors, and gave freely from her medicines. In return she received herbs and healing-lore known to the Spanish-speaking people, and also more understanding of their customs and their problems.

The Mexicans lived in perpetual fear of their hereditary enemies, the Mescaleros. And they could not understand the lack of apprehension the Jones family displayed. If a woman went to the river for water she watched for Indians. No man went to his field unarmed. Where they lived in close proximity to neighbors, as most of them did, one stood guard while the others worked. No shepherd moved his flock without danger of a surprise attack.

It was quite an experience for Barbara to learn more about the lives of her neighbors. One day, with Minnie behind her sidesaddle, and Sammie on a pillow, she rode to the *chosa* of one of her neighbors. Almost immediately a sudden storm came up. Menacing, copper-colored clouds swept over the range. She quickly took the children, left the *chosa*, and prepared to mount her horse.

"*Peligroso* — dangerous —" warned Juanita. "Do not go till the storm is over. You could be killed. Stay! I will stop it."

Juanita returned to the house, took a handful of salt from a pottery jar, and advanced into the path of the approaching hail as though repelling an enemy. From the hills came the terrific roar of crashing ice pellets as they struck trees and rocks. Juanita threw pinches of salt into the wind. She muttered strange words. Barbara overtook her and attempted to pull her toward the house. Juanita shook her head and jerked loose. A hundred yards ahead the hail battered the earth.

"It's going to hit us. Come!" Barbara said.

Juanita stood her ground with Barbara beside her. Suddenly the wall of hail stones changed its course and passed the *chosa*. It raced down the Ruidoso, missing them by yards.

"There's no more danger. Now, you see!"

"I see; but I do not understand."

"I turn it. You see."

As Barbara's mount picked its way home through pieces of ice as big as baseballs, she marveled at what had occurred. Of course miracles happen; hadn't they often intervened in her behalf? But they had come in answer to prayer, and Juanita hadn't prayed. Her mutterings had seemed more like those of sorcery than supplication. There was something very queer about it, something she had better not mention to her husband or sons. And Juanita had cautioned her not to tell the *padre*.

"Is there a church here?" Barbara had asked.

"*Si*; but a very small one. Some time we will have a *padre* all the time and build a large one."

Barbara had not previously known of the church's existence. And as for judging Juanita's act, this was not Barbara's way. As Americans, these people had the privilege of worshipping as they chose. Nor would she tell anyone what she had seen. Many things were best left untold anyway. Hadn't her mother always told her that there should be an eleventh commandment, "Thou shalt not blab!"

Shortly after Barbara had returned home, she heard a slight noise outside the door. She opened it to find an Indian woman with her baby in a cradle on her back. The woman turned slowly, and Barbara saw that the child was ill. When the mother removed the strap from her forehead and eased the *tsach* — cradleboard — to the floor, Barbara laid a hand on the baby's forehead. It was hot and dry. She wrapped the baby in a clean blanket and sat down by the fire.

"*Muy enfermo!*" she said to the mother.

The woman nodded and touched the child's chest. Barbara placed the child in the mother's arms and set about making an onion poultice. The baby made no sound. Though the mother moaned faintly, she did not protest when Barbara placed the warm poultice on the little chest. When offered food the mother shook her head. Barbara fed her own family and put the younger children to bed. Then she prepared a tea for the sick child, but the mother would not permit the baby to take it. Through the long night Barbara renewed the warm applications from time to time. If she could only talk to the woman, make her understand! Pneumonia was usually fatal, and especially in high altitudes. Would this woman realize that Barbara was doing all she could to save her baby? Might she not hold Barbara responsible if the child died? It did not matter; she must do all she could, and pray for the recovery. When she prayed she saw that the Apache woman also was praying. She pointed upward and the mother nodded.

Toward evening beads of perspiration appeared on the child's forehead. Its temperature was reduced, and it slept. Barbara felt that the crisis had passed and that the baby might live. The mother recognized the change, and she accepted the food that was offered.

Barbara kept her patient three days. During that time she taught the mother to substitute cloth for the grass in which the baby was wrapped. It had never occurred to her that the Indians had no cloth. Their babies were placed on a layer of soft, fine grass, covered with another layer, and bound in their cradles with strips of velvety buckskin. To bathe them, the mothers warmed water in their mouths and let it trickle over the little bodies. Barbara offered some of her meager store of clothing, but the Indian woman shook her head.

• • •

In February, 1871, another son was born to the Jones family and named Frank Heiskell. He lay in a hand-made cradle, hauled from Virginia, and, as babies do, he slept much. When he was a few days days old the Apache woman returned, with her child asleep in its *tsach* on her back. In her hands she carried another cradle. She proudly presented it to Barbara, and with it she gave fine, soft grass wrapped in a skin.

The cradle was beautifully made. It was built on a strong frame of hickory, soaked and bent to form a graceful arch to be used for lifting or hanging. Several inches below the arch, a little structure, woven of willow, jutted out to serve as a protection against rain, light, or falling objects. It, too, was covered with buckskin. There was a foot support of wood, moveable in order to be adjusted to growth. Along the sides of the frame, soft folds of buckskin were attached with perforations for lacing the baby in safely. The child's arms could be confined or left free. From the shade above the head dangled ornaments made of beads with which he could play when he reached toward them.

The cradle could be carried on the back, supported by a strap across the forehead or chest, or it could be laid flat. It could be hung from a limb or saddle horn, or leaned against a support.

Barbara thought how very convenient it would be when she rode, for it would leave her hands free for rein and rifle.

From then on, she had frequent calls to aid the sick. The Apaches came secretly, or so she thought, but Apaches did everything so quietly it was hard to judge. Barbara learned that the Apaches called her *Gouyen* — Wise Woman — and she felt she must not fail them. If she should lose a patient they might attribute the death to intention. Though some patients administered to by their own medicine men died, this was interpreted as the will of *Ussen* — God — but it might be different with Barbara. It was a risk she must take, regardless of consequences. And she must learn their language. Both John and Jim could talk with Apaches, and she must learn.

"They do have many plants and herbs beneficial for the ailments for which they give them," the doctor at Fort Stanton told Heiskell. "Before they had contact with the white man they just didn't have much sickness. There were no colds, no children's diseases, no social diseases. Among other blessings of civilization, so called, they got smallpox from the Mexicans and other diseases from the soldiers. Before, like animals, they had died of age or violence."

"Does the doctor at Fort Stanton take care of the Indians?"

"Scouts, maybe, if they will let him. There are some scouts at the fort."

"Does he attend births?"

"An army doctor? Heavens, no! No Indian woman would permit that; they take care of each other. They know almost nothing of cleanliness; but they seem to be little the worse off for that. Still, it's a wonder the babies don't all die."

"When do you suppose the Apaches will have doctors and care?" Barbara asked her husband.

"We haven't had them, either, Miss Barbara."

"No. But I know how to take care of us. And you're a good nurse, Heiskell."

"We've never lost one of our children. That's because of you."

"The soldiers kill Indian babies," said Jim. "I saw one take a baby by the heels and crack its head on a wagon wheel — just because it cried."

Heiskell frowned at the boy, but the story was out.

"Why would anybody do such a terrible thing?" asked Barbara.

"Oh, they're just Indians; soldiers don't think they're human."

"God help those poor people. It's a shame and disgrace to people who claim to be Christian and civilized that they permit such things."

"People forget that the Apaches are just returning a little of the terrible treatment they've undergone for a long time. So long as they weren't molested they didn't kill white people, but when mistreated they retaliated in kind. And, like the people in the Old Testament, they believe in revenge. Their customs require that if a member of the family is killed, another member must avenge that death."

The Issue House

5

When Heiskell Jones and Jim first assumed the responsibility of butchering beef and issuing the meat to the Apaches, no other food was being furnished the Mescaleros, who were in pitiful condition owing to soldiers having killed off the deer about Fort Stanton. Without game the Apaches lacked clothing and coverings for tepees. Accustomed as they had been to spending the winters in Mexico where it was warm, they now suffered excessively from cold. So distressing was their plight that even the agent was moved to ask that blankets be given them.

The situation that confronted Heiskell was difficult. His ability to understand a few words of the Apache language was of great value to him. The Indians had been promised that if they would remain near the fort and make no trouble they would be fed and clothed. They had scrupulously kept their part of the agreement; but, as frequently happened, the government had not. When the first cattle were brought in, they were given chase and shot with arrows. The supply of beef was quickly exhausted, and the Indians were half-starved before more was provided.

An order went out requiring each individual to present himself at the fort to be counted and recorded. They went in, expecting food.

HEISKELL JONES, *emigrant to New Mexico from Virginia, had promised his wife Barbara when they came west that never again would he engage in fighting. The Lincoln County War found Heiskell compelled by this vow to carry on everyday life while his sons were active participants in the bitter and dangerous conflict.*

They received none but were told that thereafter one member of each family might come each Saturday and be given meat for his group. Because not all had come to register, the aged, the ill, and the wary found no provision made for them.

Heiskell sensed the friction existing between the post commander and the civilian agent. Their animosity did not contribute to the security of his position. He debated warning Jim as to the hazards confronting them and found that the boy already had a definite understanding of conditions.

They left home before daylight Friday morning and rode up Devil's Canyon, over the ridge, and down to Fort Stanton. They found a bunch of thin, scrawny steers in the corral. They butchered them and cut the meat into portions, so as to give each family some of the more desirable cuts.

"We'll be as fair as we can. Try to give each bunch some of the tender meat, and some of the brains. They need brains to tan hides. They'll soon catch on that we're not playing any favorites."

Jim nodded.

"And, remember, no matter what happens, we'll stand hitched. If once we show the white feather, we're finished."

"I know."

"It may not be easy," warned his father.

Again Jim nodded.

"When I watered the horses at the Bonito yesterday I saw Magoosh. He'd spent the night with John. He told me what to do. When he comes through the line tomorrow we are not to recognize him, but he'll be there in case anything happens. I feel a lot better since talking to him. It beats all how he likes John. But it's lucky for us that he does, for he can be of help in case of trouble."

The line formed and started toward the crude tables upon which lay piles of meat. The trader arranged the Apaches in alphabetical order, provided each with his ration ticket showing the number for whom he was to draw food, and gave its duplicate to Heiskell Jones. Distribution proceeded smoothly until a brave attempted to take two portions. Heiskell reached across the table and drew the second one from under his arm. The Apache whirled and looked him steadily in the eye for a long time. Then he walked away without making further effort to take more than his allotted share.

Heiskell and Jim had left their six-shooters in the office and had no arms other than the knives in their belts. The end of the line appeared before another effort was made to take an unfair amount of meat. The Apache passed Heiskell and stopped opposite Jim to reach for a second portion.

"No!" said the boy preemptorily.

The word may not have been intelligible, but the intention was. The boy's hand dropped to his knife, the Indian's hand to his belt. A long pause ensued before the Apache dropped his eyes and went on. The next in line patted Jim's shoulder and said in Spanish, "Good boy! Good boy!"

The sun was setting as father and son mounted and started home.

"It pays to stand your ground, just as John said. If we get in a jackpot again we'll try it; there's nothing we can do but try. If we don't, we might as well give up the job now. If they bluff us just once we're through."

"I know it, Pa, and I was scared to death."

"So was I. But I really think the worst is over. Let's not mention this at home, Jim. No use worrying your mother."

"She thinks all we need do is be kind to them."

"In a way she's right. We were kind today. If we had let one take more than his share somebody would have gone without. As it is, the two are angry, but they respect us. No matter who you deal with, respect is the foundation of friendship. That's true of all relationships. That's what your mother says," he finished lamely.

"Sounds just like her."

They rode in silence for some time.

"Would you have fought him, Jim?"

"Don't know, Pa. Didn't have time to think."

They arrived late at the *chosa* on Eagle Creek, weary and hungry. To their surprise no supper awaited them. Barbara was making swift preparations for it but they could see that it might be an hour or more before the meal was ready. They asked no questions but went about the evening work. When the meal was served there was an awkward atmosphere, very unusual in the household. They ate in silence. When they had finished Tom announced, "They was 'Paches here today."

"Was? Men?"

"Yes," said Barbara, shortly. "I took the children and went to the turkey trap. When we returned two Mescaleros were bending over the hearth. They had upset the kettle of stew on it and were picking out and eating the bits of meat. That's why supper was late."

"They bother you?"

"No."

She went hurriedly about clearing the table. Heiskell knew she was disturbed, but he asked no questions. He got out the ox yoke he was finishing and went to work on it by the firelight. Barbara took her knitting, and they worked in silence for some time. Several times he considered questioning her but decided against doing so. When she told the younger boys to go to bed, he said to them, "Go on — the Indians won't bother you."

"No. Mother won't let them. Today she ranned them out of the house with the ax."

"You didn't, never!"

Barbara nodded and burst into tears.

"I'm mighty proud of you, Miss Barbara. You did exactly right. They'll never do anything like that again — not any of them. The word'll get around."

"After all I've said to the boys," she sobbed, "I don't know why I did such a terrible thing."

"It was exactly the right thing. They'll respect you for defending yourself."

Barbara wiped her eyes.

"If you don't want them to come in, all you got to do is lean a stick across the door. That's their way of tellin' people they're not wanted. No stick — come in! But they won't bother you again. I'm sure of that."

His prediction was verified both at home and at the fort. On Issue Day a man put a hand on Heiskell's shoulder and said, "Good man! Good woman! Good woman, *mucha brava!*" Then he laughed, took his meat, and left.

•   •   •

Thereafter no Indian entered Barbara's home uninvited. Those who came did not rap, for they thought that impolite. They stood in silence until noticed and bidden enter. She offered food to each, as she did to every other individual who came. She spoke a few words of their language and asked names of objects so that she might increase her Apache vocabulary. Her attempts at learning their tongue pleased them; and they never laughed at her efforts.

Once she noticed sly smiles and meaningful glances at the ax by the fireplace, but she gave no indication of having seen them.

Barbara bought buckskin from the women and paid them in food. From the skins she made jackets and gloves. Her workmanship was good. She used sinew instead of thread, and it wore well. When the men in the valley saw the garments that Heiskell and Jim had, they asked Mrs. Jones to make similar ones for them. There were said to be few along the Ruidoso who did not have garments of her making.

Heiskell was equally industrious. In the evenings, as Barbara sewed, he whittled out the pieces of his ox yokes and scraped them smooth. With a long bolt heated in the embers he burned holes for the bows. They were of hickory and six feet long. He carefully rounded the ends. Then he passed the piece through the hot ashes until it would bend easily. He shaped and tied it. When it was cold it retained the curve made to go under the neck of the ox.

No member of the family was idle. The boys and Minnie sewed carpet rags to be woven into rugs by their Mexican neighbors. They kept and used every scrap of cloth large enough to be used in piecing quilts. They picked burrs from wool, to be used for mattresses, and this was an almost endless task. By the time one mattress was completed, those in use needed refurbishing because the wool had matted and had to be pulled apart to restore its resiliency.

Barbara followed the lead of the Mexican women in gathering herbs for medicine and plants for dyes. Black walnuts grew wild, and the hulls made excellent coloring. She learned other sources of dye, bought unbleached muslin by the bolt, and colored it to suit her purpose.

The only people Barbara really feared were the soldiers at Fort Stanton. The officers often stopped for meals and she welcomed them. Had the Negroes come she would have fed them at the back door as she had in Virginia. Sometimes they passed the house, but not once did she see one dismount. Nor did she hear of their having molested any woman, either Mexican or white. But when she asked Heiskell how the enlisted men treated the Apache women, he was evasive. It was not until a girl fell against her door that Barbara understood the terrible indignities the Apache women suffered at the hands of the soldiers.

She drew the frightened girl inside, bolted the door, and got her Winchester. The girl, when she was able to speak, explained reluctantly that she had been on her way to get medicine from Mrs. Jones. She had slipped quietly through the bushes, kept hidden as well as she could, and watched for dust that might indicate a rider. Within two hundred yards of the house she was sighted. She slid down a bank that a horse could not descend. A man — a white *Capitán* — had followed.

"And he did not catch you?"

"Yes, he did. But I use this. It is all we have."

She drew a buckskin bag from beneath her skirt, a bag containing sand. It was this, Barbara learned, that the resolutely chaste Apache women used in an extremity. Discovering the trick, the *Capitán* had kicked and beaten her.

Barbara threw open the door and looked up and down the canyon, but could see nothing of the officer.

Heiskell told her that, of all women, the Mescaleros were considered the most chaste. Officers who had been on duty at the Bosque Redondo, including Major Lawrence G. Murphy, testified to Washington in his official report that he considered them so. And to think that such a disgraceful attempt should be made by an officer, and at her very door!

She got the medicine wanted by the girl, saddled her horse, and with her rifle across her arm and the Indian girl mounted behind her, returned the child to her people.

Heiskell rarely made the trip to Fort Stanton in the wagon because the trail was almost impassable. It was steep, winding, and rocky. When he had to haul back supplies he took Bill with him and let the Apache women keep him overnight. When he did not give his permission, Bill ran away and went to the tepees. This occasioned Heiskell and Jim little concern for they knew the child would be cared for and returned in the morning.

When they went to the corral at dawn to begin their work they found a Mescalero examining tracks in it. "Big Mouth," murmured Jim. They joined him. The cattle were gone. No tracks of horses were found. The thieves had worn moccasins, and had driven the cattle to the river, and then down it for some distance. Big Mouth pointed to the tracks, some of which toed in, but the most of which were like those made by a white man. "*Indah* [white man]!" he said. And Heiskell agreed. The thieves had worn moccasins to throw suspicion upon the Apaches. Heiskell reported the matter both to the post commander and the trader, but neither seemed to attach much importance to it. He began to wonder if one or both were not aware of the disappearance of the herd, or even responsible for it.

The supply of beef ordinarily issued was sufficient for about three days. That week the Indians received nothing. Beef was supplied by John Chisum on the Pecos, and if a message were sent to him he could not get a herd to the fort before the coming week. Hunger had no chance against regulations, and if a few Indians starved, what was the difference?

"Couldn't they have been given meal or flour?" asked Barbara. "Some time ago they promised to issue sugar, flour, meal, and coffee."

"When did the government ever keep its promise to the Indians?"

She shook her head.

"Could it be it's been sent and they didn't get it?"

"Could. But it's dangerous to say so, even if we could prove it; and we can't. Nobody's going to go into court and tell it. I get mighty disgusted sometimes. Even think about quitting. But if I do they'd put somebody in my place who'd steal the beef, too. I wouldn't be helpin' the Apaches any; I might even make it harder for them."

It was ten days after the theft that more steers were put into the corral. Heiskell wanted to butcher them that day and feed the hungry, but he was not permitted to begin the task till Friday. When he began shooting the animals, there was not a steer in the corral that had either ears or tails. The Apaches had promised not to kill the animals, but had made no commitments as to appendages.

Why had not the Indians butchered enough beef to stay their hunger? They had given their word, and they had kept it.

When would the white people begin keeping theirs?

Smallpox   6

John came for one of his infrequent visits, and his mother washed clothing and bedding, baked bread, and prepared for his return to the Hondo. As John was putting his gear on a pack horse, a stranger rode up and hailed the Jones home. Barbara invited him to get down and have breakfast.

"Cain't, I reckon, Ma'am. Come by to tell you they's a fambly down on the Hondo with smallpox. Newcomers. They're all down, and if they don't git some help they're goin' to die. Not many folks ever gits over smallpox."

"I'll go. My husband's at Fort Stanton, but he'll be home by noon. I won't wait for him. Who are these people?"

"Don't know their name, but I can tell you where to find 'em."

"Mother," John protested, "you can't go down there. Smallpox is almost certain death. I'll go."

"You'll stay here with the children. This is going to take an experienced nurse — or two of them. Saddle my horse while I pack some clothes for the baby and get some medicine ready to carry with me."

"But you can't go, Mother!"

"How would you feel if it were us and nobody came to take care of us?"

45

"You don't even know who they are."

"They're people, and they're in distress. Must I saddle my horse myself?"

Reluctantly the boy obeyed. When he led her mount to the door she was ready with Frank in his *tsach* on her back. John filled her saddle bags with the supplies she had collected, helped her to mount, and handed up her Winchester.

"I won't need it," she told him.

"There's queer doin's down the Rio," he said. " Better take it."

"You stay here with the children. When your father gets home, see that he eats before he comes. Put this pile of bedding and clothes in the wagon — those boards, too. Get the hammer, saw, and some nails. We may need them. Then load the bedding on top."

Mrs. Jones went on, "And don't worry about the cattle. The Romeros will look out for them till you get back."

The boy did not reply.

She stooped and kissed him. "I have no choice, John."

She rode down the Ruidoso and turned east at the Hondo. When she reached the stricken family she tied her horse to a tree and hung the cradle on a limb. The messenger had not exaggerated the need for help. The family was bedfast, and some of them were very ill. She filled the big black kettle in the yard and built a fire. She cut beef into small pieces and put it to simmer in the fireplace. One by one she bathed the patients and changed the beds.

When Heiskell arrived at sunset the broth was done and he helped her give food to those who could take it. When they had finished their own supper he told her to bathe and change her clothing. She was to go to sleep on a pile of blankets in the wagon.

"Not till I've hung the clothes out. I've washed and boiled them and the bedding."

"I'll do that. You take care of the baby and both of you get some sleep. No tellin' how bad you'll be needed tomorrow."

"Will you call if you need me in the night?"

"I will."

"And don't stay in the house, Heiskell. Leave all the doors open and stay outside. Fresh air may keep us from getting it."

That terrible siege on the Hondo always seemed unreal to Barbara Jones. There were days and nights when neither she nor Heiskell slept more than a few minutes at a time. The big kettle required much wood to keep hot water available. They were constantly washing clothing and bedding. They handled both with a stick.

Before the end of the week Heiskell made three crude coffins and dug one wide grave. The mother was not conscious of the death of her children, and for that they were thankful. Barbara prepared the bodies for burial and repeated the Lord's Prayer beside the graves as Heiskell filled it.

Ten days passed before the parents were sufficiently recovered to be told of their loss. That, Barbara Jones felt, was the most difficult of all the tasks they performed. When they thought it safe to leave the family, they returned to their home on Eagle Creek.

When Heiskell went to the fort he found that the Indians had learned of the illness in the country and had fled to the mountains.

"What will they do? Where will they go? How will they get food?" Barbara asked.

"Nobody knows. But anything's better than smallpox. They learned that at the Bosque. The cavalry was afraid that if the Indians continued to camp up the Bonito they'd get it, and they'd pollute the water supply. I suspect they ordered the Apaches to leave — just to get out, go anywhere — the further away the better. But, of course, they'll report that the Indians ran out on them."

"They promised to stay on the reservation."

"But nobody knows where the lines are. None have ever been designated. The Indians won't go far because of their promise. When this scare is over the cavalry will round them up and drive them back. Where they'll put 'em I don't know. They say the old camp is too dirty to risk their being there."

"Dirty! The soil of the earth isn't dirt! It's white people who are unclean with their diseases. Things that can't be seen are much more dangerous than the soil. Why the Apaches never had smallpox before the white people came!" Barbara was scornful.

Hart

7

When John visited the family he sometimes took Jim's place at the Issue House so that his younger brother could hunt. Except when necessity caused him to kill game, John cared nothing for hunting. But Jim liked it and liked going with the Apaches and learning their methods. When Barbara questioned John he was evasive.

"But there must be some reason you dislike hunting."

"When we need meat I kill to satisfy our hunger. But I can't stand seeing an animal wounded and left to suffer. I try to hit a vital spot so that it dies quickly. If you'd ever followed a wounded deer and had it look at you with its big soft eyes you'd understand."

"I do. I never take a turkey from the trap without dreading to kill it. But we have to have food."

"A bullet's a merciful thing. I'd much rather die of one than of sickness. I'd hate to lie and suffer and be a lot of trouble to you. I'd hate to be a care to anybody."

The boy was so earnest that Barbara suspected that there was something behind his words. She knew that if he wished her to know of it, he'd tell her, so she asked no questions. That evening she seated herself before the log fire with her knitting, and he threw himself at her feet and stretched out on the buffalo skin. She waited.

"There's a white boy out in the *rinconada* [hiding place]."

48

"How do you know?"

"Saw him. I was ropin' wild horses with Magoosh."

"Well?"

"I've got to get that boy, Mother."

"What will Magoosh do?"

"I don't know. He's my friend, but whether he'll let anyone interfere with anything that concerns the tribe, I don't know."

"And if he won't?"

"I must try, anyway. To go against the orders of the chief is a serious thing to Apaches. I just hope he doesn't give orders."

"How do you know this boy is white? Couldn't he be a half-breed?"

"There just aren't any 'breeds'."

"Is it possible that a white boy is held without the agency knowing about it?"

"The less the agent knows, the better it suits the Apaches."

"John, they're worked up over not getting the food they were promised. It's not the time to risk antagonizing them."

"This has to be done. I've considered everything, Mother. I just have no choice in the matter."

"If Magoosh doesn't support you it means death."

"That's a chance I must take."

"What will you do with this boy?"

"Take him to the Hondo with me."

"You'll do no such thing. If you get him you'll bring him home. I'll look after him. Anyway, why can't the cavalry do this? What are they for, anyway?"

"You know the answer, Mother. The Indians know what the cavalry is going to do a week before they know themselves. They couldn't get the boy, anyway. And I may not, either."

"This just isn't your responsibility."

"If it were one of us, wouldn't you want someone to rescue him from the Indians?"

"That's different."

John smiled up at her but did not answer.

"When will you be back?"

"When I get him. Give me five days. If I don't return by that time, don't let Pa nor Jim follow. If I can't get him there's no chance that anybody else can."

"Then we'd better go to bed, John. I'll get up early and pack some food for you. You mustn't risk building a fire on the mountain."

• • •

Barbara Jones lay awake. She told herself that she needed strength for the ordeal ahead, and that she must sleep. It was late before she did. She was awakened by the good odors of bacon and coffee. How she appreciated John's getting breakfast when he was at home! And how he enjoyed doing it!

Barbara got the food she'd intended for John to take with him. She drank coffee while John ate his breakfast. No mention was made of his mission until he mounted his horse.

"How do you know he'll come with you?"

"That's another chance I must take."

"He may not even be white; suppose he's Mexican?"

"With light hair and blue eyes?"

"Even so —"

"I have to do it, Mother." He leaned and kissed her.

She went about her household tasks as usual. When she had thoroughly cleaned the house, she bathed the children.

"Going to boil us, too?" asked Bill.

"It might help," she said, "but this kettle of water isn't for you. I'm going to make some dye. Get those walnut hulls and put them in it. I've been intending to color some of that last bolt of cloth your father got."

"What you goin' to make?"

"Some dresses for Minnie and me."

She worked early and late, feverishly pacing the floor with her knitting when she could find no other task to perform. If she could only become sufficiently exhausted to sleep! Five days!

Three days had passed when toward midnight Barbara heard a horse approaching — John's! It was coming very slowly. Was Magoosh bringing his body? She ran out into the dark.

"It's all right, Mother. And here's Hart."

A slender form beside John shrank back.

"Come inside."

"Just as soon as I've unsaddled and fed my horse."

"Now!"

He dropped the reins and led the strange boy inside. "This is Hart, Mother."

She extended her hand, but the boy shrank from her. He held up his arm, with the palm toward her. Through dirty buckskin she could see muscles quivering. Her heart went out to the frightened lad.

"Hart, *bueno!* I'm glad you're here. John, you can't know how thankful I am."

"So am I. Now, I'll look after my horse. Hart will follow me. Don't try to stop him. I'll bring him back."

She filled plates and placed them on the table. John took them and seated himself before the fire. Hart dropped beside him. Barbara shuddered at the obvious hunger of the lad and at the way he wolfed his food. She refilled his plate and tried not to watch him.

"Any trouble, John?"

"Not a bit. I didn't even see an Indian, but I felt their presence all about me. Hart came willingly. Once he understood what I wanted, he made no objection. We camped one night — then we rode out, slowly. We didn't even look back. I didn't want them to know that I was scared."

"Magoosh?"

"Nobody else would have been able to do it. I didn't see him, but I knew he'd given orders, or I'd never have got away. I just hope they don't hold it against him. He's a real friend."

"You must get to bed, but first you must have baths. I'll get soap and towels. When you're finished you'd better sleep here before the fire. You'll probably have to wash him as you did 'Migo."

The boy patted his chest and said, "Hart."

"That's his name, Mother."

"His real name?"

"I don't know. He calls himself Hart."

"He's quick. What'll we do with him tonight?"

"I'll bring my bedroll in for him."

"But he must have a bath."

"I've already shared my blankets with him; another night won't make any difference. Tomorrow I'll try to get him to wash. I'm pretty tired, for I haven't slept much since I left."

How John managed to get Hart to submit to a bath, Barbara never knew. She left them with hot water and lye soap; when she returned Hart was wearing some of Jim's clothes, his face was shining, and his hair was clean. He was, as John said, unmistakably white. His skin was tanned but light under his clothes. His eyes were blue. She could hardly believe that such a transformation could have been effected by a bath and a change of clothing. A stranger might easily think him a member of the family.

"His hair, John?"

"No lice, Mother. I looked. Magoosh doesn't have any either. No Indian does till he gets them from the soldiers."

•   •   •

Hart was gentle and unobtrusive about the house. He picked up words and phrases easily. He watched and imitated John in everything he did. When John used a fork, Hart watched closely. He was clumsy, but he never attempted to use his fingers when a fork would serve. He was gentle with small children and helped them. When Barbara spoke he invariably answered, "Yes, Ma'am."

"Thinks Ma'am's your name, Mother."

When John left for the Hondo without him, the boy was obviously distressed. He pointed down the canyon inquiringly. Barbara shook her head. She tried to explain that John would return, but she could not make him understand. Gradually he responded to her kindness and overcame his shyness. He endured the romping of the little boys patiently and became the self-appointed guardian of Minnie.

"Never heard of an Apache molesting a white woman or girl," said Heiskell. "Their deviltry takes other forms. Still — he's white. Can't tell what he'll do."

"Hart wouldn't harm anybody. He's the most modest person I ever saw. He wouldn't undress in John's presence. We need have no worry about him. In fact I'll feel much better for having him here when the others start to school."

"School!" Heiskell looked at his wife in amazement. "What in 'tarnation are you talkin' about, Miss Barbara?"

"There's a school at Lincoln Town. It's not a free school — you have to pay the teacher. I've meant to talk to you about it. We could take the children over in the wagon Monday morning and see about starting them. After that Jim could do the driving four days a week. I could go Friday morning when you leave for the Issue House."

"Got it all figgered out?"

"Well, don't you think it would be a good thing?"

"Reckon so. We generally pull together, don't we?"

"Yes. That's why we get along so well."

"Who's teaching this school?"

"A young Mexican that Major Murphy had educated; sent him to a college somewhere. The man's name is Saturnino Baca."

"I hate to send our boys and not Hart. But until he learns more English it wouldn't help him much."

"The worst trouble is that it's such a long way to Lincoln — twenty miles by wagon road through Hondo. If we could take the horse trail over the mountains it's about seven."

When the plan was announced to the children it was met with significant silence. They sat and looked protestingly at their mother. Finally Jim spoke, "Sure glad I'm too old to go."

"But you're not too old; you're not but fifteen and you're to go."

"You wouldn't make John go."

"If he were here we'd want him to have the same chance as the rest. I've always been sorry John didn't get an education."

"He's getting an education," said Heiskell. "He's getting the kind a man needs in this country if he wants to stay alive and get along. He has friends among Indians and Mexicans. He's the best shot in the country. He knows cattle and horses. What more does a man need to know?"

"Those things are necessary; but the boys need reading, writing, and ciphering. I'd like for them to know history and geography. Times are changing. Just look how much money those officers at Fort Stanton make. And the traders —"

"If I thought book learnin' would make our boys like them I'd be sorry to see 'em get it."

"Education is a good tool. Like a knife or gun, it can be used for good or for bad. Everybody needs good tools."

•   •   •

Long before daylight the next morning Heiskell set out with the small children huddled under a buffalo robe in the back of the wagon. He and Jim shivered on the seat with a huge basket of turkey and fried pies at their feet. His errand at the school accomplished, Heiskell went to the Murphy-Dolan store to purchase supplies. He declined the owners' invitation to lunch and ate at the Patrón home. At four o'clock he stopped at the school to collect the children.

"But, Señor, they are gone. They left shortly after you did. I tried to keep them, but they would go. They took their food and left."

When Heiskell got home after dark the children were all asleep. They had taken the short-cut over the mountain, with Tom on Jim's shoulders. At the summit they stopped to eat. Jim selected that spot because the trail was visible from both directions, thus affording safety from surprise.

Heiskell asked Barbara what they were to do.

"If they can walk home they can walk to school. But we can go against nature just so far. It seems we've reached the limit with Jim. And the little ones can't go alone; Bill's too small to protect them."

"I know you're disappointed, and I'm sorry."

"We'll do the best we can to teach them at home. I just hope that in future years they're not handicapped by our failure to send them to school."

"Maybe I should lick 'em. I got so many beatings when I was a boy that I left home the first chance I got. I don't want our boys to feel as I did. My father said the proper way to raise children was with a bed slat, and frequent. Could be he was right —"

"I don't know, Heiskell. I can't feel that way. But I want so much to do what's right for them that if you think whipping will help we'll do it."

"There might be things that call for it, but I don't figger that this does. Take Jim, now; it would be hard to find a better boy."

"What do you call a good boy?"

"Well, for one thing, if he's sent after a horse he comes back with the horse. He's good help at the Issue House. He can look at a steer and tell within ten pounds of what it will weigh. That's more'n the scales at the fort can do. Maybe he'll get along in the world without much book learnin'."

"I'll continue to do all I can at home. Even Tom can read a little."

There was no further discussion of school till John came for a visit. Ash Upson, he said, was back on the Hondo, living with the Caseys, and teaching their children to read.

"I'd like to see Mr. Upson. Of course I couldn't ask him to come here if he's teaching another family; but I do wish we could find someone to live with us and help educate us."

John interrupted her to say, "I'll tell him. When he gets all their liquor drunk up maybe he'll move in with you. We wouldn't have to pay him anything, just keep him in whiskey."

"He used to say he liked it too well."

"That's once he told the truth," said John. "He don't exactly lie — he just stretches everything."

Hart's delight at seeing John was both amusing and annoying. Barbara told her son so. "He's never seen you but a few times, and I've worked months trying to civilize him."

"He loves you, Mother. He follows you about like a dog."

"I don't want him to act like a dog. I want him to be like the rest of you boys."

"He's learning fast."

"While you are at home, try to find something about his people. I can't talk Apache well enough to understand what he tries to tell me."

Hart knew little about his early life. He remembered vaguely wagons and white faces, an attack, and the burning of the wagons. He remembered horrible shrieking and being carried on a horse. Then came an Indian camp where a woman had taken him to her tepee and been kind to him; he remembered her death and then another Indian mother. He had been obedient and had been treated kindly.

When there was food he shared equally with other children; when there was none he had gone hungry. All Indian children were obedient, and all were treated kindly. None were ever beaten.

There were hardships necessary for survival to which all were subjected. A child's crying might betray their hiding place and endanger all. A hand placed over the mouth prevented that and Indian babies learned early to keep quiet. Apaches were used to being hunted like wild animals, and they learned the importance of silence.

Both boys and girls were taught to run long distances with burdens on their backs and water in their mouths. When they returned to the starting point they were required to spit the water on the ground; thus they learned to breathe properly. Speed and endurance were essential to preservation. They broke the ice and waded across streams. They went long hours without food. But none of these things seemed unreasonable to Hart, though he did dislike the long wait in hiding for game. The Mescaleros surpassed him in that, and also in trailing. Barbara thought his ability to track little short of miraculous. She was amused, and a little repulsed, when Hart scented a garment to identify its owner. But when Sammie ran away, as he frequently did, she was grateful when Hart sniffed about, looked for tracks, and invariably found the child.

When John embraced his mother Hart pushed gently between them.

"My Ma'am," he said.

"My Ma'am," the boy repeated. "My Sir, too?"

"Your Pa Jones, too, Hart. You're our boy now and we love you."

"See, Mother? It's you he loves best."

Because Hart addressed Barbara as "Ma'am," others started using the term. Neither Heiskell nor John like hearing comparative strangers use what they considered a familiar address, but Barbara realized that there was no intentional disrespect, and she permitted it. She had a gentle dignity that inspired respect.

Hart was her faithful attendant. Knowing how the Apaches regarded women's work, she did not require his help about the house; but he offered it. Her sons might not keep the wood box filled, but Hart did. He carried water. He anticipated her needs in many ways that she appreciated. And she was unfailingly patient and kind to the boy.

He disliked bathing except in the river in summer. For that matter so did her own children. And perhaps for the same reason they disliked Sundays, which she insisted be observed by cleanliness and religious study. From Barbara Jones' point of view the odor of sanctity was closely allied to that of soap. When she faced a row of faces to instruct them upon Biblical subjects she expected them to be scrubbed and shining. Perhaps that was asking too much of any growing boy, but she felt it an obligation she must not shirk.

Rumblings

8

Barbara spent the night with a Mexican family and delivered a baby. It was a difficult case and she was weary. When her horse stopped at the door, John came to lift her from the saddle and welcome her home. He introduced a dark, handsome young man who took the name from her son's lips, "Marion Turner, Ma'am."

She responded courteously but did not offer her hand. She entered the house and took the chair Hart offered. As she sank into it John brought coffee. Hart put her bonnet on its peg, and dropped to the floor beside her. "My Ma'am," he said, "My Ma'am."

"Yes, Hart."

"And mine?" asked Turner.

"That remains to be seen," she replied, curtly. Then, regretting her abruptness she added, "Meanwhile you're welcome."

That assurance came so late that John was obviously puzzled. "I've been making him at home, Mother; made him wash the dishes."

There was an awkward silence which John broke by asking, "How is Mrs. Sánchez?"

"All right; at least she is so far."

"Bull or heifer?" asked Turner.

There was no reply. Barbara stood and spoke to John as though there was no one else in existence. "I see you've had your breakfast. Take the children out of doors for awhile. I'm very tired. I'll have a bath and lie down. Call me in an hour."

That evening John spoke to his father of the occurrence, and especially of his mother's attitude.

"That was no way for a man to talk before a lady. It's bothered you, but I don't see that it's had any effect on Turner."

"She doesn't like him."

"Your mother's as good a judge of men and hosses as I ever saw. Never knew her to be fooled on a hoss, and just once on a man. Lucky thing for me she was. If she don't like this one it's because there's something wrong with him. I hope he don't stay."

He did not. While he remained the atmosphere was strained, although Turner seemed unperturbed by it. He did most of the talking, and Barbara admitted to herself that he was adroit in his attempt to rectify his mistake. Never again did he offend her with coarseness. In fact, she could not complain of his behavior in any respect. He had better manners than most of the men who stopped at the house, but she could not rid herself of her instinctive distrust. She hoped he would not accompany John to the Hondo. What his business was nobody could ask, of course — nor his destination. It was with great relief that she saw him ride away alone.

The next arrival afforded the family much pleasure. Lib Rainbolt rode in to spend the night. The family was delighted.

"Did you move to the Hondo, Mr. Rainbolt, as you planned?"

"We did. And we're very happy there. Several of my kin came, too. We've been there three months now. And like you told me, Ma'am, we found good neighbors."

"You brought good neighbors, I'll be bound."

"We tried to."

"And you're there to stay?"

"I hope so. My uncle and one brother went over to the Feliz and built a little house for a horse camp. They're stayin' up there. And there's been a "rep" from the Circle W stayin' with them."

"A rep?"

"That's what the cowboys call a man who represents an outfit."

"I see."

"This is a right clever man, but pretty old. Tex must be all of forty-five. Some folks think he's on the dodge, but then they think that about all us Tejanos — that's Texans, Ma'am."

Barbara wondered if Marion Turner were a Tejano.

"The Rangers has been makin' it hot for hoss an' cow thieves.

It's gettin' so that stealin' cows is serious, now that they's a sale for them. Lots of rustlers has been hittin' for these mountains, they say. They's been some killin's, and a lot of stealin'. Rustlers can do 'most anything and blame it on the Apaches. As long as a man has a hoss and ammunition he can hide out in this country for years and not get caught up with. So far nobody's bothered us except to leave a jaded hoss and ride off on a fresh one. That don't matter much, for when it's turned loose it comes back home."

"Nobody will take one of ours," said John.

A glance from his mother silenced him.

"This man stayin' with my uncle is still much of a man for his years. One mornin' Tex saw four men comin' over the hill. He could tell by the way they rode they was give out. He sent Bill after the remuda, thinkin' to get shut of them. Then he started breakfast cookin'. Time they rode up he had meat fryin' and coffee boilin'. They got down and commenced overhaulin' their saddles. He howdyed and asked them in to eat.

" 'Got any horses?' they asked.

" 'Down the canyon; boy's wranglin' them.'

"They turned their mounts in the trap and et. As they come out Bill brought in the remuda, not knowin' they was anybody there. He tried to turn 'em back, but they went on into the trap. They was a fine black that he tried to keep out, but he was too late.

"Tex tole them to take their pick 'ceptin' that black, on account that's Aunt Becky's mount, and she takes a sight o' pride in him. They didn't say nothin' but he suspicioned what they aimed to do.

" 'Hang yore line on the black,' the leader said.

"Now, this here Tex ain't no outlaw, but they don't nobody step on his toes.

" 'That's my hoss!' the leader said.

"Tex stated meaningfully, 'I'll shoot any man that throws a rope on him.'

"The leader made his loop; the hoss came 'round in a swing and ran his head through it. Tex shot, and covered the others.

" 'Now you climb yore hosses and git!'

"They did. Then Tex told my brother, 'You saddle that black an' lope over to Picacho. Tell 'em what happened. If they's a law there I reckon you better bring him.'

"Bill reported it to Jim and Ed Rainbolt. They went to see Juan Chávez, the *alcalde,* and a good one. He listened. 'You don't need no law,' he said. 'You just dig a hole and roll him in.'

"Us Rainbolts hated it on Tex's account. If he wasn't already on the dodge he would be, unless this man he killed was an outlaw hisself. Nobody wants no breshes with the law."

"Where's this Tex now?" asked John.

"Back with his outfit, I reckon."

"Did you have any idea who the men were?"

"They's a Ranger on the Hondo lookin' for Johnny Ringo. Some thought he might have been one of them."

When Lib Rainbolt left, John rode with him. Not until they were gone did Barbara mention Marion Turner. "I'm sorry that young man ever came here."

"I noticed you didn't like him."

"I didn't. I can't tell you how I know there's something wrong, for I don't understand it myself. I just know. It wasn't his vulgar speech alone. I don't know what tells me, but whatever it is I dare not disregard it. I had this feeling so strange that it frightened me."

"How can you be sure without proof, Miss Barbara?"

"That's what I ask myself. I can't explain it, nor how I got it; but it's a warning not to be disregarded."

"If I hadn't seen it happen many times before I might question it. Whatever tells you has the right answer, and that's all that counts."

"I was afraid you'd think me foolish."

"I'd never think that, even if one of these warnings fail."

"That's good of you, Heiskell."

"But don't worry. Turner may never come back."

"I'm afraid we haven't seen the last of him."

•   •   •

That summer there was an influx of horsemen and wagons to the Hondo and Ruidoso valleys. Wagons crawled up the divide and slid down into the valley of the Tularosa. Rumors of trouble over homesteads and water rights came to the Jones family. The Indians were restless, for the coming of the emigrants meant encroachments upon their land, the boundaries of which nobody knew. They claimed the land from the Río Grande to the Pecos, and they bitterly resented being deprived of the river valleys.

Hart explained, "This is all Mescalero land to both rivers; but the soldiers say just a little bit ours. They make Apaches camp close to Fort Stanton when they leave the Bosque Redondo. And they promise meat, but don't give much. Not for long time till Pa Jones come, do we have meat. They promise blankets, but not any. After a while a few — not many, not good. Promise many things; do nothing. Then the *Nantan* [chief] say, 'You got to move back on the Tularosa

or somewhere 'way from the Fort. It don't matter if white people
there already. It all your land. Go 'way — you make water bad for
soldiers.'

"Three chiefs go to the Fort; talk to the *Nantan*. Natzili and
Gregorio go — he Medicine Man, too. Román Grande go. They make
talk. Soldiers tell us to pick out our place anywhere away from the
fort because they don't want Indians camping on the Rio Bonito. If
they do somebody be sick."

Hart went on to explain that Gregorio began gathering his men
and continued until they were assembled for a council. He told them
the cause of their coming together and the necessity of their selecting
another home. He reminded them that on the Hondo and Bonito there
were many deer, and that both river valleys were theirs, or had been
until the white people took the farm land along the rivers and pushed
off the real owners.

Then Natzili, the Buffalo Chief, spoke. He reminded the Apaches
that they might take refuge in the Guadalupes and on the Pecos. Good
land was available there as well as on the Peñasco. The Sacramentos,
too, belonged to the Apaches. The agent had said that they were
eventually to have all their land taken from them by the Great White
Father. But Natzili thought the white people wanted it for themselves. In fact, every place the Indians suggested using as a home
was now occupied by white people.

Román Grande spoke last. He told the previous speakers that
they should make their own decisions, but as for him and his band
he preferred remaining on the slopes of the Sierra Blanca. It belonged
to the Mescaleros, and there they should stay. There were also other
advantages. Both the north and south forks of the Ruidoso were good
hunting grounds. The western slope of the great mountain was well
watered and had good grass. Living near the Mexican settlement at
Tularosa was not ideal, but anything was better than living near the
soldiers.

Román Grande had decided upon the Tularosa for his band. Now
that the Apaches had established trade with the people there, they
could exchange skins and jerked meat for ammunition and blankets,
as well as for corn and beans. The Mexicans would sometimes take
game and skins in barter, too.

The Apaches agreed that Natzili's idea was good. When he
reminded them that there was no mescal in that area, they recognized
that he had not withheld the disadvantages. He continued to recite
the abundance of good water and of wood. If they went to the Pecos,
he said, they would soon consume the supply of wood. The older
people would not live much longer, but their children and grand-

children would face the certainty of an exhausted supply of fuel. Soon they would have only twigs, and then weed stalks to burn.

Besides, all knew the taste and effect of Pecos water. To those accustomed to drinking water from the melting snows, the prospect was very unpleasant.

But how about Dr. Blazer? He owned the mill and some land on the Tularosa. Would he be permitted to stay?

Natzili reminded them that Dr. Blazer had been a friend to the Apaches. When they were hungry, he had fed them. When they were cold he had taken them into his store and seated them before the fire. He had even given blankets to those who had nothing to trade.

Like Heiskell and his sons, Dr. Blazer had treated them as men. They — Blazer and Heiskell — were unlike other white men who lied to the Apaches and stole from them. Let them stay. What had become of the food and clothing sent to them by the Great White Father? Had not the agents stolen those things and sold them for money?

•   •   •

But even on the Tularosa, some of the Apaches were dissatisfied and wished to go to Mexico. Before the coming of the white man, they had always migrated with the seasons, spending the summers in the mountains of New Mexico. After they had killed enough deer in the fall to supply dried meat and skins for the year, they had mounted their horses and gone south to the warm lands, not stopping until they reached a place of mild winters and an abundance of fruit and other foods.

They were determined to go again.

But they had no horses and few guns. And they must take everything and everybody. What about the aged and helpless? The infants and children? The supplies they had so laboriously acquired?

They must not do anything to excite the suspicion of the cavalry. Things must be secretly packed and prepared. On the eve of their departure, men must remain in camp to keep fires burning until the encumbered people could, on foot, get a good start. Once across the line in Mexico they could get horses, as they had always done.

They slipped away in the dark, taking care to separate into small groups so that if one were overtaken the others might escape. One old woman, entrusted with a group of children, camped under an overhanging rock ledge and built a fire where it might not be seen. She had very little food but cooked a small amount and gave each child just a few bites. Though they wanted more they did not ask for it. They were Apaches. Nor did they talk, for they had been taught the dangers of being overheard. They noticed that the woman did not eat. They saw that she took her blanket from about her shoulders and motioned for them to lie down beside the dying fire. She warned them, then, that they must not protest, for if they did "the soldiers might find them and chop their necks off." Cold and hungry they huddled together till morning. They could not awaken the grandmother who had given her life for them.

On the fourth day the soldiers found them, rounded them up like cattle and drove them back to Fort Stanton. They overtook the braves and told them it was best for them to return to the fort. Natzili replied that there was no place on earth left for the Apaches. There was, Natzili said, nothing left for them to do but die.

The soldiers promised the chiefs that if they would return to Fort Stanton the troops would protect them, and they agreed to do so. They promised the Indians that a wagon would await their arrival at Three Rivers with food. Though the Mescaleros were hungry, they were refused anything to eat until they reported at the appointed place. That was one occasion upon which the promise of a white man proved good. When the starving people got within sight of the wagons the women and children began running toward them, but the men had too much dignity to do so. Though they were almost starved, they did not quicken their pace. When they arrived the food was being distributed to the non-combatants — beef, bread, and coffee.

The weary Indians, having gorged, lay down and slept. Then they followed the cavalry and wagons to Carrizozo, turned east to Nogal Canyon, climbed over the divide, and struggled on through the snow to Fort Stanton. On the way a baby died. A sick boy fell and was put into a wagon. Upon their arrival at the fort the mother found him dead.

Big Mouth was a very young man at the time. He had been old enough to ride a horse when the Mescaleros were taken to Fort Sumner, and he had escaped when they fled unceremoniously from that hated place. He had attempted to influence his people to return to Fort Stanton, but he was poorly rewarded for his advice. The captives were given some beef upon arrival, but the next consignment of cattle was missing from the corral when the Apaches went for them. The Indians were accused of stealing them but suspected that the cattle had been sold by the trader and that he had pocketed the money.

Again they were cold and hungry. They had neither horses, food, nor arms for making a second attempt to get to Mexico, and they settled into the apathy of the hopeless.

Complications *9*

Heiskell Jones hoped that the change in the personnel at the agency might be beneficial, but he soon saw that, if anything, conditions were worse. The conflict between the military and civilian authorities was nearing a break, thereby increasing the miseries of the Apaches. By the time both were satisfied, little was left for the Indians for whose benefit, presumably, the agency was maintained. Godfroy wrote repeatedly to Washington and requested a change of location. At last he was permitted to rent an office from Dr. Blazer, on the Tularosa, to serve as his headquarters.

"I think things will be better now," said Heiskell, "but it's too far for us to go every week. Looks like we'll have to move again."

"Do you think Dr. Blazer would rent or sell us a house near the mill?"

"He don't have room enough for his employees. But there's a house I can get, a little adobe, by Dowlin's Mill on the Ruidoso. 'Bout twenty miles from it to Blazer's."

"Still a long trip."

"Only place I can find."

"Then we'll go there."

"Got a chance to sell this place. Met a Tejano over to Lincoln,

64

name of Horrell. He wants to buy. I told him I'd talk it over with you and let him know. He'll be at the agency tomorrow for his answer. He'll pay a fair price, and if we let him have possession at once he'll throw in a wagon."

"We don't really need another wagon, but if one of the boys marries, he will."

"Marries!"

"Yes. Heiskell, do you realize that the only white girls our boys have ever seen are Minnie and Mr. Godfroy's niece who came to the Mescalero Reservation to teach school?"

"There's Mexican girls."

"And Apaches." Barbara added. "Both make good wives and mothers. As far as character is concerned there are few women as chaste as the Apaches. Many of the Mexicans, are, too. The boys could do worse."

"John's but seventeen!"

"I married before I was seventeen," replied his wife.

"I know. But a man is different. I was twenty-two. Besides, I don't know about the boys marrying Mexicans."

"Nearly all the men of the California Column did. And from my point of view their wives are much too good for them."

"You're right about that. 'Cordin' to my tell they're a bad lot. Some of 'em's been kicked out at the fort. They've already built a store at Lincoln; got the lumber from Blazer's Mill. And I reckon they're cheatin' an' stealin' from people there like they did at the fort. They're runnin' the Mexicans out by gettin' them in debt and takin' their land for failure to pay on the date due. Given a little more time to sell their cattle or hay, the Mexicans might have been able to meet their obligations. Oh, they're taking it legal, but it's dishonest just the same. Nobody else to buy from. Charge things for a year, but at the store's price. And sell at the store's price, too. Don't keep no accounts. The Mexicans are trustin' people, and honest. At the end of the year they're always in debt. Bad off as slaves."

"If there were another store that treated people right, would it pay?"

"Bound to."

"We might put in a little stock of goods at Dowlin's — or has he got one?"

"Did have. But he don't have time to run it. Might be glad to sell us his stuff — a little food, clothes, tobacco, ammunition, and whiskey — mostly whiskey."

"I wouldn't like selling whiskey."

"No. But men won't go a long ways to trade unless they can get it. Whiskey and ammunition they're goin' to have."

"You'll trade with Mr. Horrell, then?"

"Looks like the best thing I can do. And we'll move right away. Have to if we're going."

•   •   •

A few days later at Dowlin's Mill Barbara recorded the birth of another son. She wrote the date in the Bible but left a blank space for the name. She had not sufficient energy to decide upon one. She lay and looked with distaste upon the dirty, crumbling walls of the adobe room. Of one thing she was sure: just as soon as she could, she would collect limestone on the mountain, bake it as she had seen Juanita do, pulverize it on her *metate* and make paint for those walls. Then she'd clean the *vigas* (beams) and level the dirt floor. With a shovel heated in the fireplace, she'd smooth the floor. There was nothing more attractive and cozy than an adobe house kept in good condition. And there was nothing warmer in winter and cooler in summer.

She'd finish the exterior, too, when the boys got through digging the bullets out of the walls. They had enough lead on hand to melt down for bullets for months to come.

"I'm sorry I can't get your meals," she told the boys, "but you are all good cooks. I never tasted better baked potatoes or beef stew than you prepared last night. When I get up I'll make you some dried-apple pies. If your little brother is a good boy like the rest of you, I'll have much for which to be thankful. He will be another strong twig for the bundle."

"And a good citizen?" asked Bill.

"Above all, a good citizen."

When the little citizen was three weeks old Barbara had transformed the dingy little building. When two strangers rode in and sought hospitality she was proud of her home, but she apologized for being unable to ask them to sleep in the house because of the size of the family. She told them of a little vacant house nearby that they might occupy. Food was not a problem — they must take their meals with her.

"We can do our own cookin'," they protested. "Old cowboy — used to doin' it. I'm Charlie Siringo and he's Charlie Nebo. You got any chores to do while we're here we'd admire to do 'em for you."

After eating one of Barbara's good meals they made no more

protests, but appeared regularly for food. They gave no intimation as to their business or the length of their stay, and no one asked.

"What you goin' to call this fine boy?"

"I haven't decided, and I must. He's in the Book, all but his name. I just haven't found one that we like."

"Why don't you call him Charlie? We'd both be plumb proud to have a namesake."

"Then make it Charles Nebo," said the other. "The Nebo'll be for me. You'd think Siringo is the only Charlie in the world to hear him talk."

"Charles Nebo is a big name for a little tyke like this," said Jim. "We'll just call him Nib, for short."

When John came to see his new brother, the strangers were still at the mill. Barbara told him that she cooked for them but that they repaid her many times by doing the work outside.

"Wonder how long they intend to stay?"

"I have no idea. We can't ask things like that."

"There's supposed to be some detectives snoopin' around huntin' for cattle thieves. It could be these men."

"Well, even if it were, it doesn't concern us."

"Not unless they're spyin' on our friends. If they'd come out and say they are I could have some respect for them; but if they're detectives sneakin' around tryin' to get people into trouble, I can't."

"People who get into trouble have only themselves to blame, John."

He shook his head.

Just then Sammie burst into the house and shouted. "Come, quick, Ma'am. Ben Havens got his arm cut off in the saw."

John started for Fort Stanton to get a doctor, Hart kept the baby, and Barbara hurried to the mill.

"Ain't you goin' to put his arm back on?" Sammie asked.

Barbara shook her head. She administered first aid as well as she could, and when the doctor arrived she had her patient lying flat with the stump of his arm elevated, and a tourniquet controlling the bleeding. She watched the treatment of the arteries and the dressing of the wound. The doctor gave her instructions as to the man's care.

"You did a right good job, Ma'am. I could use a good nurse like you at the fort."

"I don't know of anything I'd rather do than work with a doctor. Though I don't suppose any woman ever was one, I'd have liked to be a doctor."

"You'd make a good one."

"I never miss a chance to learn what I can. It's remarkable that all people seem to have remedies; even the Apaches have taught me many things. They use herbs that really help. I've found that some of their remedies are good."

"Really?" The doctor seemed surprised.

"Yes. And the Mexican women have some effective medicines. You'll think it funny, but I learned from them that a moulded bread poultice is more healing than one made from fresh bread."

"How 'bout them usin' sheep marble tea for the babies?" asked Heiskell.

"I don't approve of that, of course." Barbara said.

"And that awful mess they gave the boy with lung fever?"

"That just happened, I think. The boy was very sick and I thought it impossible for him to recover. His mother insisted on using her remedy, and who was I to object? She gave him cockroach tea each half hour, and he recovered."

•   •   •

A few days later a tall man and three cowboys stopped at the mill overnight. Mrs. Jones fed them. When they were ready to leave, the tall stranger praised the food and insisted upon paying for it. Mrs. Jones was indignant. The stranger reminded her that she accepted money for uncooked food. What was the difference? Many people would be eating her meals — people willing and glad to pay. At Lincoln, he told her, people paid for their needs, and willingly.

"But so much of our food costs nothing."

"Nothing?"

"Well, we raise the beef, and we shoot the deer and turkeys. We raise corn and have it without buying it."

He placed some money on the table and left.

"Know who that was?" asked Sammie. Without waiting for an answer, he said, "That was John Chisum."

"How do you know?"

"They threw a herd in Carrizo Creek. Had the Long Rail brand and the Jinglebob ears."

"How do you know to whom they belong?"

"I asked one of the men."

Sammie overhead more news. He brought the rumor that Major Murphy was forced to leave Fort Stanton and the trader's store because of his dishonesty. When questioned, Heiskell Jones made no reply. The following day he cautioned Barbara about listening to idle tales. But she had no hesitancy about listening when strangers at her table discussed Marion Turner.

One said, "He's been swingin' a pretty wide loop, and he's gettin' off too easy."

As the food was placed before them the conversation ceased. Barbara asked if they'd heard of a stage line to be in operation soon from Puerto de Luna to Lincoln.

"Yes, Ma'am, reg'lar route up the Hondo to Lincoln. Lots of folks comin' into the country."

"May come here."

"Won't bother you for breakfast, Ma'am. Leavin' early."

"I'm always up. Come over for breakfast before you leave."

"If you'll let us pay."

"Never in my life have I charged anybody for a meal or for spending the night!"

Now Barbara felt that her intuition regarding Marion Turner had not been unjust. Shootings were sometimes justifiable, but these men said Turner had killed a Mexican just to see him kick! And now, the story was, he'd tried to elope with Mr. Godfroy's niece. They'd ridden all night, but it was said that the agent had caught up with them at daybreak and brought the girl back home. It might also be true, as she had heard, that he worked with Murphy and Dolan to steal from the Indians. But Barbara thought it more likely that he didn't share the ill-gotten gains.

Jim had known about Turner's actions, and he thoroughly disapproved of them. John's liking Turner was hard to understand.

It was gratifying to know that Jim was usually on the right side of whatever problem he faced. He had been present when the treaty was made with the Mescaleros, guaranteeing them their land about Fort Stanton, if the federal government ever ceased using it. He had, in fact, had a remarkable lot of experience. Barbara realized that it was good to have a son as honorable and dependable as hers.

The Hunt   10

Barbara fed every traveler who came, and there were many. One evening as she prepared supper two men sat before the fireplace talking. There was, they said, a new agent at Mescalero. Godfroy had been permitted to resign. These men estimated that he had sold over ten thousand dollars worth of merchandise intended for the Apaches.

"How about the new one?" asked Heiskell.

"It's plain he don't like soldiers," one of the strangers said. "If he's honest he may do well, but it don't seem like an honest man has any place in the Indian Service. I sometimes think that if I were an Apache I'd glory in every wagon train I ever ambushed and every white man I sent to the hereafter."

"I hear that the Apaches staked them out over ant hills," said the other.

"If we'd been treated as they have we might have done as bad."

Heiskell saw that Barbara was disturbed, and he interrupted to tell her that some of the Apaches had passes to go to the Guadalupes hunting, and they had asked if Jim might go with them.

"How long will they be away?"

"The pass is for two weeks; they'll probably stay that long. But if they kill enough game before the time is up, they'll come back sooner. They've always taken good care of Bill when I let them take him for the night."

"Bill never told me that he spent the night with the Apaches."

"Beatin'est thing the way that boy holds his tongue; he's like an Indian. I wish Sammie would get some of it."

Barbara went on, "You know that Jim always thinks John gets the best of everything because we leave him at the Hondo. Jim says there's no excitement at the mill. And you know how that boy loves to hunt."

She asked Heiskell, "Will Magoosh go?"

"I don't know, but whoever does will take care of Jim. He can take care of hisself, for that matter."

"When do they leave?"

"Day after tomorrow. They won't start out afore daylight. You know how they are about the dark."

"I'll bake some bread for him to take along. They'll have meat. And I'll send coffee and sugar; they never have enough. How many are going?"

" 'Bout forty. Twenty men got passes, and I figure they'll take that many women. Better count on fifty, because some children will go too. The way they like your bread they'll eat a lot."

Barbara made ten loaves of light bread, using the starter with which she baked biscuit. She also baked two floursacks of the sourdough biscuit her family liked. The Indian women would make fried bread, but all would enjoy her contribution.

Jim carried the food on a packhorse. He was the first to reach the feast ground where they were to assemble. They went through Elk Canyon toward the Pecos. At noon they ate handfuls of jerked venison and pulverized mesquite beans, but did not stop traveling.

The halt came at sunset, and the men went down to the little stream to hunt. They killed two deer, which the women dressed and brought to camp. When the fire had burned down to coals, they put pieces of venison on to cook. Jim proudly produced his biscuits, and every one was eaten.

During the night he became violently ill, and the next day the Apaches remained in camp. A woman hunted through the undergrowth and returned with herbs from which she brewed a tea. The attack of dysentery was quickly relieved and the following day they resumed their journey. The meat, Jim thought, had been well cooked. Indians did not like it rare. Why should it have caused the sickness? Or had he just over-eaten?

They followed the Pecos south till they reached the foot of the Guadalupes. They rounded a point and rode to a spring (Rattlesnake Spring) which fed a small lake near the mouth of a canyon. On the ridge above, Big Mouth said, was an opening in the earth — a deep, dark hole, very deep. He said it was a forbidden place, the Abode of the Evil Ones. (Later, of course, this was to be known as Carlsbad Caverns.)

"What are the Evil Ones?"

"I cannot say. I do not know. But they live there."

"Why don't we go down into the hole and find out?"

"Those who enter that place do not return. It is a death hole. If it opens for you, you are swallowed. Only the Evil Ones come out."

"Can they be seen? What do they look like?"

"Like smoke, filled with countless tiny things, specks like birds. I have seen one; it was the scout who came first from the cave to look about and give the signal for the rest. Soon it will come from the earth and fly upward in circles, looking all around. If the scout thinks it good, the Evil Ones will follow, many as the leaves of grass, and the scout will lead them upward like smoke. And they will go to the far away."

"You have seen this?" inquired Jim.

"I have seen."

"An Apache never lies," said the white boy, "but I would like to see it myself."

"Then we wait."

"Can't we go closer?"

Big Mouth shook his head. They lay in a mescal pit on the mesa and waited. The sun sank behind the mountains in flaming glory.

"*Mire!*" Big Mouth whispered. "He comes!"

"That's just a bird," said Jim.

"Watch!"

The solitary speck mounted in spirals, going higher and higher. After an interval it was followed by others, separately at first, then in groups, until a smoke-like spiral rose above the mesa and disappeared in the distance. In fact, it was a flight of bats.

"You see!"

"Yes! Does this happen every evening?"

"Every time I am here."

"Let's go down into the cave."

"It is forbidden."

"But they're gone now — whatever they are."

"Who knows? But maybe more down there; those who go do not return."

"Have your people tried it?"

"Long time ago, maybe; not now. *Muy malo!*

"It may be bad," thought Jim, "but I'm going to try it."

When they returned to camp the Mescaleros were cutting mesquite and building fires in the pits that dotted the mesa. The women
had collected huge piles of mescal heads and were cutting vegetation
with which to line the pits. Jim watched them cut away the outside
leaves with their long sharp thorns. In the center, like a cabbage,
was the thick meaty part used for food.

When the wood had burned to coals they covered it with vegetation and placed the heads on it. A second layer of green stuff was
added. Long leaves of the plant were put in upright with the tips
projecting and could be pulled out for testing the cooking. Then the
whole was covered with earth. All night the pit was watched so that
if steam escaped, more soil could be added and tamped down. The
third day it was opened. The outer leaves of the mescal were peeled
off, revealing the pulp encrusted with a sugary coating; it had a
delicious odor. Jim found it very palatable — a pleasant change from
a meat diet.

But the work was not yet finished. The women cut the mescal
pulp into slices and put them in the sun to dry, much as they did
jerky. The huge quantity prepared would be stored for the winter, as
the meat was.

At the first indication of dawn, the men stationed themselves in
thickets encircling the lake and commanding the game trails leading
to it. Jim crouched beside Big Mouth. The women, too, placed themselves in hiding around the banks, each equipped with a piece of
red cloth fastened to a stick. Soon some antelope slipped warily down
the trail toward the water. They came in single file, and when one
had drunk and lifted its head, a red flag was gently waved. The
animal walked toward the object of its curiosity until distracted by
the motion of another bit of cloth. One after another circled the pond
to investigate. Not an arrow had been fired, and Jim's curiosity made
it almost impossible for him to keep still as he'd been asked. Were
they going to let the animals escape?

When there were perhaps a hundred of the beautiful animals
circling the lake, the arrows began to fly. One by one the animals
dropped. The slaughter continued until not one was left standing.
The men cut the animals' throats to let them bleed; then they left
the skinning and butchering to the women. Jim tallied and found
that they'd killed ninety-eight.

"Why didn't they run? They could have got away — anyway, most
of them could."

"They have much curiosity," replied Big Mouth. "Besides, they always leave the drinking hole by the path by which they approached it."

"Why?"

"I don't know; I guess because *Ussen* made them that way."

Big Mouth tried patiently to teach Jim to use an arrow as skillfully as he did a bullet, but the boy found that impossible. At close range Jim could do fairly well, but many of the warriors could shoot accurately at a hundred yards. Some could send an arrow three hundred feet, and before it fell to the ground they would have six in the air.

Oak, Big Mouth told Jim, made the best bows, but it would not hold up well with constant use. Wild mulberry, from a mountain on the reservation, was durable. Locust was strong, and bois d'arc, excellent. The Comanches used it, and Big Mouth had traded arrows for a bow made of it. Wild choke cherry, or Apache prune, Big Mouth said, was excellent for arrows. Flint was good for points, but the Apaches preferred metal. How did they get it? The rims from barrels carried on wagons — Big Mouth did not finish.

"When we hunt buffalo we ride close and aim for the kidneys. Sometimes we tie a knife to a lance and cut the cord in the leg. Then the buffalo can't run. But the agent — we can't hunt buffalo any more."

How well Jim knew!

"Once we come to this place. A man put the skin and head of a deer over him and pretend to graze among the bushes. He moved the horns as if the deer were feeding. Another hunter creased him, right across the stomach.

" 'Hey! Why you shoot me?' The man asked.

" 'Anybody shoot you; you good deer.' "

Big Mouth made his point. "If you want to be a good hunter, hide; watch for dust. Keep up wind. Be very still."

Jim did not find that easy. Like Hart, he found waiting monotonous and tiresome. When they packed the meat on horses to return to the reservation, he had not yet made a kill with bow and arrow.

Around the fire at night Jim asked for stories of the long ago and was told that summer is not the time for them. "In winter, when the snow comes, then our people sit about the fires in the tepees and the old men tell the stories. Come to us in cold weather and you may listen to their talk."

Lincoln Town   11

"I've got to go to Fort Stanton in the morning, Miss Barbara. How'd you like to take the children to Lincoln Town?"

"Very much."

"There's a man ridin' down the Hondo. He might could get word to John to meet you at Lincoln."

"Fine. And we need a few things."

"Got plenty of money for you to do the tradin'. Get what you need; get some clothes for you and Minnie. Anything else?"

"Medicine. The Indian herbs are really good for some things; but I need others. Maybe I can get them from the doctor at Stanton."

"The trips you've saved him, lookin' after his patients, he oughta give 'em to you."

"And they say Mrs. Bolton has come all the way from Ireland with her children, and that they are living at Lincoln. I've wanted to meet her since I heard that she was there. We'll camp the wagon, cook our own food, and make no trouble."

"Not in Lincoln, you won't. That town's full of our friends. Everybody on the Hondo and the Ruidoso has relatives there — and you know how the Mexicans are. If they have only one bed they give it to you and sleep on the floor. If you refuse, they're hurt."

The surgeon at Fort Stanton gave Barbara medical supplies. She drove to Lincoln where her wagon was speedily surrounded by welcoming villagers.

"Will you honor my poor dwelling, *Señora?*"

"My house is yours; stay with me."

"You see," said Juan Patrón, "you have only to choose. Every *casita* in the village is at your disposal."

"Tonight we make fiesta at the Patrón home," said a smiling woman. "It might be better for you to stay with me. I am just across the street from them."

"Mrs. Bolton may expect me."

"Her house is small; and in one room Mr. Bolton has the post office."

"And there are so many of us."

"Let me take the two older boys."

"And me the little *señorita.*"

Barbara assented, but kept the younger boys with her. Before she was settled, people thronged to welcome her. Beneath the cordial gayety she detected an undercurrent of tension. When she was left alone Mrs. Bolton came, and Barbara asked the reason for the unrest.

"It's the Horrells, Mrs. Jones. You may know of them."

"Yes. Mr. Jones sold our Eagle Creek place to one of them some time ago."

"Frank Reagan wanted that place, and he was resentful about not getting it."

"We didn't know."

"At first the Mexicans made every effort to welcome the Horrells and to be friendly. But you know how shy they are if rebuffed. These newcomers were a queer, unfriendly, clannish people. From the time of their arrival they dodged every effort at neighborliness. They kept strictly to themselves, except for their own gang."

"Are they Anglos?" asked Barbara.

"Anglos? What's that?"

"That's a term used to designate white people not of Spanish descent. I'm Dutch and you're Irish; the majority of people here are Mexican, but they dislike that name."

"The Horrells call them 'Greasers,' and they dislike that even more."

"I shouldn't wonder."

"For awhile it was a case of armed neutrality. Now it's armed hostility."

"I'm sorry to know it."

"So am I. To add to it, the Horrells act so 'biggety' that they'd be disliked, anyway. It's said they're refugees from Texas. Over near Lampasas they killed a man. Then the whole family took their cattle and left."

"That might not be held against them if they were friendly. The one unpardonable sin in this country is acting as though you thought yourself better than your neighbors."

"I like that," said Mrs. Bolton. Then she continued, "Ben Horrell rode over the mountain from Eagle Creek and got to drinking with Jack Williams and an ex-sheriff, David Warner. They became quarrelsome and objectionable. They brandished their revolvers and threatened people."

"That's not uncommon when men are drinking," Barbara commented.

"Somebody went for the officers. Three Mexican deputies came and disarmed them. They said no Mexican could arrest them. The deputies told them it was not a matter of arrest, provided they quieted down. They didn't. They got six-shooters somewhere and started in again. When the deputies returned there was a free-for-all. That's what my husband called it. Three white men and one of the officers were killed.

"The other Horrells came over and tried to have the deputies indicted for murder, but that was out of the question because the officers had acted in the line of duty. The Horrells swore revenge. They killed some Mexicans, and now almost every time a man rides in from the Hondo he brings word of a killing. They say the Horrells kill Mexicans on sight. And they threaten white men who've married Mexican girls."

"Who else is there for them to marry?" Barbara asked.

"Down at Picacho there's a good Anglo family — the Rainbolts. You might know them."

"Yes, we do."

"Near them lived a young man who was recently married to a beautiful Mexican girl. The Horrell gang broke into their home and killed them both. The Rainbolts buried the couple on the bank of the Hondo by their grandfather's grave."

"Lib Rainbolt?"

"He died last winter, of smallpox," Mrs. Bolton said.

"A week after the couple was killed," Mrs. Bolton went on, "four Mexicans from the Chisum Ranch started up the Hondo with an oxcart full of corn to be ground at the Casey Mill. At Missouri Plaza they were attacked and two of them killed. The Rainbolts hid the others and enabled them to escape. One of them told my husband that the Tejanos came, forced their way in, and searched the house. They ransacked every place up and down the Hondo looking for the men. They didn't kill anybody, but naturally it stirred up a lot of resentment. Four days later the wagon was found with the oxen still unyoked. Now the Horrells have told the white people to line up with them or leave the country. There's no staying out of it. If you're not for them, you're against them. Hadn't you known of this?"

"A little," replied Barbara. "But Heiskell and the boys may know more. Perhaps they think they're being kind by not telling me."

"The Rainbolts say they're determined not to become involved. They and some other families are quietly preparing to leave their homes and return to Texas, but they want to harvest their crops and gather their cattle first. Some of the Anglos refuse to go. Last week they sent their families to the Casey Mill for safety. A man rode in and told Ham Mills — he's sheriff now — that the Horrells had besieged the mill. He deputized a big force and rode to the rescue. The Horrells left and fortified an old adobe with very thick walls. The sheriff demanded their surrender, but they told him to go to hell. He camped and held them there two days. Then he came back to Lincoln. Now what do you think of that?"

Barbara answered evasively, "Lincoln is beautiful and you couldn't ask for better neighbors."

"Yes; what they've done for me is unbelievable."

"That's because you are a good neighbor, yourself."

Barbara expressed her fear that the tension was not over.

"I think perhaps it is. To celebrate we're having a dance tonight at Juan Patrón's. Everybody's cooking. I've baked a turkey and a cake. And it's about time to get dressed for the *baile*." Mrs. Bolton got up and started to bustle about.

"I see you're picking up some Spanish," Barbara said.

"But not as fast as my children are."

"They learn effortlessly. You should hear the jargon mine speak — mostly Apache and Spanish. They even use a little English."

•   •   •

The village consisted of adobe houses lined up along the one street. After she had changed her dress, Barbara got her knitting and sat facing the window to watch for John. If he came he would ride in from the east, and he would come if it were possible. If only he could be kept out of this trouble! He wouldn't seek a fight, but neither

would he avoid one. She thought of the sense of security she had
when he was with the family.

Not all of this feeling of security was the result of Magoosh's
friendship for them, she well knew. Part was, as John said, a tribute
to his own skill with a six-shooter. If John were here nothing could
happen. Then Barbara smiled at her own estimate of the prowess of
her son. He was one of many brave men.

Suddenly he was dismounting in the street. She ran to him
questioningly.

"Mrs. Bolton has sized the situation up correctly, Mother. But
I've never even seen one of the Horrells," he continued. "You've always
said that most of our troubles never happen. Now I'll spruce up and
take you to the *baile*. You'll be the most beautiful lady there."

"How did you know about the dance?"

"I just saw two women go into the Patrón house carrying baskets
of food."

Barbara was proud of her family's appearance. Minnie, with her
long black braids dangling over her new red dress, was beautiful.

Across the street, in gay clothing, men were assembling outside
the Patrón residence. With serapes across their left shoulders they
squatted on their heels and rolled cigarettes. Inside, a group was
tuning violins and guitars. Suddenly the men sprang to their feet.
Some drew knives, and a few brandished six-shooters.

From the west, horsemen dashed down the street. Barbara saw
no more, for John lifted her up· bodily and put her down flat on the
floor. As the boys rushed toward the window, John thrust them down
beside Barbara. There was a volley of shots, and then the noise of
departing horses.

"What is it, John?"

"The Horrells must have decided to even the score. They've
threatened to."

"They're all gone?"

"A mile away by this time."

"There's a man lying at the Patrón door. There's three! Get my
medicine bag from the bedroom."

Barbara bent over a prostrate form. "There's no pulse; he's dead."

"It's Juan Patrón's father," John said.

"This man is shot in the leg. The other one is dead."

John slit the cloth and Barbara applied a bandage to the wounded
man's leg. Meanwhile women gathered, sobbing and shrieking, about
the fallen. Barbara worked calmly while people tugged at her and
begged her to flee to the Torreón. Men lifted a wounded man. Bar-

bara examined a fourth victim, and John helped carry him, unconscious, to the tower.

"We must get fresh water from the river. There's plenty of wood. Somebody go to the Patrón house and bring the food."

Inside the tower she knelt beside the wounded man.

"Where are the children, John?"

"They're all here. Can I help you with this man?"

"Take his wife away. And get a candle."

There was blood on the man's shirt, and she examined his chest. "The bullet's gone through, but so high that I don't think it penetrated his lung. The blood doesn't look as though it had. I'll plug the wound and stop the bleeding. Get a stick and bring me a spider web."

When she had finished applying bandages she became conscious of those surrounding her.

"My father-in-law — he lies in the patio," a voice said.

"They've gone to get him," said John.

Men began checking for absentees. Only John Bolton was missing. His wife said he had gone to Fort Stanton and would not return till late.

"How late?" asked Barbara.

"He didn't say — just late."

"Now, while things are quiet perhaps we should feed the children. Perhaps everyone should eat now, in case the Horrells come back," Barbara continued. Food was distributed to the nervous refugees.

A man spoke, "The Horrells took the short-cut over the mountain. They won't return without re-enforcements. That'll give us three hours, at least. When they get back, we'll need strength. Go ahead and eat while you have a chance. And those who can sleep, might as well. This may be an all-night ordeal."

"He's right, Mother," John agreed. "It will be safe till ten-thirty or eleven. You get some rest. I'm assigned to guard the ground floor, so I'll be here with you. The women and children are to go to the second floor, and sharpshooters will be stationed on the third. See if you can get the women to go upstairs. They can help best by lying down and keeping quiet."

"Who else is to stay with you?"

"Several men, all good shots."

The wives of the dead and wounded refused to leave them, but the other women ascended the winding steps to their allotted places. There were four stories in the Torreón, the highest being the roof. The walls were very thick. There were no portholes and no windows.

The stairway was made of cedar posts tied with rawhide. The only door was of very thick wood reinforced with iron bars.

Barbara's quick ear caught the sound of hoofs; then came a pounding at the door.

"Who's there?" asked a guard.

"John Bolton. Let me in."

The heavy bolt was drawn, and Bolton entered.

"Is John Clark here?"

"Yes, he's on the upper floor."

Clark came down.

"Will you deliver a letter for me, John?" Bolton asked him.

"I'll try to."

"Then saddle your horse and come back. While you're gone I'll write it." Bolton took a pencil and scrap of paper from his pocket, squatted on his heels, and wrote a brief note. He took his Masonic ring from his finger and wrapped it in the paper.

When Clark returned, Bolton gave instructions: "Ride up the short cut and try to reach the summit before the Horrells get there. Wait for them. When they come, their horses will be winded from the climb. Hail them and give them this note and ring. I don't know that it will go any good, but there's a chance it may."

"Men," said John Bolton, "I have an explanation to make. Some of you may be Masons. The Horrells are — or at least one of them is. He came for his mail one night after we'd gone to bed. When I handed it to him he thanked me and we shook hands. He gave me the Masonic grip. Masons are pledged to help each other. For the first time in my life I'm asking for that help. The Horrells are rough men, but they might be influenced to spare us. I don't know, of course, but it's worth trying."

Señor Baca spoke for the village. "We appreciate the effort, but we must be prepared for attack. I have a list of names for guard duty. Each man is to stand guard three hours and then be relieved. We've decided to put John Jones on the top floor with the sharpshooters. If they can prevent the mob reaching the door we may be able to hold them off."

The night passed quietly. Toward morning a solitary horseman rode to the Torreón, waving a white cloth. John Clark had reached the crest before the Horrells; he waited and delivered his message. One of the Horrells struck a match, read the note, and examined the ring. He talked with his followers, and the ring was passed among them. It was then returned to Clark, and the Horrells turned back.

•   •   •

Women wept and gathered their children preparatory to returning to their homes. Men began digging graves. Crude coffins were made and the dead were buried. There was no resident priest, but prayers were said for the fallen.

Mrs. Bolton told Barbara that John Clark had come from Fort Stanton with Major Murphy when he was deposed from the commissary there. Murphy, she said, had been educated for the priesthood, but had never been ordained. Both Murphy and Clark were Masons.

After John had carried the sleeping children back to bed, he said goodbye to his mother.

"You're going? Without breakfast?"

"There'll be no more trouble. I'll just have some coffee."

"But you expected to buy supplies. Won't you have to come back?"

"Yes, I will. Perhaps I should stay. I felt that I just had to get back, but it'd be foolish to make a second trip."

She looked closely at John.

"You aren't expecting more trouble?"

"No, Mother. I really think that for awhile things will be quiet. But I must get back to look after the cattle. And you must get home as soon as you can. Don't go by the Hondo. Take the road to Fort Stanton and over the ridge."

Clouds

12

Heiskell had news of the Rainbolts. Suspecting that they might be the next victim of the Horrell's, they had left their home. Nobody who stayed on the Hondo could remain neutral, and the Rainbolts refused to become involved in the controversy. With several other families, they made up a small wagon train and began the trip back to Texas. Years later the Jones family learned the details of the flight.

When the Rainbolts got through Hondo Gap near Riverside they circled their wagons to camp. In the center they dug a hole for the women and children. Though they anticipated attack by the Horrells, it was the Apaches who followed them. At daybreak the Indians circled their camp and fired a few arrows. Why the arrows were fired, the settlers could not determine, for the Apaches had never previously molested them. The Indians may simply have wanted to intimidate the white men so they would not return.

Each morning the Indians appeared, rode around the camp a few times, and then disappeared. They maintained their vigil until the wagon train had crossed the Pecos at the Horsehead. After that they did not appear. Had they wished, they could easily have killed everybody in the train.

The settlers then felt so sure they would no longer be molested that they ceased exercising much caution.

Meanwhile the Horrells took their families to Roswell and returned to resume the conflict. Ben Turner, one of their men, was killed at Picacho. A few days later a group of Mexican freighters were waylaid and killed on the Hondo. The Casey Ranch was searched for Frank Reagan, but the Horrell party did not find him. So great was the fear of the Horrells that several more families quietly abandoned their homes and returned to Texas. After several weeks had elapsed without anyone seeing the Horrells, people gradually relaxed their vigilance and returned to their routines.

"I declare," said Barbara Jones, "I just can't believe it's the same country. People live in fear. I'm surely glad the Tejanos who caused the trouble are gone and that we have peace again. How I long for the old days before the outlaws came, when there was nobody but the Mexicans and Apaches. We were safe and happy then."

"It sure has changed," said Heiskell. "Over to Lincoln there's bills out for hundreds of outlaws. Seems like every man on the dodge makes for these mountains. Used to be a stranger's coming was something to enjoy. Now you just don't know who you're takin' in. Better be careful, Miss Barbara."

His wife assented.

Heiskell mused, "How come the 'Paches didn't kill the Rainbolts and the rest? Reckon John had anything to do with it?"

"He couldn't have, except through Magoosh. John did seem in an awful hurry to get out of Lincoln that morning. But he may not have known that those families were takin' out."

•   •   •

During that summer there was heavy westbound traffic up the Ruidoso. Settlers flocked into the valleys of all the little streams. The Mexicans, despite the abundance of timber, used adobe. The Anglos preferred logs, but bought lumber from Dowlin's Mill for doors and window casings. Some even used lumber for floors. Those who went to the mill bought other supplies, and the Jones trading post prospered.

Travelers going west made the post their stopping point. These people were the only source of news, especially from the Pecos. John Chisum had brought in great herds of cattle and eighty cowboys. He had a contract to supply reservations and military posts with beef. He considered the Pecos Valley his exclusive range. People suspected that small settlers — squatters, in Chisum's terms — may have been intimidated into leaving their claims. But proof was lacking.

A Mormon Colony had settled on the Pecos. Mexicans, too, had gone there and built little adobe houses. Now, with a few exceptions, they, too, had left. Yet John Chisum was a genial, kind sort of man, rich, but not "uppity." All who stopped at his ranch were treated well. He was friendly and sympathetic. He never carried a weapon. When a poor settler came to report the loss of his few head of cattle Mr. Chisum always promised to help recover them. But none were ever found.

When one of the Chisum herds was driven out of the country nobody dared cut it to find cattle not bearing the Long Rail brand. It was asserted that cattle of many brands were in his herd, but Chisum said he owned them and had bills of sale for them. He sometimes drove cattle to Fort Bayard or to the San Carlos Reservation, in Arizona. He had stopped once at Dowlin's.

Ma'am recalled his staying overnight. Sammie had described the brand and distinctive earmark of the cattle. The ears were split so that the outside half flapped down, leaving the other upright. It was a mark easily distinguishable in a big herd.

Some of the trail drivers came to the trading post, and with them was Marion Turner. Whether or not he was an employee of John Chisum, nobody asked. Barbara fervently hoped that he would not spend the night in her home, but he did. Turning anyone away was unthinkable. Keeping Turner there was better than having him with John. In spite of his ingratiating attitude, so irritating to her, she could not find fault with either his manner or his conversation. She rebuked herself for her previous reactions toward him, until he began criticizing John Chisum adversely.

"He claims the whole Pecos Valley. Those who left went because Ol' John had 'em run out. They's nothin' much the matter with him except he wants all the land that touches his'n."

"Are there no other ranches on the Pecos?" Barbara asked.

"Hugh Beckwith has one, down toward the mouth of Seven Rivers, but his herd is mighty little 'long side of the Jinglebobs. Everybody knows the Beckwith Ranch; it was there long before Chisum hit the Pecos. Some say Beckwith had a contract to furnish beef before Chisum began selling it to the government for the Indians and forts. Might be why Beckwith hates Ol' John. Chisum claims that Beckwith started his herd with a yoke of oxen and sold three hundred steers his first year. An' Ol' John thinks that everybody on the Pecos got his start from the Jinglebobs.

"Beckwith alleges that when a Chisum herd leaves the range it includes every critter along the way. The little fellows can't do nothin'. Chisum says all they need to start a herd is a good ropin' hoss and a lariat. He don't worry none about brands till he sells the steers, so long as he's got 'em. Changes brands then."

"Hugh Beckwith's the only man with the nerve to buck Chisum. That man ain't afeard of hell nor high water. Maybe his foreman wasn't, neither. Dick Smith got in a ruckus with the Jinglebobs, and Jim Highsaw, Chisum's range boss, killed Dick right in Beckwith's own corral when he come down there huntin' evidence that Beckwith was stealin' Chisum's cattle. Now Highsaw's on the dodge. Chisum didn't do nothin' to back him, neither. You don't ketch Ol' John protectin' nobody."

Mrs. Jones made no comment.

"Ol' John was at Cruces, and Beckwith was away, too, when the Jinglebobs pulled that raid on the Beckwith place. Beckwith's house is a reg'lar fort. Corral's got high adobe walls. The Beckwiths stood off the whole Jinglebob outfit till Smith was killed. Then they beat it into the house. Highsaw didn't find none of Ol' John's cattle, but claimed they was a pile of Jinglebob ears in the corral. But nobody believed it."

Barbara remained silent as Turner went on.

"An Ol' John didn't do a thing to help Highsaw, after him riskin' his life to pertect Chisum's property. Shows what he is. Naturally Highsaw expected his boss to back him. Ol' John's lookin' out for hisself, not his cow hands. That's why he don't carry a gun. He lets somebody else do his fightin'. And he knows nobody'd shoot an unarmed man. He's a mean old cuss."

"Does he have a family?"

"Don't know except they's talk of a niece comin' to keep house for him."

"And Mr. Beckwith?"

"He married a mighty fine lady. Real Spanish, granddaughter to old Nicolas Pino, sheep king of the Estancia Valley, up toward Santa Fe. Some say she's a niece; some say a daughter. Pino has a reg'lar hacienda there."

"Do they have children?"

"Got some mighty pretty girls and a boy or two."

Barbara arose and ended the conversation.

It was her habit to analyze situations and people after she went to bed. That night she gave fervent thanks that they had not remained on the Pecos, that Heiskell and Jim were doing well at the Issue House, that the little trading post at Dowlin's was thriving, and especially that they were so far removed from the disturbing occurrences about them. So far there had been little trouble at the mill. There had been accidents of course, the worst of which was Ben Havens' loss of an arm.

•   •   •

On Heiskell's next trip to Fort Stanton the doctor gave him a book for his wife. It was written for the laity and suggested medication obtainable at the fort. Barbara was delighted. She studied it whenever she had a few minutes for reading.

Again a Chisum herd was driven west. And again the owner insisted upon paying for the meals served to himself and his men. He told Ma'am Jones that Major Murphy and Jimmie Dolan were "coining money" at Lincoln and that everybody was beginning to charge for meals. She talked the matter over with the family. Though they did not like the idea, they did not oppose it. She reminded them that Murphy and Dolan were charging.

"They do a lot o' things I wouldn't," said Heiskell.

"What do they do?" Barbara asked.

Sammie spoke up: "They're gettin' control of the whole country. They get people in debt and take their cattle and hay. Hay's awful high; they sell it to the cavalry. The store gives the Mexicans credit and charges anything they please. They keep the people in debt all the time; and they won't let nobody else put a store in at Lincoln."

"Sammie! Where do you hear these things?"

"At the mill, and from everybody that comes along."

"Talk can be dangerous; you must never repeat these things."

"Everybody knows it, anyway. They're robbin' people just like they did at Fort Stanton. That's why they got run out."

"How long have you known these things?"

"Long as Jim has. He says when you work for a man you work for him. You don't go 'round tellin' his faults. But I'm not workin' for 'em."

She quizzed Heiskell.

"It's 'bout like Sammie says. I've seen a lot, but I keep my mouth closed. They must be some rich fella' backin' Murphy — somebody at Santa Fe, likely. If I tole, I'd lose my job. The next man to take over would rob the Indians, and they'd be worse off and so would I. The ones that's doin' the stealin' — it wouldn't bother them none."

"It's no news to me," said Barbara. For a long time I've known that the whole situation was dishonest. Now I'll know what subjects to avoid when they're mentioned."

Lightning

13

"Mr. Jones, what do you think about my riding down to the Hondo in the morning and taking some things to John? I've made him two shirts. And he needs clean bedding and some other supplies. I could take the baby and Sammie and Frank. Hart can take care of Tom and Minnie till you get back from the Issue House. And I'll be home by that time."

"Don't know 'bout you makin' that trip without one of the older boys."

"Haven't the Horrells left the country?"

"That's what's bein' told, but — "

Marion Turner interrupted with an offer to accompany her, and she could not refuse his escort. Before daylight they set out down the Río Ruidoso with Nib in his cradle on her back, Frank clinging to Turner's belt, and Sammie riding the pack horse. The water rippled over the stones, in keeping with its name — Noisy River. The world was waking as the sun's first rays lighted the tops of the mountain, but the canyon was still in darkness. Deer fled across the trail ahead of them. Birds chirped. Turkeys gobbled on the hillside. Turner slipped from his horse, dropped his reins, and disappeared in the pines; there was a shot and he returned with a fine, fat hen.

It was a long ride from Dowlin's to Picacho, and it was after dark when they arrived at the *chosa*. When John approached Barbara, his welcome obviously lacked warmth. He kissed his mother, but she sensed something she could not interpret. Sammie shrank from his kiss and John gravely shook hands with the child. "You think you're a man, Red Neck, don't you? Not till you get trousers. Shirt-tail boys are just children."

"I'll get supper as quickly as I can," Barbara said. "Brought a turkey for dinner tomorrow. I'll make cornbread tonight, enough so we'll have some left for stuffing. You give Nib something to chew on; he's cutting teeth."

"I'll unload my six-shooter; they've all cut their teeth on it."

John got a bucket and went to the Hondo for water. Turner followed him. They were gone so long that Barbara became impatient. But when they returned John was so cheerful and courteous that she forgot the coolness of the reception.

Sammie wanted to sleep with the men in a bedroll outside, but John curtly forbade that. He gave the boy a buffalo robe in front of the fire. Barbara lay in the bed in which Sammie had been born and watched the flames. She made plans for securing a farm for each of her sons — perhaps a place where they could run cattle. But she and Heiskell must have a larger house, at least four rooms, and big ones. Minnie must have her own room. A combination living, dining, and cooking room would be convenient. A bedroom for themselves would, of course, be necessary. She wanted a nice home before the older boys married and left. None of them should live in a home he didn't own, for only poor white trash did that.

John hadn't seemed very happy about their coming. Was she becoming supersensitive? Could she be getting childish at thirty-eight? And this lying awake — could it be a sign of senility? She'd always been able to sleep, and especially when exhausted. She planned to get up very early and have breakfast ready when John came in. He had done his own cooking so long that he'd enjoy her breakfast. How fortunate she was to have such a son! She was lucky, lucky . . .

John bent over her with a fragrant cup. "Coffee for my best girl! Drink this, and I'll keep Turner out till you're dressed. I've got biscuits and bacon cooking."

Before they rode out with the cattle, John told her they would return at noon. Usually he went without food till evening, but his mother was determined that he should have a good midday meal. She watched while he and Marion Turner mounted Spanish mules and rode away. She must remember to ask John why he preferred mules

JOHN JONES, *eldest of the nine sons, was a forthright defender of personal rights and a self-reliant homesteader on his own, even in his teens. Just at the age to be caught up in frontier troubles, John took part in many of the individual gun battles sparked by embittered feelings in the wake of the Lincoln County War.*

to horses. He did, she knew, for he always used them. She'd heard him say that a good horse will go till he drops, but that a mule is too intelligent for that.

She suspended the turkey over the coals. She washed the potatoes and put them aside to place in the ashes later for baking. Surely there were none better than those grown along the Ruidoso. The frijoles had been soaked overnight. She put them into a kettle to which she would add salt pork later. From a string of chiles suspended from the ceiling she took one pod, removed the seed, and put it beside the pork. She made some fried pies of dried peaches, and she used cold biscuit and cornbread for dressing. Fortunately she had onions. That afternoon she would wash John's clothing and bedding. How she loved making things clean and comfortable for her family!

And what a wonderful future lay ahead! With each of the boys owning a ranch and cattle, nothing could prevent their having a full and happy life. Tom, she reflected, might not want a herd. He had strange ideas; he was always picking up bits of stone and attempting to find the ledges from which they had been broken. He'd told her that some of them had tumbled down stream from the very peak of Sierra Blanca. Could that be true? When the little *río* was in flood it was amazing how huge boulders rolled down the bed of the stream.

She went to the door to look at the sun to determine the approximate time and saw a man riding toward the house. He was middleaged and unkempt. Few men were so careless of appearance as this one. As he approached she saw that he was unshaven and dirty.

"Howdy, Ma'am. Lookin' for John Jones."

"He'll be in for dinner in a few minutes. I'm his mother. Get down and eat with us. If you want to wash I have plenty of hot water. I'll bring a towel and soap." She set a basin on the bench outside the door. The stranger used it. Then he squatted on his heels until John and Turner rode up.

"Howdy, Riley."

"Howdy, John."

"This is Marion Turner."

"Heard of him," replied the man, shortly.

Barbara called that dinner was ready.

There was little conversation during the meal. She attended to the children first. Then she heaped food upon plates for the men. Riley ate ravenously. John arose to refill the stranger's plate and that of Turner. John himself was not eating much, and his mother was disappointed, because she had prepared some of his favorite foods. She could not restrain herself from comparing his table manners with those of Mr. Riley. And she had to admit that Marion's were not bad.

"Won't you have another fried pie?" she asked Riley.

"Don't mind if I do, Ma'am. Never tasted anything so good in my life."

"John?"

"No, thank you, Mother."

"I want some more," shouted Sammie.

"Hold on, Red Neck," his brother said. "Eat what you have on your plate first."

John poured coffee. When they had finished he thanked his mother for the meal and praised the food. Then he turned to Riley and said, "Want to finish that business now?"

"That's what I come for," replied the man, shortly.

John nodded to Turner. Marion went to Barbara, took her arm, picked Nib from the bed, and led her out the door and down the bank of the Hondo. Frank toddled at their heels, and Sammie lingered briefly at the door.

• • •

"Ten steps?" asked John. He and Riley were at the doorway of the *chosa*.

"Suits me."

"Then start counting."

Riley said nothing.

"Any other way to settle this?" asked John.

"No."

"Then start counting."

Standing back to back, they began walking away from each other, stepping and counting simultaneously. As they said "ten," each whirled and fired. John dropped his six-shooter and ran to Riley, who had fallen. He bent over the man and unbuttoned his shirt.

Riley looked up. "Oh, John, I forced this on you," he said. And he closed his eyes.

When Barbara and Marion reached them, John stood by the body sobbing. Barbara placed her fingers on Riley's wrist. She opened his shirt. There were three bullet holes over his heart, so close together that all could have been covered with a playing card.

"Do you know who this man's friends are?" she asked.

"I do," replied Turner.

"Go to them. Tell them to bring a wagon and to come unarmed. Tell them I said so."

"John, put some wood under the kettle and fill it with water. This man must be prepared for burial."

She set about packing. She sent John to round up the cattle and horses. While he was gone she bathed and dressed Riley. She attempted to put one of John's new shirts on him, but it was too small.

Her son returned with the stock.

"Mother, I'm not running. I'm going to face those men."

"We both are. Saddle the horses. Get out the old pack saddles, and get things ready to start. We're taking everything to Dowlin's."

It was almost dark when they heard the rumble of wheels. Not a word was spoken as Riley was lifted and laid in the back of the wagon. Silently Barbara offered a blanket, and silently it was accepted. The men covered the body and drove away. John stood with his hat in hand until they had gone out of sight.

"Marion, take the pack horses and start on with the children. Put the bedding on behind them. Everything's rolled and ready. I'll wrap the food and put it in the saddle bags. You'll be hungry before we reach the mill."

John lifted her to the saddle and they set out.

Flight

14

In fall of 1877, the little caravan left Dowlin's Mill, with Barbara Jones driving a team of Spanish mules to one wagon and Heiskell walking beside the oxen at the other. John, Jim, and Marion Turner drove the cattle and remuda. They wound up Carrizo Creek, over the divide, and down to Mescalero. There they stopped for Heiskell to inform the agent of his leaving.

They camped for the night at Blazer's Mill. "Hate to see you go, Heiskell," Dr. Blazer said. "You've got a good start here; you've many friends besides the Indians. There's very few white men they'll accept. Don't you think you're making a mistake?"

He waited for a reply.

"Might be. Think we'll try our luck at Tucson, though."

"You won't like that desert country, not after living here. If you decide to come back, there'll be work here for you and the boys. My family's coming out soon. I'd like them to have you for neighbors. And this place has a future, now that the Mescaleros are away from Fort Stanton. I'm doing well here, and there's no reason you shouldn't."

"You and I have never had any trouble with the Apaches."

"Your mill's been burned, ain't it?" asked Turner.

"But not by the Indians. I've never known who set it on fire, but

I know it was not the Mescaleros. It could have been Comanches, but more likely it was white outlaws. Since I haven't any evidence I say nothing about it."

At La Luz they filled the barrels on the sides of their wagons and began the long trip across the desert to Organ Gap. They found the waterholes along the way empty and made dry camp. Near the top of the divide there was a spring and an abundance of water. The next day the wagons jolted down the long slope to the Río Grande.

They followed the Butterfield Trail to the Continental Divide. At each station they received warnings from the keeper. The Apaches were on the rampage; why not stay until a wagon train came? Regardless of danger they refused to remain, but continued on their journey. Just when they crossed into Arizona they did not know; but Hart identified two peaks as Dos Cabezas. The Jones family knew there was a possibility of being attacked, but they preferred dealing with the Indians to being involved in the faction with which Riley had been identified.

Concealment was impossible. The Indians probably knew exactly where the Jonses were every minute of the time. Keeping a man on guard at night was useless. Apaches did not attack at night.

While the family was cooking their supper one evening, three Apaches rode through their camp and, with their lances, upset the pots and scattered the coals. A hundred yards away they turned and hurled insults at the party. Turner's hand dropped to his six-shooter, but John's fingers closed around it and prevented his firing. The Apaches began circling the camp. John called to them in their own tongue, and they stopped. He and Hart held a parley with them. They rode away, but only for a short distance.

"They won't bother us again, Mother."

"Why didn't you invite them to eat with us?"

"I did, but they refused. They said they wouldn't come back again."

•   •   •

The remainder of the journey was uneventful. The little party camped on the river near Tucson. Compared with the lush grazing land they had left behind, this country was barren and desolate. Barbara saw that the boys were disappointed and tried to encourage them to look for better surroundings, to the south, perhaps, on the San Pedro.

No work was available, and idleness increased this discontent.

Had Sammie not become very ill, Barbara could not have held them there. Fortunately there was a doctor at Tucson, and he examined the child. He told her frankly that he could not diagnose the illness by name. It was some kind of fever, not uncommon on the desert, and often fatal.

By the time the boy was able to travel, another obstacle to their leaving occurred. Barbara recorded the birth of a son — Henry. She told the family that in one week they might leave. When the new baby was three days old they started, with John driving Barbara's wagon, and the baby on a pillow.

About the fire at night the men discussed the future. They assumed that the family must return to the Ruidoso. The country there was undoubtedly the best they'd ever seen. The men obviously hoped for Barbara's sanction, but she said nothing. John felt responsible for their having left and decided that when he was driving the wagon for her he would make some explanations.

"When we get back we'll sell what's left of my steers and keep yours and Pa's. It's because of me that he and Jim lost their jobs and made this trip. It's been a bad thing for everybody. We sold more than half our cattle to buy food at Tucson. But there's still enough left to make another start. I don't aim to let you lose by it."

Barbara said nothing.

"I didn't want to leave the Hondo, Mother. I did it because you wanted it."

There was still no reply.

"You never asked me any questions, but I want you to know exactly what happened. Riley came to our *chosa* and ordered me to take the cattle and get out. He said if I didn't he'd take them. I went to Lincoln and talked with the *alcalde*. He said that if a man builds a home, or even lays four logs down to outline the walls of one, the place is his. That's the custom. Riley knew that. He was more'n twice my age, and he figgered he'd bluff me. If I'd let him, everybody else would've been tryin' it. He kept tellin' me I couldn't hold the place because I'm not of age, and he said if I didn't pull out I'd have to shoot my way out.

"I told him there must be other ways to settle it, legal ways, but he wouldn't listen. What good's the law that's thirty miles away? Take two days to get him there. I told him I had some things to attend to before we could settle. I owed the Romeros for a horse, and the Chávez family for two days' work. I had to take care of those things first.

"I told him to set the day, and he did. Now, I'm going back and stand trial."

"And become involved in a feud with his friends that will not stop so long as one of them or of us lives?" asked his mother.

"I don't think so. If I stand trial I'll be cleared. I have witnesses in Lincoln who'll testify that I came there to find out what my legal rights were."

"That won't stop Riley's friends from killing you."

"I'm willing to take my chances on that. But I don't want the other boys mixed up in this. What do you want me to do?"

"Stay with the family. We'll hunt for a range somewhere away from Lincoln County."

"Where?"

"Anywhere but there."

"The Peñasco is a good valley. I like it."

"Too close," Barbara said.

That evening Turner talked confidently of their return to the Ruidoso. He spoke as though the decision were a matter of his choice and not to be questioned. Barbara kept still, happy to see that John resented Turner's attitude. Heiskell looked questioningly at her, but she remained silent. She went to the wagon after the dishes were washed. And the next morning she took the reins and pulled out ahead of the slow oxen. All the way to the Río Grande she avoided talking of their destination. As they neared the parting of the trails she debated going north up the Rio Grande, or south toward Franklin (the town that afterward became El Paso). The later she announced her intention, the less time for opposition. When they camped on the east side of the river, she still preserved her silence.

•   •   •

The next morning Barbara climbed to the seat, checked to see that the children were in the wagon, and pointed the tongue south. Without a backward look she drove steadily toward Mexico. At midday she stopped, watered the mules, and fed the children. At sunset she camped, cooked a bountiful supper, bathed the children and herself, and waited beside the fire. A white spot appeared on the northern horizon and she cooked more food. When the wagon drew near she put coffee on. The oxen stopped and the late arrivals seated themselves without comment and without looking toward her. She fed them generously, went to the wagon, and did not return.

They kept in sight of her the next morning until they reached the village of Franklin, across the river from El Paso del Norte. They drove by the scattered adobe houses and along the river until the road left it; then they struck out along the long, weary trail toward the Horsehead Crossing of the Pecos, and arrived finally in Fort Stockton.

There, incidentally, Nib got the whipping of his life; in fact, he got two. His father had sent him, with Frank, to grub mesquite roots for fuel. They returned without wood, and his explanation was, "Grubbin' roots is hard work. I saw a lot of palin's around a house. Didn't look like nobody lived there, and I began pullin' 'em up. A Mexican woman snuck up on me. She grabbed me and frailed me with a palin' till she 'most beat me to death. I 'pologized and offered to put 'em back. Pa come 'long 'bout that time, and he beat me, too."

"Served you right," said Barbara. "If he hadn't, I would. I'm not bringing up children to be thieves. You're going to be good citizens if I have to whip every one of you every day. Now, go get me some mesquite roots."

The abundant water and lush grass of West Texas lured the Joneses to think that this night be a desirable place to make a home. The possibilities of farming were attractive. By now the cattle were footsore, and the group needed rest. They learned that the Army was paying sixty dollars a ton for hay and that water for irrigation was available.

"Comanche Spring," said Heiskell. "This is where the buffalo herds come to drink. Or anyway, they did before so many were killed for their hides. The Comanches lived on the trail of the buffalo, and the Apaches came out to hunt when the herds migrated. Now most of the buffalo have been killed, but there's still some strays, and their hides are valuable. What would you boys think about living here?" Heiskell asked his older sons.

"Pa," said Jim, after a long silence, "none of us boys is ever goin' to farm. We're going to run cattle. If you and Mother want to stay here, John and I will go on to the Concho. We can get jobs as cowboys till we get ranches of our own. There's good range over there, and we've got a start of cattle. Marion and Hart can stay with you or go with us, as they like. It's not far, but there's no water on the way, so we mightn't get back to see you very often."

"Got it all planned, haven't you?"

"Well, we're old enough to look ahead. But I know Mother doesn't want to split up the bundle."

Barbara spoke, "It's not what's best for you and me, but for the boys, Heiskell. What's good for them is good for us, also. If you can get work, they'll herd the cattle till we get some place of our own. Then it'll belong to all."

"I'll throw in with you boys for the Concho," said Turner.

That was bad, but Barbara could keep her eye on him.

Around San Angelo the boys found a demand for cow hands. One rancher employed John and took Bill as wrangler. Another hired Jim and Turner.

Hart stayed with the family. They lived in the wagons, near the fort. Heiskell got work hauling supplies for the cavalry, and Barbara managed with one wagon. Tom and Sammie herded the cattle, and all looked for a waterhole where they could establish a home.

"Beats all how that Sammie can ride," chuckled Heiskell. "The soldiers are bettin' on him to ride any outlaw bronc in the country. An' him just a little boy."

"Never been th'owed," boasted Sam.

"Better let somebody else tell that," said his mother. "Pride goeth before a fall."

"What's pride?"

"A failing that causes people to brag on themselves."

"Tom can't ride as good as me. Neither can Hart, and he's older."

"Both are better ropers than you; so is Frank. Of course they practice constantly, but so do you."

"Yes. Soon as Frank can lift a saddle and throw it on a horse he can get a job as wrangler. And Bill's boss has promised him a job as cowboy if anybody quits. That'll give Frank his job."

Heiskell put his wages in heifers. The boys took their pay in them, too. And they roped wild calves out of the brakes. Because their employers forbade their having brands of their own, the boys turned the calves over to Heiskell.

"Where'll we ever sell cattle, except one now and then?"

"There's pool herds going up the trail. We'll join them till we have enough steers to make one of our own."

Barbara's skill with a needle brought much mending for people at the fort. She began to feel at home and that there were possibilities for a future on the Concho, but she had forebodings. It seemed to her that every time they prospered and could see security ahead, something happened to prevent realization of the dream.

•   •   •

Shortly after midnight Jim rode in and called his father from the wagon. When Heiskell returned he said, "Miss Barbara, how long will it take you to pack?"

"John?"

"Yes."

"Where is he?"

"Gone. The Rangers are holding Bill. He wasn't there when it happened and wouldn't talk if he had been. Lucky he don't know; but he wouldn't talk if he did. They'll find that out and turn him loose. Jim said it was a fair fight and forced on John."

"Where's Jim now?"

"Roundin' up the cattle and horses."

"If you'll tend to filling the barrels I'll awaken the children and we'll get the other wagon ready. It won't take more than fifteen minutes. We've got to load the big black kettle; better do that first. But I hate to leave without Bill; he's just a child."

"Plenty able to take care of hisself; he'll get loose and follow. He's got a hoss, six-shooter, and bedroll. He'll make out all right."

"John'll hit for the Peñasco. All the way from Arizona he talked of that country. Bill will figger where he headed and follow him. Bill's long-headed."

"What was it about, Heiskell?"

"Calf — worth maybe three dollars. Each claimed it for his outfit. John tried to get Burks to settle some other way. He thought John was just a boy and could be bluffed. He just hadn't been knowin' John."

"Do we owe anybody anything here?"

"No. I got a little coming from the fort."

"That doesn't matter, but we couldn't leave any debts. As soon as Jim comes in with the cattle we'll hitch the mules to my wagon and start. I've packed everything we can get in the wagon."

"Head for that bright star till you hit the trail; then follow it west. Hold the mules up, and when it gets light enough, camp and fix breakfast. We'll keep as close as we can. We can make several miles before daylight. Jim and Hart will bring the cattle and hosses."

She nodded.

"Got your star?" asked Heiskell.

"The biggest and brightest?"

"Yes."

"I'll head for it."

Seven Rivers   *15*

The Jones family struck the Pecos, not at the Horsehead, but at Pope's Crossing. Barbara had no doubt but that they'd find John on the Peñasco. She looked forward to being reunited with him and Bill.

They drove north up the Pecos. Attracted by their campfire one evening a man rode close and hailed them. At their invitation he dismounted and approached them. From the darkness came a familiar voice, "As I live, the Joneses!"

"Ash Upson!"

"The same. Where've you been, and what're you doing here?"

"We're looking for a place to settle. Get down and have some supper. What you doin' here?"

"I'm surveying this land. The government has made a few laws requiring settlers to register on land they claim. They have to file on it, put in some improvements, and live on it three years to get a title. Then it's theirs and nobody can take it from them."

"You have to do all that now?"

"Yes, you do. And I know the very place for you. Up the river where seven small tributaries come together and form Seven Rivers before flowing into the Pecos, there's a big adobe house. There's six or seven rooms, and one is big enough for a trading post. Half a mile of ditch already made. Be a good place to live and run a store."

"Who does it belong to?"

"Nobody. All you got to do is move in and turn the water loose on your land."

"But who owns it?"

"The land? Why, you do — if you file on it. All you need is a piece of paper with your John Henry on it. That's all it takes."

"Somebody must own the land, or there wouldn't be a house and ditch on it."

"Somebody undoubtedly did. But that somebody didn't file on it, so he's no longer the owner. Must have been a Mexican family built it. The Mormons didn't come down this far. There was an Anglo down this way for awhile who might have run the Mexicans out and took it. I think he's been gone some time, maybe a year. If you file first nobody can do anything about it."

"That doesn't seem just right," said Barbara.

"It's the law."

"Besides, somebody's already filed on your place on the Hondo. I looked that up recently."

Ash continued, "There's a good place with good water, where John could file. Where is he?"

"He went ahead of us to the Peñasco."

• • •

Heiskell was delighted with the land, the house, and the surroundings up the river. He decided to take Ash Upson's advice and let him attend to the application for the land.

"There's no land office closer than Mesilla," Ash explained. "I'll send your application there. Just as soon as John signs his, I'll send it also. That'll hold the quarter section where you spent your first winter in New Mexico. Your old *chosa's* about gone, but two little adobe houses have been built."

When Heiskell returned from accompanying Ash Upson to one of the little adobes on the Hondo, he found both Bill and John with the family. As Jim had anticipated, Bill knew nothing of the shooting. As soon as the Rangers were satisfied of that fact they released him.

The family set about establishing a home in the big adobe. It was a huge structure with walls two feet thick. The rooms were large, and two were equipped with fireplaces. The *vigas* were of peeled cottonwood logs. They were overlaid with poles and covered with a layer of adobe a foot thick. Around the roof was a wall four feet high with rifle rests. A ladder inside the house led to the roof. The building undoubtedly had been designed for defense.

"I'm goin' to sleep on the roof," said Jim. "It'll be wonderful in summer. I've never liked sleepin' inside where the air is stuffy. I love to lie and watch the stars."

"The wind will be the worst feature," said Barbara. "But when we can have a house like this without either buying or building it, wind is of little importance. I've always wanted several rooms. With a family the size of ours we need them."

There was good water, soil, and grass. With a trading post, they could buy at wholesale prices and Barbara could serve meals to travelers.

From the storeroom and from Barbara's bedroom, which adjoined it, narrow slits, shoulder high, commanded the one entrance. Over each she kept a rifle hanging. The door was deeply recessed, and it had a heavy latch. It was reinforced by a bar made of oak, which could be laid across supports.

They swept the earthen floor, leveled it, sprinkled it with water, and heated shovels at the fireplace to smooth the surface. It became slick and hard. When they had finished scrubbing and scouring, the storeroom was cozy and attractive. Heiskell built a sturdy table and benches to seat twenty people. The fireplace served not only for heating and cooking but created an atmosphere of comfort and hospitality.

Ma'am Jones began making a list of supplies they would need for operating a trading post. Heiskell would go to Las Vegas, take both wagons, and two of the boys. They would drive cattle, for they had no money with which to buy merchandise. They would return with barrels of flour, brown sugar, and meal. Arbuckle coffee came in hundred-pound sacks, and with each was given a cup and saucer. All other commodities — kerosene and whiskey, for example — were sold in barrels.

Jim was enthusiastic about the country.

"Such grass, Mother! All up and down the Pecos it's belly-deep to a horse. A few miles south there's an arroyo comin' down from the Guadalupes. It's sheltered, well watered, and has wonderful grazing. Guess we'll name it Rocky Arroyo. Ash says everybody's afraid to settle in the canyon because the Apaches go through it to raid the Pecos country."

"Did they ever raid this country?" Barbara asked.

"They have at times, usually just for horses," Jim replied.

"Ma'am, up Rocky Arroyo is where I'm going to start a ranch when I'm old enough," said Bill.

"That's a long time ahead."

"When I'm fourteen ... "

Barbara smiled but shook her head.

"The Beckwiths ain't far off," said Turner. "They got plenty of nerve, but they don't fool any with that Rocky Arroyo country."

"Perhaps they're wise in that."

"There's already two or three men down here with herds, but none of them's got families here. There's Hank Harrison, Tom Gardner, and Rufe Segrest. Segrest's an old Indian fighter and buffalo hunter. He's got a scar on his neck from an arrow; I saw it when he was shaving. And he said that 'bout twenty miles south, at McKittrick Spring, somebody else has a herd."

•   •   •

Barbara Jones knew that the time for the birth of another child was near. She thought it would be less trouble if she and Heiskell were to leave for a few days than to make arrangements at home, as many travelers came to the trading post now. The two set out one morning in the wagon, and at Blue Water, in 1878, their ninth son, Robert Bruce, was born.

Neighbors

16

The Jones family's possession of the Seven Rivers place was never contested, but John's filing on the Roswell claim was refused because of a prior application — Marion Turner's. What adjustment was made the family never knew, but John and Turner opened a trading post in one of the little adobe houses, leaving Ash Upson in possession of the other, which he used as a postoffice.

The two young men put in a small stock of merchandise, consisting primarily of whiskey and ammunition. Heiskell freighted for both trading posts. He used a bump wagon — one without springs. From the beginning the store at Seven Rivers was profitable; that at Roswell was less so. Heiskell was away much of the time because of making the round trip to Las Vegas. As a reward for good conduct he would sometimes take one of the younger boys with him on his trips.

Jim went to work for John Chisum. Because of his superior ability with cattle, his good marksmanship, and his dependability, he became trail boss for the Jinglebobs. Another asset that contributed to his promotion was his friendship with the Apaches. With Jim Jones ram-rodding the drive, no herd was molested.

Conflicting reports came to the family regarding Mr. Chisum, reports upon which they could get no information from Jim. The code of the range was that if one worked for a man, he worked for him. He fought to protect his property, and he refrained from discussing his employer and his business.

In return, the cowman tacitly assumed responsibility for the defense of his cow hands. If one fought in his behalf he expected to be defended in case of need. Jim soon learned that he could depend on nothing from John Chisum. He was expected to defend the Jingle-bob interest, but if he were held accountable for risks taken in Chisum's interests, he could not look to his employer for aid. A trail boss's responsibility was great and entailed risks. Jim longed for the time when he could accumulate enough cattle to justify giving full time to his own herd. Besides that, he was apprehensive about his mother's being at Seven Rivers with his father and older brother away.

When a stranger stayed overnight at the Jones home he was invited to share the boys' room. Sleeping on a bed was such a luxury that men gratefully accepted the hospitality. As for fearing strangers, the idea never occurred to Ma'am Jones. Had she been alone she would have had confidence in any stranger who sought shelter for the night. When a man entered a home he automatically became its defender. Any man who violated that code would know that his days were numbered. She had never known of its having been done.

Year after year men who drove herds up the Pecos looked forward to staying at Seven Rivers. Ma'am's hospitality and good food became famous. Her welcome was gracious, her prices fair, and the whiskey good. Seven Rivers was known from South Texas to the terminals of the railways in Kansas.

Ma'am never charged for meals until she found that men were leaving more money on the table than she considered fair compensation for their food. If they asked prices she named a low one; if not, she did not ask for money. They usually bought enough supplies that the profit was sufficient, anyway.

Bill, Tom, and Sammie herded the cattle. They left early in the morning and came in late at night. They had no noonday meal. At times they were away for weeks and carried food with them, as all cowboys did.

Ash Upson, operating an unofficial postoffice, visited them to arrange for Minnie to run one at Seven Rivers. It was only a question of time, he said, until the government would legalize the offices and Minnie would receive a salary. They might even get a mail carrier. Minnie was twelve, wasn't she? And could read and write? Of course she could read and write! Well, then, she could operate a postoffice. All the equipment needed was two sets of saddle bags. The size used by officers for their sidearms would be ample. Anybody riding up the Pecos would carry the one containing letters going his way. If he turned off the trail he could hang it on a conspicuous limb and the next passerby would carry it on. In time it would reach either Pecos or Roswell. Those who rode by could open it and if they had letters, take them.

Incoming mail was dumped on the counter, and all comers sorted through it and took theirs. The important thing was to collect for the letter when it was mailed — say twenty-five cents for each letter. If people were cantankerous enough not to be satisfied with his methods, let them send their mail by special messenger, as did a "biggety" lawyer named McSween who had recently come to Lincoln. Easterner. Distrusted everybody. Sure, there was rustling going on in the country, but who ever heard of letters' or money's being stolen? There was nobody in the Territory low enough to do that.

"And would you believe it, Miss Barbara, the sheriff at Lincoln's got bills for five thousand criminals — all supposed to be on the dodge in Lincoln County?"

"I would not. There's not that many bad men in the world. There's plenty of Tejanos coming in, but they seem to be good men. I ought to know; I see and feed plenty of them."

"Everybody says your judgment of men and horses can't be beat," replied Ash. "Is it true that you can ride as well as the boys?"

"No, of course not. I seldom break a horse anymore; don't have to. After one's been ridden three saddles anybody should be able to ride it. And the boys do that now."

Ash never drank intemperately in the Jones home. Nobody did. But it took only one toddy to loosen his tongue, and Ma'am could not refuse him that. He knew every family on the Pecos, and he knew all that occurred. He had worked years in the newspaper business and had the knack of getting information. His knowledge was in some cases a liability, for he talked entirely too much, and especially did he become confidential when he was drinking.

●   ●   ●

Except for the Beckwith family, everybody in the country was friendly and came frequently to the trading post. Ma'am was a bit curious about their aloofness and encouraged Ash Upson to talk about them. He had lived with them for some time and acted as tutor to their children. He told he what he had gleaned while at the ranch:

"In 1875 Captain William H. Johnson and Wallace Olinger drove a herd into the territory. As they neared the Pecos, below the mouth of Seven Rivers, they found three wagons under attack by Comanches. They rode to the rescue and thought they had turned the tide of battle, until Johnson was struck by a bullet. He fell from his horse. Upon finding that his leg was broken he continued to fire but realized that his situation was desperate. When he heard a volley from the north he hoped that reenforcements had arrived.

"Hugh Beckwith, with some of his cow hands, had heard the shooting and come to investigate it. They routed the Indians and loaded Johnson into one of the wagons. Olinger followed with the herd to the Beckwith Ranch. There Captain Johnson was cared for by the women of the family.

"The addition of two competent fighting men was a welcome one to the Beckwith forces. But Hugh Beckwith was shocked when Captain Johnson asked permission to marry his daughter, Camilla. He was the nephew of Sir Marmaduke Beckwith, and La Señora's father claimed descent from Spanish nobility. Grudgingly Beckwith considered the request. Having been born in Virginia, he was pleased to learn that Johnson was a native of that state. He asked few questions, but among them were these:

" 'Did you see service in the War between the States?'

" 'I did, Sir.'

" 'Your rank?'

" 'I enlisted as a private and was discharged with the rank of Captain.'

"Beckwith assumed that Johnson's military service had been in the Confederate Army. So did Camilla. William Johnson felt that before their marriage he should inform her of the facts, and he did so. His father, Dr. William Johnson, was a graduate of one of the best medical schools in the United States. During a visit with his family in Virginia he fought what he believed to be the last legal duel occurring in the United States. Public sentiment was so strongly opposed to dueling that he decided to leave and begin medical practice in Marion, Ohio. He said nothing of his southern background and when Abraham Lincoln called for volunteers to serve three months, the doctor was requested to make a speech for the purpose of recruiting. He was so successful that his first volunteer was his son.

"Captain Johnson was discharged in East Texas and wandered west. He got work on a ranch, and though it was new to him he soon became adept as a cowhand. On this range he met Wallace Olinger, and when the latter was stricken with smallpox, Johnson nursed him to health.

"As was the custom, the cowman paid his hands when he sold

his cattle. Instead of driving his steers to market, he informed Johnson and Olinger that he was so deeply in debt he could not get payment for his cattle. The only means he had of paying them was to turn the herd over to them. Before daylight they headed it west.

"For Camilla's wedding the family went to Galisteo. The women went in a hack with an escort of the Beckwith men and their cowboys. The ceremony was performed in Santa Fe, and the party returned to the Pecos.

"But," Ash added, "Captain Johnson and Wallace Olinger don't work for Beckwith. They own their cattle in partnership. And they have separate brands.

"Johnson wanted to build a house for Camilla, but La Señora insisted that they live with her. Johnson ate with the family, but Olinger remained quietly in the bunkhouse and acted as though he were one of Beckwith's employees. And Old Hugh is lucky to have two such fighting men around."

"Twigs," commented Barbara.

"Twigs, Miss Barbara? Don't you think we'd better have a log? It's getting cold outside."

"Please, Mr. Upson. I was thinking of something else."

When Ash came back from getting wood, he resumed his conversation: "Mrs. Beckwith has high-faluting ideas of education. She wants her daughters to have finishing school training. She wants them to learn to dance, pour tea, paint on velvet, and make hair wreaths and wax flowers. But she liked the improvement they made in English under my teaching."

"And her sons?"

"Oh, the usual — arithmetic, mostly."

"Who lived in this country before we came?" asked Barbara.

"Hard to say, but the abandoned *chosas* show that somebody did."

"Did somebody run those people out?"

"That's something that can't be proved. Just figure it out for yourself, though. To whose advantage was it to have them leave?"

That she knew very well. And she hoped that Mr. Upson might not be there if Jim came for a brief visit. Jim, because he was in the employ of Chisum, would resent criticism of the man, regardless of whether or not it was merited. Anyway, neither he nor John liked Ash Upson.

•   •   •

Both trading post and herd were bringing profits to the Jones family. But Ma'am was apprehensive about prosperity. It seemed always to precede a catastrophe.

Ma'am was determined to strengthen the bonds uniting her sons. They were becoming a bit resentful of her supervision; she must refrain from letting it be felt. She no longer asked questions about their absences, but she did insist that they maintain a standard of cleanliness unusual on the Pecos. Not infrequently they broke the ice to bathe in the river, because they disliked carrying water.

Each Sunday morning the family assembled in the store room for religious instruction and to "make their manners." Minnie or Ma'am played the role of a visitor. One of the boys met her, lifted her from her horse, opened the door and ushered her to a chair. The others stood until she was seated. One took her mount to the corral.

At the meal, the boys carved and served and carried the plates to the tables; they also refilled cups. But because of the many who came and who were served at irregular hours, Ma'am had not required that grace be said before meals. She had let the younger boys drift into the habit of reaching for dishes instead of asking for them. Good discipline required that she correct some of these omissions.

Sunday morning John cooked breakfast.

"We're going to say grace before being seated. You boys will take turns. John will start."

He bowed his head and said the grace he had learned from his Mexican friends.

"Just Sundays?" asked Bill, hopefully.

"Every day."

"What'll we do when there's folks here?"

"The same. They'll respect good people."

"Everybody knows we're good people without that."

"And you are not to reach for anything. Ask and the food will be passed."

"The rule is," said John, "that you keep one foot on the floor. Sammie reaches across the table with both in the air."

"If I didn't, Faustino [Bill] would get every biscuit on the plate."

"That's why we must do these things. I don't want ill-mannered children." Barbara insisted. Then she announced that they'd have the Bible lesson.

"Before we wash the dishes?"

"Yes, and before you leave the house." Ma'am replied.

They sat in grim silence.

"Now, we'll see how much you remember. What was the name of Mary's husband?"

"Joseph," came the reply in chorus.

"What did he do for a living?"

No reply. Sammie guessed: "Wasn't he a cowpuncher?"

"He was a carpenter. Now, what was the occupation of Jesus?"

"He was just a damn sheepherder."

"Sammie Jones!"

"Well, it's in The Book, Mother. I saw his picture, wearing a dress and carrying a lamb."

She saw a twisted smile on John's lips and began an explanation of the symbolism, but she knew that he was not convinced.

She hastily began a discussion of the admonition to turn the other cheek. The boys stared at her in silence. She went on, "It's not right to fight. It's better to trust in God." More silence. "He's always with you, and He will protect you."

"Like John," said Hart, admiringly.

"No, not exactly. He's — "

"I'd rather have John," insisted Hart. "Can't see *Ussen*. He not do your fighting for you, anyway. He expect you to do it yourself. Much better John."

That was positively sacrilegious, but how was she to make the boy understand? Or her own sons? She must continue to try.

•   •   •

That night John sat with his mother after the rest had gone to bed.

"Mother, there's something I have to say, and I hardly know how to go about it. You told the boys that if they were struck on one cheek they are to turn the other."

"That's what Jesus taught."

"Times must have been different. If He'd ever punched cows on the Pecos do you think He'd have said that? He'd have had His head knocked off if He had."

"Why, John!"

"Well, He would. He wasn't so easy-going as He sounds, anyway. Didn't He rope the thieves and drag them out of the Temple?"

"No. He drove them out with a piece of rope."

"Shows He would fight, no matter how He did it."

Tears came to his mother's eyes and she looked helplessly at him.

"You don't want the boys killed, do you Mother?"

"You know I don't, John."

"They believe everything you tell them because you've never lied to them."

"They respect me because I'm their mother."

"They respect you because you're worthy of respect. Some time they're going to figure that these things you tell them are all right for women because they can't fight, anyway."

"Then what am I to do?"

John bent his head and laid his lips on her forehead.

"Even when you're wrong you're right. You hold your twigs together. Hart worships you. Much as you dislike Turner he pays more heed to your judgment than to mine. This country's in for trouble, and it's not far in the future. I've never contraried you since Sammie was born, but I have to warn you of what's coming. Your bundle of twigs must be ready; and it must be ready to fight, if necessary."

"Mr. Upson's more than hinted of trouble. I'm beginning to be afraid. Tell me what to expect. I don't like being kept in ignorance, like a woman."

John laughed.

"You're a mighty smart woman. I'm beginning to see just how smart you are. You can outguess any man."

Barbara was distressed. "You've said too much; or maybe you've said too little. You know I can keep my own counsel. Shouldn't I know what is going on?"

"It's something I am not sure about, myself. I can smell trouble. When I know what it is I'll tell you."

And he bade her good night and went to the roof.

Billy Bonney 17

Infrequently Mescaleros slipped down to visit the Jones family, but never when there were wayfarers at the trading post. The Indians brought gifts of buckskin, jerky, and venison, and little bags or quills filled with gold dust to trade for ammunition. Barbara limited the number of bullets to each man; she had misgivings about letting them have ammunition but felt that a small amount might prevent entanglements. It was still occasionally reported that the Apaches had attacked emigrants primarily for the purpose of securing ammunition and metal for making arrow points. The latter they obtained from the hoops on water barrels.

Barbara kept her accumulation of gold in a buckskin bag until she had about three ounces. Then she asked Heiskell to use it for the purchase of a trundle bed in Las Vegas. It would serve the two younger boys and could be pushed under her bed during the day. She made a calico flounce to match her bedspread and to conceal the presence of the small bed under hers.

"Where do you suppose the Apaches get gold?" she asked Heiskell.

"Don't know," he replied. "There's stories of both hidden treasure and gold mines in the Sacramentos. It's said that Indians worked five mines there years ago but that no Apache ever dug gold, although they might pick up coarse dust from the sand in the beds of streams. Before their time other Indians might have mined. But Apaches are super-stitious about gold — think it has something to do with the Sun God. To them it's sacred. Ever see an Apache wear a gold ornament?"

"Come to think of it, I haven't — or very little silver, for that matter. The Mescaleros made bracelets out of copper wire. They'd cut the telegraph lines to Fort Stanton, just for the wire to make jewelry — but gold, no."

"What surprises me is that they'll even handle it," said Heiskell. "They hate prospectors worse than ranchers because they burrow in the earth for minerals."

"People say there's a lot of gold and silver around the White Mountain, buried there."

"It's been told that the Mescaleros killed a man taking the payroll to Fort Stanton, and that they hid the money. It would have been silver dollars, of course, if it's true."

"You can hear almost anything," said Barbara. "But if any money was stolen I'd believe that it was taken by the cavalry rather than the Indians. They're always stealing and laying it onto the Apaches. You know that all the time we lived up there we never knew of the Indians stealing anything."

"That's right," Heiskell affirmed. Then he cautioned: "There's an interpreter at the Agency now, José Carrillo, a Mexican. Captured by the Navajos when he was a button. They trained him to be a warrior. When he was about grown they came down to the Capitans, hunting. The boy tried to escape and go to the Mexicans on the Hondo. They trailed him; they stoned him and left him for dead under a pile of rock. Some Apaches came by, heard him groanin' and dug him out. He married an Apache girl and lives on the reservation. Speaks Spanish, Navajo, Apache, and English. 'Pache and Navvy's lots alike. He's a big help to the agent — soldiers, too.

"And that goes to show that the Apaches aren't so bad," Heiskell went on. "They saved his life. And did you ever hear of them killin' any of the white settlers 'round the reservation? Nobody else didn't, neither. These folks down here on the Pecos think the Mescaleros are reg'lar demons and are scared to death of 'em. And they think it's queer if white people are friendly with 'em."

"I can understand why the Tejanos might have that idea," said Barbara, "but I can't see why people who live close to them would. You needn't worry about their coming here. They don't if there's a strange wagon or horse around. When we're alone they slip in quietly, usually after dark, molest nobody, and leave without being seen except by us. I can't see any harm in their coming."

"There ain't none. But there's other Apaches at Mescalero now. They was run outa their own country around Ojo Caliente and took refuge with the Mescaleros. They're fightin' devils, much more warlike than the ones we know. It might be that some of 'em will wander down this way lookin' for horses," Heiskell pointed out.

"I went down to the *chosas* on the bank of the Pecos yesterday looking for one of the Feliz women to do the washing for me. They warned me of the Warm Springs Apaches. The Feliz family came here from the Río Grande and knows about them," Barbara said.

"Been wantin' you to quit doin' that washin' a long time. Sure glad you're stopping it."

"I wouldn't mind so much if the women would come here and do the work, but they won't. I can't supervise them when I can't be with them. Then they just dip the clothes in the river, lay them on a flat rock, and beat them with a paddle. I had the boys take the big iron kettle down for them, and I told them that when they'd finished washing in the river they are to boil the clothes with soap and rinse them well. I'm to furnish the soap."

"Can't they make soap?"

"Oh, I suppose they could but they let the grease get rancid, and I'd rather make it myself."

"I sort o' dread leavin' this time, and I don't know just why."

"Not worried about the Indians?"

"No, not exactly."

"I'm not, either. Go right along; we'll be all right."

"How 'bout takin' Sammie with me?"

"Bill needs him to help with the cattle. He'll do twice as much work as Tom. Tom's not lazy, but he just doesn't seem to take to cattle."

"Tom'll do anything that's to be done."

"Yes, but he'll take his time about it."

• • •

After the boys had brought the herd to the corral they unsaddled and started to the house. Sammie ran through some mesquite, tripped, and fell. His face struck a broken bottle and the jagged piece cut deep, doing terrible damage to his eye. The eyelid hung by a shred of skin.

"Quick, Minnie! Get a pan of warm water. Bring the bandages. I'll have to wash some of the blood off in order to see how badly it's hurt."

Barbara examined it. "Sammie, I'm going to have to do some quick sewing to save your sight. It's going to hurt bad."

"Go ahead, Mother. I won't beller."

"That's a boy! There! I believe it will be all right." Barbara deftly applied bandages.

"Now Sammie, you better get to bed. You're a real man. You never whimpered."

"Can I see outta this eye?"

"Not now, of course; but I hope in a week or so you can."

"Then I want some supper first."

"And you shall have it."

Then Ma'am turned and saw that Minnie was crying.

"I don't want Sammie to be blind."

"He's not going to be, Ewe Lamb. It's all right now. Get the things on the table. I expect the biscuits are burned. I forgot all about supper. No — they're just right. Everybody get washed and come to the table."

"Sammie might suffer from that eye tonight. Think I'll have him sleep in my room so if I hear him I can get to him and look after him."

"I can stand anything, Mother, just so my eye is all right. I can sleep with the boys."

"In my room, Sammie. Hart can have your bed."

"John not here. I sleep by your door," said Hart.

"No, Hart. There are no strangers in the house, and I may have to be up. Put another log on the fire, and see that there's plenty of water. Then stay with the other boys tonight."

•   •   •

At times Sammie moved restlessly, and several times he moaned, but each time Barbara went to him she found him asleep. Barbara herself had a bad night. It was, she thought, largely because of her anxiety for Sammie. He must not go out after the cattle in the morning. And she could hardly spare Hart. But Bill would have to help. If only she could get to sleep. Perhaps she should have let Hart stay outside her door as he wanted to.

Suddenly she sat up in bed, tense. Had she heard something? If so, there was no repetition of the sound. She arose, threw a robe about her, and got her Winchester from the pegs. She lifted the cowhide over the slit in the wall and listened. It was, she judged, later than three, for she could feel the approach of dawn. No horse had come in; she was sure of that. Could there be Apaches outside? Any Mescalero would have called to her had there been. Then from the corral came the sniff of a horse. There *was* something outside. In the dim light she saw movement in a mesquite bush.

She thrust the rifle through the slit and sighted.

"Come out of it," she ordered.

A slender boy arose and stumbled unsteadily toward the house. Ma'am dropped her rifle, unbolted the door, and ran to meet the boy. She half-carried him to the kitchen and eased him into her big chair before the fire. When she had a good blaze she put the kettle over it and turned to find the boy tugging at his boot. She knelt, took it in her hands — a very small boot — and pulled it off. Then she removed the other. He wore no socks and his feet were raw and swollen. How foolish to wear boots too small! Those blisters! He'd never got them riding a horse. He'd walked, and he'd walked a long distance.

"There! Isn't that better? Now I'll get a basin and we'll bathe those feet; it will take the soreness out." She hesitated and added, "While you're at it, better take a bath. I'll bring soap and towels."

When she returned with them the boy's face was so white and drawn that she asked, "When did you eat?"

" 'Bout three days ago."

"I'll fix something for you. Keep that blanket around you."

She brought milk and heated it. The strange boy sat hunched in the blanket with his feet in the water. She held the cup to him.

"I don't like milk."

"Drink it. Later you may have some food, but not now. It's bad for you to eat before you're rested a little."

There was no reply.

"Do you want me to hold your nose and pour it down you?"

He took the cup. When he tasted the milk he made a wry face, but he drank. He drank greedily. Ma'am took the cup and told him to sip the milk. He obeyed.

"Now, I'm going to put you to bed. You're worn out and need sleep."

"I can sleep right here."

"You can sleep better in a bed."

When he stood, Ma'am thought he looked better. There was color in his face. He'd filled out a bit. He followed her to the room where the boys slept. There was a double bed in each corner. She turned down the blankets in one. When she had tucked him in she said, "Good night, Son." He reached up and touched her cheek.

"Sleep as long as you can. You're worn out."

• • •

Barbara was awakened by the good odors of bacon and coffee. John! She dressed hurriedly and went to the store room. He met and kissed her.

"Why did you come, John?"

"How's that for a welcome? I wanted to see a lovely lady."

Ma'am laughed. "Just wait till you do!"

"Good morning!" said a strange voice.

"Oh, yes! How're you this morning?"

"Hungry."

"And your feet?"

"Sore."

"We'll do something about both. Let me see those feet."

"Breakfast's ready, Ma'am, and he's starved."

While she was dressing the lad's feet, Sammie came into the room. "How'd you get your feet sore?" he asked.

Ma'am's warning glance stopped further inquiries. Under no circumstances did one ask a guest's name or business. She glanced at the strange boy, but in his face there was no resentment. He was nice-looking, with blue eyes and rather prominent teeth. He could easily have passed for one of her own blond sons.

"Let me tell him, Ma'am. I walked from the top of the Guadalupes."

She glanced at John.

"You didn't know the country?"

"No Ma'am. They warned us at Mesilla to come through the reservation, but we wanted to see the country. We came the south way, through the Salt Flats. When we got to the top of the ridge and saw the stream below, I left O'Keefe with the horses and went down to fill the canteens. Just as I started back, the Indians struck. I waved O'Keefe to ride out of it, and I hid. I stayed under cover till dark and then worked my way downstream till it began to get light. For three days I lay out in the daytime and walked at night."

"See any Apaches?" asked John.

"No, but I saw smoke and knew they were looking for me."

"Accounts for the signal fires we've been seeing," said Ma'am Jones.

"You were lucky," said John to the stranger.

"Never run from an Indian," Sammie told him. "If you just stand hitched they won't hurt you."

"Right!" said John.

"Do the Apaches know that?" asked the boy.

"They do," replied John. "Nib, go get a pair of my moccasins for —"

"Billy," said the boy, "Billy Bonney. And I thank you."

Billy was there several days before he spoke of leaving. Jim spent Sunday at home and tried to teach him to braid quirts, but Billy was inept and turned the work over to Sammie.

"The Apaches taught Jim," Frank informed him, "and they ain't no White Eye can plait as good as Jim. He can make bridles, too."

"I'm leavin' before daylight in the mornin'," said Jim.

"Leaving?" Billy questioned.

"For the Jinglebobs. I 'spect you could get a job with 'em if you want it; that is, if you're a good shot."

Billy shook his head.

The boy helped about the house and romped with the small children. He helped Barbara dress Sammie's eye and seemed pleased over the healing. There was no awkwardness over the religious observances that Ma'am Jones exacted of her family. He sat quietly courteous but did not participate.

When the boys went to the yard for target practice Billy joined them. They cleaned and oiled their six-shooters and set up cans for targets.

John looked over Billy's weapons, for he carried two, and commented, "No notches."

"No notches." Billy assented.

"Me neither."

"Makes us even." John was contemptuous of men who notched their guns.

When they had tired of shooting at stationary objects, John saddled a Spanish mule and placed hand-forged bits in its mouth. He mounted and rode in a circle, firing at targets thrown into the air. He scored five, but when he missed the sixth he dismounted in disgust and invited Billy to shoot. When a tie was scored, neither felt that he had done well. They sat on a log in the sun and talked.

"You're pretty good," John told the guest. "You're mighty nigh as good as John Middleton, and he's the best shot I ever saw."

"Not so bad yourself," said Billy. "I'd sure hate to have to shoot it out with you."

"How's your left hand?" asked John.

"Not so good. Sometimes I hit, but if I was in a jackpot I'd use my right."

"Me, too." John said.

"Sammie says you're not afraid of Apaches nor nothing."

"Sammie talks too much. Besides, there's no reason to be afraid of the Indians."

"The way they followed me, I thought there might be," said Billy.

"If they don't know you they might attack you."

"Your mother doesn't think so."

"She thinks everybody is good."

Ash Upson

18

In December, Ash Upson prepared for a trip to Seven Rivers. John encouraged his going in order that Upson might return before Jim made his visit home to spend Christmas.

"Taking some butternuts to your mother," Ash said. "My niece sent them to me." Ash knew that Ma'am would probably plant them as she did the chestnuts somebody sent her from Virginia. She loved to grow things.

"Yes, Ma'am wants an orchard, so the boys are going to plant trees along the acequia where they'll get water. There's half a mile of ditch, and things planted along it will grow well with little trouble."

Ash remarked, "You Joneses are the only people in the country who ever think of planting trees and making a permanent home."

"You forget that the Mexicans on the Hondo do," said John. "They're real homemakers. And they have peach trees, many of them."

Mr. Upson found the Jones family busy. They seldom sat down to eat until a tableful of hungry pilgrims had been fed. Mrs. Jones was always cooking and baking, but with the assistance of every member of the family. Minnie was deft and efficient at housework. As Ash watched her flitting about the place with her long braids wound about her head, as were her mother's, he thought the resemblance remarkable.

121

He, too, settled easily into the routine of the household. He built fires, washed potatoes for baking, churned, and told stories to the family.

"John Chisum claims he's losing a lot of cattle here lately and that it's not the Indians who are stealing them. A few years ago he put in a claim for a herd run off by the Comanches. Others lost herds, too, but Old John collected for his. That man started out hoeing cotton when he was eight years old, and now look at him — Cattle King of the Pecos. Got the biggest herd in the world, I reckon."

"He certainly has lots of cattle," Ma'am agreed.

"He contracts them to the government for a good price. Then he buys them up cheap. Raises them on almost nothing, you might say. All he's out is the wages he pays his cow hands, that and his chuck. They live largely on beef, and probably steal enough cattle for their feed. 'Course he has to buy flour, bacon, beans, and coffee. And he doesn't pay any taxes."

"What's taxes?" inquired Sam.

"Money you pay to support the government," Ash explained. "This is a big county, biggest in the world, I believe. Takes in nearly a fourth of the Territory. And there's a county government to support. Of course Chisum doesn't own much land, but he uses an awful lot of it. He's going to elect a sheriff next time or I miss my guess. Up till now Murphy and Dolan have owned the sheriffs, but Murphy deeded his business to Dolan and went to his ranch."

"Don't people vote for the county officers?" Barbara asked.

"When one person controls close to a hundred votes he can elect his man. Not that many more votes cast in the county. So Chisum has the election sewed up."

"You don't think much of the Dolan faction?"

"Neither does Old John Chisum. They've a monopoly on the business at Lincoln — have had for years. They can charge and pay as they please — as you know. Now a store's going in at Lincoln; it belongs to an Englishman who has a ranch on the Feliz. This Tunstall came in and bought cattle. He built a store and freighted merchandise from Vegas. It's said that McSween is in on it, but I doubt that he has the money. They're even starting a bank, supposedly with Chisum's backing. You can just figure out how the Dolan bunch likes that."

"Mr. Chisum hires our boys and pays them fair wages. We expect them to be loyal to the outfit they work for."

"And they risk their lives for him every day. Does *he* take any chances? Not Old John. He doesn't even carry a gun."

"I wish nobody did. Then there'd be no killing."

"But it shows that Old John is playing it safe. It takes a low sort of man to shoot an unarmed one."

"It shows that Mr. Chisum wants peace."

"In this country every man has to defend himself."

"If weapons were discarded that wouldn't be the case."

"And Old John's on the warpath because the cowboys are branding mavericks."

"Mavericks?"

"Strays. In '75 Chisum branded close to six thousand: now he's after the little men who rope a few strays out along the Pecos. Calls them cattle thieves."

Ma'am thought it time to change the subject.

"Has the government done anything about establishing regular post offices?"

"No, and I'll be glad when it does. I need the salary. Minnie does, too. I'm doing a lot of surveying, too, but finding it hard to collect for it. Of course, most of it's for Chisum hands; he buys their claims in order to keep the real settlers from having access to water. And he doesn't pay for the surveying."

"Doesn't it require five years to prove up on a homestead? And isn't it illegal to sell before one has a title?"

"It is. But if Old John elects a sheriff —"

"He can do as he likes?" Barbara asked.

"Exactly!"

"I'm glad we're so far from the county seat. If there's trouble it's apt to be at Lincoln. It's several days' drive in a wagon. It's a long trip horseback, for that matter."

"And there's trouble brewing. In fact, it's already under way," said Ash.

Ma'am kept on knitting.

"Tunstall did a lot of looking before selecting a location," Ash continued. "He's been to the sheep country in California; he's considered Albuquerque and Santa Fe. He came down here with young Juan Patrón. Said he didn't think much of the Mexicans around Santa Fe — that those at Albuquerque are a much better class. And he thinks Juan Patrón's the best educated one he's met."

It was amazing the things Mr. Upson knew.

"What became of the Bonney boy?" Ash asked. "Heard that Tunstall hired a boy a short time ago; he was riding a horse with John's brand on it. Hope Billy Bonney didn't steal it."

"He didn't. John lent it to him. He'll return it."

"I doubt it. He's just a gambler. This is probably the first job he ever had."

"Possibly, but I don't think he'd steal anything."

There was a prolonged silence before Barbara continued.

"I'm glad Billy has a job, and I hope he'll stay with Mr. Tunstall — especially if the Englishman likes him."

"He does, but no man counts with Tunstall like a horse. He thinks more of them than of his hands."

Two tall, blond young men entered the store. One was dressed in fringed buckskin and had long hair. The other glanced at Ash Upson and nodded. The first man bowed elaborately to Barbara and introduced himself, "Bob Olinger, Ma'am — Pecos Bob." She invited them to eat; dinner was on the table, but Wallace replied that they were expected at the Beckwith ranch.

"It's good to have neighbors, Mr. Olinger. Glad you stopped by. Come again."

Bob thanked her effusively, but Wallace quietly led the way to the door.

"That was Bob Olinger —" Ash began.

"And Wallace. I suspected that the other was his brother."

"Bob Olinger's a would-be bad man, always swaggering."

Barbara nodded. She returned to the former topic.

"I'm glad to hear good news of Billy Bonney. He was as well behaved as any boy I've ever had about."

"He's always so with ladies. The Mexicans love him and welcome him to their homes."

"They're courteous people and appreciate good manners."

"But, Ma'am, in spite of his manners, that boy's a rascal."

"In what way?"

"He's said to have killed a man over near Silver City. And Indians. He's been in jail and broke out. He's a tin-horn gambler and always lined up with the wrong kind of people. Anyway, he was till he came here and Tunstall took him in."

"I hope he stays there. It seems to be a good opportunity for him. Some boys get off on the wrong foot when they're very young, and then nobody will give them work. It is hard for them to get out of that predicament, and they take to the wrong things. This job may enable Billy to realize his possibilities, and he's a smart boy and could amount to something."

Retaliation   *19*

Barbara sent Hart to the Feliz home on the Pecos with a huge bundle of clothing. It was his habit to tell her where he was going, and when he would return. Though she did not question him she appreciated his thoughtfulness. It was amazing to her that Hart was as loyal to her as to John. When Heiskell was away the boy always spread his buffalo robe and blankets outside her door and slept there. Her own sons rarely anticipated and supplied her needs as Hart did. People seldom failed to comment on his courtesy to her. And possibly because he was called Hart Jones, they accepted him as a member of her family.

There were several pilgrims, as Ma'am called them, at the trading post, and she was busy selling merchandise and preparing the noon meal for them. It was not until the food was on the table that she became concerned because Hart had not returned; not, she thought, with self-reproach, until she needed wood did she miss him. She set the younger boys to washing the dishes and she dressed for riding. As her horse was brought to the door John arrived, with a turkey.

"You're going somewhere, Mother. Who's sick?"

"Nobody. It's Hart —"

"Hart?"

"I sent him to the Feliz place this morning with the washing. That was hours ago, and he isn't back yet."

"Maybe he stayed to dinner."

"He never does that. It's not like him to go away and not let me know. And I'm worried."

"I'll saddle a fresh mule and go after him."

John took the trail. He followed the tracks of Hart's mount to the Pecos, down the trail, and to the two little *chosas* partially recessed in the bank of the river. Nobody responded to his calling and he dismounted and entered one of the rooms. There was evidence of its having been hastily abandoned.

Outside he found wagon tracks leading down the Pecos. There had been several horses, and one of them was Hart's. The Feliz family had left hurriedly. A long *ristra* (string) of dried chilis had been dropped and not retrieved.

John had not eaten since four that morning. He was weary, and he considered going back to the store for food and his bedroll. His ammunition was low. But if he took time for these things, the Feliz families — there were really two families of them — might get far ahead of him. If there were not such positive evidence of a hasty departure — and of Hart's having ridden away with them —

John took the trail.

Hoof prints were deeply indented in the sand. They had driven hard. He reached a level spot where their teams had galloped. That was strange, unaccountable. But they'd stop and make camp for the night; when they did so he'd overtake them. At sunset they had not camped so he followed until darkness made trailing difficult. John felt that there must be a reason for their traveling constantly, perhaps a sinister reason. He would follow the Pecos, as they had done so far, but when the moon came up he would ride harder and attempt to overtake them. Meanwhile his mount needed water, and he would get a little rest. But he would not sleep.

When the moon rose he recognized landmarks. He was approaching a big bend in the river. He made sure that the wagon was still following the bank, and then cut through to intercept it. The route was sandy and his mule made little noise. Shortly before he reached the river he stopped and listened. He could hear the rumbling of the wagon over the rough trail. He studied the terrain, tied his mount in a thicket, and selected a spot for ambush.

As he had anticipated, the Mexicans were watching the back trail, and he took them by surprise. Undoubtedly they expected pursuit, but not by a lone man. They obeyed his order to throw guns and knives into the Pecos.

He ordered the men and boys to get down, stand with arms upraised, and to face him. One by one he made each of them advance, submit to search, and return to the line. Then he told them to lie on their faces while he searched the wagon. Hart's horse was tied to the end gate. In the bed of the vehicle women and children huddled on the floor, obviously attempting to conceal something. He made them climb out and join the men.

He found Hart's saddle, smeared with blood. A bedroll contained his clothing, wrapped about a bloody ax. No body. What had they done with it?

They refused to talk.

He made one man unsaddle the horses and throw the gear on them into the river. The animals began crowding into the water to drink. He forced the dozen or more people to get into the wagon and turn back toward Seven Rivers. They refused to tell where they had left Hart, until John threatened to take them back to the trading post and hang every one of them.

They had not stopped until nearly dark. They had dug a round hole, deep enough to contain the corpse. They had doubled Hart up with his knees under his chin and set him in the place. Over the body they had heaped dried chilis to prevent its being exhumed by wolves.

"Take him out, and straighten his body," John ordered.

"*Señor!* It is stiff."

"Straighten him out!"

They did so.

There was light in the east.

"Get your serapes and wrap him in them."

"But, *Señor*, it is cold."

"Not where you're going."

They used the ax with which they'd killed him to dig the grave. And when they had finished they placed the body in it and began covering it with earth.

There came a voice from across the Pecos — that of Billy Weir: "That you, John?"

"Yes."

"What you doin'?"

"Burying Hart. The Mexicans killed him."

"Accident?"

"Murder."

"Are you sure?"

"Absolutely. Did it for his horse and saddle. Hit him in the back of the head with an ax."

"Horrible!"

"Come over and help me kill them."

"I'm sick, John, almost got pneumonia. I don't dare get into that cold water. But I'll keep them covered. And, look, John, there's seven men and big boys. Got two sixshooters? You can't reload, you know."

"Got two."

"Then I'll keep you covered and I'll witness for you if it ever comes to trial."

When the seven lay on the ground, John told the women and children to get into the wagon. They obeyed, wailing and moaning. He turned the team to the south.

"Now, get going, and never come back."

Billy Weir called, "Now, what you going to do, John?"

"There's just one thing I can do — give myself up. I'm going back to Seven Rivers and do it."

"Don't forget that if you need help, Billy Weir's your witness. I'm headquarterin' at Monument Spring. Just send one of the boys over and I'll come."

"There's not any law at Seven Rivers, but I'll talk to the men. If they think I ought to go to Lincoln and stand trial, I'll ride in and report myself. I'll go by their judgment."

Both men sat their mounts till they could no longer hear the rumbling of wheels.

• • •

Ma'am heard two horses come in and uttered a prayer of thankfulness. The younger boys ran to take the mounts and she sank into her chair beside the fire. No wonder Hart trusted John as she did God. Hadn't he rescued him from the Indians? And hadn't he gone to his aid now? What would the family have done all these years without John?

He bent to kiss her. Then without a word he knelt beside her and buried his face in her lap.

"Hart?"

"I couldn't bring him back to you, Mother. I was too late."

"Is he gone?"

"He's buried beside the Pecos."

With head bowed Barbara Jones sat in silence. Finally she arose and turned to the children. "John's very tired. He must have some food and go to bed. Minnie, fill a plate for him. When he's eaten we must all go to bed."

"Mother, I can't eat. And I can't sleep. Before I do either I must talk to the neighbors. If the men think I should go to Lincoln I'll be back for clean clothes and some food."

"They'll be in bed before you get to the first house. Have a bath and go to bed. Early in the morning you can start to see them. It isn't right to awaken them tonight."

Within a radius of twenty miles there were only three men at home. Others were away with cattle. Each of those with whom John talked approved his action unreservedly and urged him to keep his own counsel. If he should ever be apprehended for killing the murderers, each of the three men would testify that John had consulted him and that he had been advised not to report what he had done.

Even Ash Upson approved both the slaying of the men and the judgment of the neighbors. It was, Ash said, the decision of a jury of his peers. Let well enough alone. John had done what any real man had to do under the circumstances.

And Billy Weir was never asked to give evidence.

War   20

During 1878 the Jones family heard strange and conflicting reports
of occurrences at the Lincoln County seat. So varied were they that
Ma'am wondered if there were not a different version for each inform-
ant. Of one thing she was certain: there was no neutrality. She was
thankful for the distance that separated her sons from the scene of
strife, and she discouraged discussion of the situation.

In addition to the conflict between the traders and the military,
there was a growing resentment on the part of the small ranchers
and farmers along the Hondo and its tributaries toward the Murphy
faction and the trading post at Lincoln. The Mexicans were not in
peonage, but their indebtedness to the traders placed them in a
position little better. They were, to a great extent, illiterate; they had
an income only when they sold their cattle or crops of hay. Ordinarily
they had money once a year, and when they did, what they owed the
store was usually greater than their cash incomes. Very few attempted
to keep any accounts. They purchased what they needed without
asking for copies of the statements. Had there been alternative markets
available, there might have been some purpose in asking or protesting
prices, but distance precluded trading elsewhere. The store could and
did purchase at its own price, and thus the proprietor could keep his
customers in debt indefinitely.

But the man who owned a big herd and employed many cowhands was in a position to send wagons to El Paso, Albuquerque, or Las Vegas, and buy in quantity at lower prices. He, too, paid once a year, and he kept books. Few if any transactions were effected by check, and banks were nonexistent. Receipts could be misplaced, and the trader's records were accepted if there was a question as to accuracy.

Ma'am Jones was well aware of the situation and kept books upon which purchases were entered. Transients paid cash, but her neighbors had charge accounts. They were never known to question either her prices or her totals.

Only where water from a stream was procurable for irrigation was farming profitable. The Mormons who had once lived along the Pecos were as expert in watering their crops by running water through ditches as were the Mexicans who had settled along the little streams. But the amount of land that could be supplied with water was very small. The canyons were narrow, and in the broad Pecos Valley the banks of the river were steep, and there were few places where irrigation was possible. There were no tributaries from the east, and it was those flowing from the mountains in the west that furnished nearly all the water used for growing crops.

For years after the Jones family arrived, few of the people who came to establish homes attempted to farm. Many brought in cattle, and if they found a waterhole upon which they could file and had enough cattle, they could survive. There was yet another condition: they must be able and willing to defend their little herds at any cost. When he became an old man Sam Jones said, "If a man wanted to live in this country he had to be able to defend himself, his family, and his cattle. If he couldn't do that, he had no business here."

On the Pecos, John Chisum was the only big rancher between Fort Sumner and the Texas Line. It was estimated that he had run eighty thousand or more cattle and employed as many as a hundred men. He did not own the enormous range he used for grazing, but he controlled it. The amount of land that was actually his was very small. It consisted of the South Spring Ranch, his headquarters, and small tracts — sometimes not more than forty acres — upon which water was obtainable. On the east side of the river were very few places where there was even a water-seep. One well-known spring was named the Mescalero because the Apaches had used it when going to the Llano Estacado to hunt buffalo. Infrequently there were other places to water a herd along the Pecos where cattle could reach the stream. But there were miles of watercourse with banks so steep that access to the water was impossible.

It was alleged that men in the employ of Chisum were filing on the land where the cattle could reach water and selling their rights to the boss. The settlers knew little of law, but considered this practice, if not illegal, at least unethical. Investigation of records was difficult and probably rarely accomplished because of the distances between the Pecos and the land office. If a man settled on a homestead where no water was available for his cattle, he was not permitted to let them drink from a source belonging to another man. A few discovered and filed upon homesteads well supplied with water, but this was west of the river.

As early as 1870, Hank Harrison had discovered Rattlesnake Spring at the foot of the mesa upon which the entrance to Carlsbad Caverns is located. He had brought a few cattle and held his land. Men bringing in herds for Chisum used this chance to hunt for water, and very early Felix McKittrick found and held the spring that bears his name. Others had settled along Seven Rivers and the Peñasco, and many had gone to the Hondo and the branches that unite to form it — the Ruidoso and the Bonito.

West of the Pecos, Murphy, Dolan, and Riley had extensive holdings, but it was believed that a wealthy man in Albuquerque owned the major interest in their land and cattle. Tom Catron never appeared actively in their transactions but was thought to be the silent partner. The conflicts leading to the Lincoln County War were further complicated when Catron put a herd on the Pecos. So long as Catron did not challenge Chisum's hold on his domain, there was not much friction between the two sections. But when the contest narrowed down to what M. G. Fulton described as "a struggle between two men for control of the situation, with the Pecos Valley as the prize," almost everybody in both areas became involved.

Also there was the inevitable struggle between the small and the large cattle owners. Chisum suspected, and in many instances no doubt with reason, that the squatters stole his cattle. Men who owned few cattle alleged that when Chisum drove a herd to market, he took everything in its path. These small cattlemen had neither the manpower nor the courage to attempt to "cut his herd" and therefore had no recourse. Moreover, Uncle John was a gentle person who never carried a gun. If he heard of a man's losing his few cattle he might stop to condole with him and offer to help recover them. But there is no record of his actually having helped.

The Mexican settlers in the river valleys west of the river had not come to run cattle but to farm. Many of them did begin to acquire herds, however, and again, suspicion and distrust existed between these settlers and the big ranchers.

The coming to Lincoln of an attorney, Alexander McSween —
and his subsequent acts — added fuel to the embers. McSween and
his vivacious and stylish wife, Susan, became residents at Lincoln.
McSween at first became attorney for Murphy. The connection did
not last long, and the attorney became the friend and — at least in
one business venture — the competitor of the owners of the trading
post.

About this time John Tunstall, a young Englishman, came into
the country and established headquarters on the Feliz, another tributary of the Pecos. His first idea had been to import a dairy herd in
order to supply milk to Fort Stanton. Instead he bought cattle for
beef production. He became the friend of McSween, and the two
decided to build and stock a store in Lincoln.

The attorney built a large U-shaped adobe house facing the one
street in the village, with the opening of the U above and facing on
the Bonito. Adjoining the house was erected a large adobe structure,
built much like a fort, with both wooden and metal doors and
windows. The McSweens later obtained a piano, probably the only
one in Lincoln County, and Mrs. McSween could play it.

Tunstall went to Las Vegas, bought merchandise, and superin-
tended its transportation to Lincoln. For the first time, the area had
an enterprise that offered competition to the Murphy-Dolan business.
The new partners even announced the establishment of a bank, though
proof is lacking that any money was ever deposited in it.

John Chisum became identified as a colleague of McSween and
to a certain extent of Tunstall. Perhaps because of their distrust or
envy of Chisum, the small ranchers on the Pecos "sided" with the
Murphy faction. Residents in and about Lincoln were divided, but
many more had reason to dislike Murphy than the newcomers, and
thus became McSween adherents.

•   •   •

Ma'am was familiar with the conditions and events leading to
much of the turmoil in and about Lincoln, but the situation that
arose after the arrival of John Tunstall and the McSweens was
especially difficult to understand. She knew of Tunstall because Billy
Bonney had reportedly gone to work for him after leaving her home.
But she found incomprehensible the involvements of McSween with
the settlement of an insurance claim made by a Fritz family. The
Fritz heirs were said to have sued McSween for a ten-thousand-dollar
policy and to have alleged that the lawyer had charged an unfair
fee. There had been a trial at Mesilla for embezzlement of funds.

Tunstall had accompanied McSween to Mesilla and on the way home had been challenged, but he apparently did not understand the local customs and did not fight.

If McSween had money invested in the new store in Lincoln, which was doubtful, the partnership did not include Tunstall's cattle. Ash Upson informed Barbara that Tunstall and McSween had entered into a written contract by which the partnership was to become effective when and if McSween produced the required capital.

McSween had represented Tunstall when he went to St. Louis (for the insurance) and was said to have acted as purchasing agent for cattle for the Englishman's ranch on the Feliz — but why anyone so ignorant of cattle should have been authorized to act is puzzling.

The Fritz family attached Tunstall's cattle. A posse was sent to get enough cattle to satisfy the claim but found few at the ranch. Tunstall had asked John Chisum for aid, but none came. He and his men fortified the house with sandbags. Dick Brewer, a McSween employee, left the Tunstall house to talk with the posse. He told the men that McSween had no interest in Tunstall's cattle, and that they could not take the animals. However, he would place them in the hands of some disinterested person to be held until legal ownership could be determined. He indicated that an attempt to take them would be resisted. The posse agreed to his terms and were invited into the house for coffee.

Tunstall himself was in Lincoln at the time, but the following day three of his men rode to the county seat to tell their employer of the occurrence.

Hearing these stories, Ma'am Jones felt relieved to be far removed from the scene of the conflict, and reminded her sons that they were fortunate not to have been involved. John quietly reminded her that as yet they had not been molested. Just what this remark implied, Ma'am did not know — surely not much, for what possibility was there of anyone's attacking the Jones boys?

Shortly thereafter a stranger brought a report of the brutal murder of Tunstall by the posse. Then came news that Captain William Johnson and Wallace Olinger had been deputized by Sheriff Brady. That was getting close. Ma'am admonished her sons to stay at home and attend strictly to their own business. She was firmly convinced that those who could do that quietly would always have a business to mind. The boys made no reply, and that was disturbing to their mother.

The following day as Ma'am crossed the yard to the door, a man —

apparently unaware of her presence — used his customary form of address in speaking to another. John overheard the epithet.

"You'll apologize to my mother for such language," he said.

"You don't call that cussin'?"

"My mother does. Get down on your knees and start crawlin'."

The startled man dropped and approached her. "Beg your pardon, Ma'am. I didn't see you. I'd insult an angel just as soon."

"I'm sure that's true," she replied. "Get up! And John, you shake hands with this man. I don't want any more of this."

"I'd never start a ruckus at your place, Ma'am Jones. Every man in this part of the world respects you."

"I'm glad to know it. And this is to go no further. You hear me, John?"

Her son nodded. The stranger mounted and rode away. She turned inquiring eyes to John. She knew that there was something behind this, something which she did not understand.

Her son explained: "He's a spy for John Chisum, been on the Pecos almost as long as Old John, and he's not up to any good. It gave me a chance to get rid of him without him knowing I'm wise."

"Now you've made an enemy of him, and he'll be much more dangerous than if we'd been friendly. He'll figure that we have something to hide. Is that the way for my twigs to stick together?"

"You're right, Mother. Did you know him?"

"Certainly. He's spent the night here. He asked questions and I put two and two together."

"You know how to handle people, Mother."

"I'm a mother protecting her young."

"You protecting me?"

"All of you. I don't want you mixed up in whatever is going on around here."

Ma'am was disturbed. What did John mean by his reference to one of Chisum's spies? And why should anyone watch the Jones family?

•   •   •

When Heiskell returned from a trip he told of a man's riding from Las Vegas to Roswell with him. They had spent the night at the trading post and found that Marion Turner had become a deputy for Brady. "That means he's in trouble," said Heiskell. "He figures that nobody will shoot an officer. And this man said that Billy's took up with the Coes. They're on the Ruidoso and gettin' sixty dollars a ton for cuttin' grama grass for hay. Sell it to the cavalry. Got it in for Brady. It's bein' told that Billy Bonney and Coe had a bet as to which one would get the sheriff. Put up a pearl-handled revolver for the winner. Seems like Billy won the bet."

"Billy didn't kill the sheriff?"

"Don't rightly know. Anyway, Brady's dead. Billy and some more, three or four, were behind the gate in the wall runnin' east from the corner of the Tunstall store. Brady and Hindman walked down the street and they fired. Somebody hit the sheriff. Billy says he aimed at Hindman; he died, too. Ol' Dad Peppin, who built our old trading post at Roswell, is sheriff now. The governor, on the Murphy side, appointed him. I'm afraid Peppin's not *hombre* enough to handle Lincoln County."

Heiskell went on, "The Dolan outfit's offering a hundred dollars for every scalp their men bring in, and they're out for the McSween bunch. They went out to arrest Ol' Man Buckshot Roberts at Tularosa, stopped at Mescalero to get a drink at the spring, and heard shots. Billy Bonney was on his knees at the spring; he raised up and said, 'Guess we're missing something.'

"The chief clerk at the agency rode up on the feast ground and didn't come back. The Apaches thought it was a bunch of hoss thieves. Half an hour later they rode over and got Bernstein's body. The posse didn't find Roberts at Tularosa, but later they got him. Godfroy had rented the big two-story house Dr. Blazer built for his home. Mrs. Godfroy used it for a hotel. The posse stopped to eat. Roberts rode in on a mule. He left his ammunition belt and pistol on his saddle and started in unarmed. He heard somebody yell, 'Here's Roberts!' and he returned for them. There was a fight and George Coe and Middleton were wounded. Dick Brewer and Buckshot Roberts were killed."

"Was Billy with them?" asked Ma'am.

"Yes. And Dr. Blazer's story is that Billy killed Roberts. The Coes tell it different. Dr. Blazer had reserved one room in his house for use as an office. Roberts backed into it and got Dr. Blazer's single shot .45-60. He was shot through the body, but he dragged a mattress off a cot and lay down on the floor. He killed Dick Brewer with a long shot.

"And they buried 'em both in the Blazer cemetery."

Heiskell produced a Las Vegas paper. It reported that the sheriff had deputized John and Robert Beckwith, Charlie Kruling, and J. B. Matthews. There had been a skirmish near the Fritz Cemetery, in which McNabb was killed, Saunders wounded, and Frank Coe captured. Wallace Olinger had been detailed to guard Coe but had turned him loose.

"I wish John were here," said his mother. "Roswell's much too close to Lincoln. Why don't you go back up there? If John knows that Minnie and I have none of the older boys at home he'll come back."

Then came word that the President had heard of the Lincoln County War and replaced the governor with General Lew Wallace. He had stayed at Dr. Blazer's for three weeks, and during that time he was working on a book. Later he gave Dr. Blazer an autographed copy of *Ben Hur*. At the same time he was investigating and making a list of people. Indictments were thick.

What, asked Ma'am, were indictments? Papers, Heiskell explained, charging people with crimes. Nearly everybody in Lincoln County was on the list.

Ash Upson informed her that Heiskell was indicted; and also that John and Jim were. The Olingers and Captain Johnson and the two Beckwith boys were included. Ash said that Old Man Gilbert had given Lew Wallace many of the names.

"Billy?" asked Barbara Jones.

"Oh, yes; they're after him for killing Brady."

"But he was one of five who fired."

"Sure. But they're after Billy — got to get him for something."

•   •   •

Gus Gildea, recently employed to carry the mail, made a trip to Las Vegas weekly. He reported that John Chisum had been arrested there and held for debt. Tom Catron and his partner, Thornton, represented the plaintiff in attaching Chisum's cattle, but the wily cattle king had placed his assets in the names of his brothers, Pitzer and James. Chisum was traveling to St. Louis with McSween and his wife. The attorneys used an old law providing that if a debtor were unable to pay a judgment and refused to render a schedule of his property he was subject to imprisonment. Chisum was held without bond but was permitted to stay in a hotel.

Chisum's defense was that in 1875 he had sold out for a considerable sum to Hunter and Evans. Those hostile to him had begun to plague him. A rival, William Rosenthal, had attempted to eliminate him as a contractor for beef. He bought up certain old notes from holders in Texas. He got these notes for little. Chisum explained the paper thus: While he was still a resident of Texas he associated himself with a packing-house venture at Fort Smith, Arkansas. He gave sufficient sanction to the plan to say to the others involved, Wilber and Clark, that if they could raise two-thirds of the hundred thousand dollars needed to capitalize the business he would furnish the other half in beef. Wilber and Clark were to give Chisum a decision later. His investigation of the two convinced him that he wished no business affiliation with them. Upon his return to Texas a year later he was surprised to learn that they had established a packing house under the firm name, Wilber, Chisum, and Clark. He immediately sent one of his brothers to Fort Smith to expose the imposture. The firm had issued notes totaling between eighty and ninety thousand dollars on the strength of the Chisum name.

On some of these notes Chisum was sued, but the courts gave him relief upon his denial of being a partner. He was a resident of Texas four years after their maturity. In order to accomplish the barring of the notes under the Texas statute of limitations, he established himself as a legal citizen of New Mexico. Then Rosenthal and others of the Santa Fe Ring attempted to resuscitate some of those old notes. Catron and Thornton obtained judgment on some. This action came after the sale to Hunter and Evans, which was to have brought in enough money to enable John Chisum to "roll in wealth."

"That seems to clear him of dishonesty," said Ma'am.

"Maybe," replied Ash Upson. "But it doesn't explain why he was traveling with Mrs. McSween."

"Mr. Upson! Her husband was along."

"You've hit the nail on the head, Ma'am. He *was along.* That's the best that can be said of her. Or of McSween. She's the brains of the team. And she's making a play for John Chisum."

"I don't like to hear anyone speak so of a lady, Mr. Upson."

"She's a born trouble-maker. You have no idea how she stirs up ruckuses at Lincoln."

Ash stalked indignantly away to bed.

Ma'am turned inquiring eyes at John.

"You just told Ash off for talkin'. Want me to go back on your raisin'?"

"That's all I want to hear, John."

"And people say you think like a man!" He laughed softly as he followed Ash to the roof.

There came more news: Tunstall, en route to Lincoln with Billy Bonney and another man, rode alone while his henchmen went up the mountain after turkeys. They heard shots and returned to find the Englishman's body stretched gruesomely on the trail. They took it to Lincoln and buried Tunstall north of the corner of the Tunstall corral.

Billy Bonney had sworn over the grave to kill every member of the posse.

"Billy's surely not going to try to oppose that bunch?" said Ma'am.

"He won't be alone, and he can take care of himself," replied Gus Gildea.

That evening Jim rode in with his gear. He was no longer working for Chisum, he informed the family. Ma'am told him of strangers who were frequenting the place, and he identified them from her description: Bob Speakes and John Selman. Bad men, both. Up to no good. She was to ask no questions of them. As though she would! And she must warn Sammie. No telling what he might say!

Battle   21

Marion Turner rode in and joined the boys who were milking in the corral. After bringing the buckets to the house they went to the Pecos for a bath. After they'd had supper, Turner and the younger boys went to the roof, but John lingered.

"You're one of those mind readers, I think, Mother. And you're right, as usual."

"What is it, John?"

"In the morning we ride. I want to get away by three. Don't get up; I'll cook breakfast."

"What are you going to do?"

"I don't know yet. When we get to Lincoln we'll see."

"Lincoln?"

"Yes, Mother."

"I knew Marion Turner was up to no good."

"You've always wanted us to be on the side of law and order. Well, Turner's a deputy and has come for us. All he does is deliver orders from the sheriff. We'll be deputized; we're not going because of Turner."

"What, then?"

"It's a showdown between the big ranchers and the settlers. This is John Chisum's fight for control of the whole country. If we don't

140

stand together everybody will be pushed out, just as the people were before we got here."

"That's to line you up with the Dolan bunch. And you know what they are."

"It just happens that they're on our side. We can't help that. We're certainly not for them, but we do stand with the little fellows."

"How about the Beckwiths?"

"They've always hated Chisum. They're with us, naturally."

"I see."

"Captain Johnson's going; so are Bob and John Beckwith, and Wallace Olinger and Bob, but not Old Hugh. Like Chisum, he lets others do his fighting for him."

"But this isn't our fight."

"If we want to stay here, it is."

"How about Billy Bonney?"

"Turner says he's with the Chisum bunch."

"You mean you'll be fighting against Billy?"

"That can't be helped. He has a right to choose his side just as we do. He don't care anything about Chisum; he hates Old John; says he owes him money and won't pay." And John added, "Billy's said to be after the bunch that killed Tunstall."

"Gus Gildea says Billy's a dangerous man. So does Ash Upson."

"Billy's like fifty or sixty more in this country; he's just a little quicker on the trigger than most."

"Did you ever know of his killing anybody?"

"Hindman, maybe; four or five fired at Brady and there's no way of knowing who hit him. Baker and Morton, maybe; Billy had a reason for them. And I never believed Old Ash's story of his killing a man at Silver City. Upson always was windy."

"If it comes to a showdown would you shoot Billy?"

"Not unless I had to; if somebody attacked me what else could I do?"

"Who's going?"

"Jim and Bill."

"Bill's just a child. Don't you realize that?"

"Do you think Bill'd stay out of it with everything we've got at stake? He's much like you, too much for that."

"But *is* everything at stake?"

"It is, Mother. There's no doubt about that."

"Take care of them, John, especially Bill."

"I'll take care of both of them and bring them back to you. And that's a promise."

"You'll need clean clothes; I'll get them."

She helped John cook breakfast and saw them off. Then she awakened the younger children and fed them. She told Sammie to hitch the mules to the wagon. When they arrived in Roswell Ash Upson was the only person there. He had resorted to drinking to veil the horrors he anticipated. Ma'am and Sammie put him to bed.

•   •   •

How Barbara endured the agony of the days that followed she did not know. She washed and boiled everything in the two little houses. She had the boys carry all bedding into the yard and place it by ant hills to rid it of vermin. That, she had learned from the Apaches, was the quick and easy way. She took the wool out of the mattresses, washed the covers, and set the boys to picking apart the matted bits so it would be fluffy again.

She thoroughly cleaned walls and shelves; she overhauled and rearranged merchandise. Last of all she heated the shovel and smoothed the floors.

While the children slept she walked the floor and prayed.

Six long days elapsed without word. The days seemed like weeks, months. Would the boys never come?

After dark she heard horses. Men were dismounting at the door — ten or twelve. As her three rushed toward her, John's arms closed about her. Captain Johnson, Wallace Olinger, and John Beckwith followed her into the house. Outside, in the light from the open door, she recognized Jake Owen.

"Everybody come back?" she asked.

"Everybody but Robert Beckwith; he lies by the Bonito, Mother."

"Marion Turner?"

"Not a scratch. Left him at Hondo."

"Mrs. Beckwith— poor woman!"

She began putting food on the table and others came into the house to share it. She urged all to spend the night, but nobody stayed. After the others had gone, the boys replenished the fire to heat water for baths. When they'd gone to the roof Barbara gathered up clothing and found blood on John's shirt. She called to him.

"Just a scratch," he assured her, "where Billy creased my shoulder."

"Billy?"

"He was among the first to leave the McSween house. He'd said that if he surrendered to anybody it would be John Jones. But maybe he didn't recognize me, for he took a shot at me. I yelled to him that it wasn't him we were after but the man he was working for. He ran toward the river, down the bank, and got away."

"Thank God!"

"I told him to hit for the brush, that we didn't want him."

• • •

It was years before the Jones family heard from the boys the details of the five days' siege of the McSween house. None of the participants discussed the fight with others; and when it was mentioned in the presence of Jake Owens, he cried. Bill Jones was an old man before the family got his account of what happened. He had not fired a shot but had moulded bullets and loaded guns for the older ones — not that any were really old. Milo Pierce lacked a month of being forty. Robert Beckwith was eighteen.

In the beginning, with few exceptions, the town had been divided at the McSween house, with the Dolan faction holding the upper portion and the McSween adherents the lower; but the divisions shifted and blurred during the siege.

When the cavalry came in from Fort Stanton, Bill Jones recognized Major Dudley. Wallace Olinger had gone to meet Dudley with a white cloth tied to a stick. He had told the officer that he was instructed to meet him and ask him to keep the cavalry out of the affair, because it was not their fight; and he added that if they interfered the two factions would unite against the military. The troops had camped but had not participated in the fight, though Mrs. McSween had gone to the officer and begged him to do so.

The McSween house was besieged. The inmates had scorned the parley requesting surrender, and they might have held out indefinitely had not the house been set on fire.

An adobe house burns slowly, and the men retreated from one room to another. Finally only the kitchen was habitable. When it caught, Billy said there was only one man to whom he would surrender — John Jones. He said that if anybody else tried to take him into custody, it would mean death for all the attackers. When Billy learned that Marion Turner was directing the siege, he resumed the fight.

From what the Jones family learned, Billy Bonney led the first group that attempted to leave the building. He offered to go first, attract the fire of the besiegers, and give McSween and the others an opportunity to escape while the enemy was concentrating on Billy and his companions. McSween held back; when he finally did run into the yard, he was driven back to the cover of the woodpile. In the southwest corner of the patio, the escapees took refuge and did not emerge until calling out an offer of surrender. McSween was shot by someone who was in the chicken house on the west wall of the patio, and with him fell Bob Beckwith.

Billy and others had dashed out shooting, while running toward the bank of the river. On his way he creased John Jones, possibly because of not seeing clearly whom he was attacking. John called to him to hit for the brush, that it was not he who was wanted, but the man for whom he worked.

The attacking party examined the fallen to ascertain if all were dead. Salazar, who had been wounded, feigned death and lay for hours where he fell. When he could do so unobserved, he crawled off to seek refuge. People were afraid to admit him because they feared that those who gave aid to him would be killed. He did at last find a home where he took refuge. The family sent for a doctor. Surgeon Appel was in Lincoln, at the camp just east of the Torreon. In his written report he tells of going to the house east of the Ellis place shortly after sunrise and treating Salazar's wounds. Appel's report adds that Salazar gave him the names of all those who had been defenders of the McSween home and also made an affidavit to the effect that, "The McSween group offered to surrender, and when Robert Beckwith came up, one of the party fired at him and killed him."

Joe Nash's report at the Dudley Court of Inquiry contains this account: "After the first party left, i.e., Billy the Kid and his partners, [then] I myself, Robert Beckwith, John Jones, and Andrew Boyle, stood at the gate north of the east of the house, to guard that portion of the premises and if possible to prevent any man of the McSween party from escaping. While there, someone of the McSween party called out to us to know if we would take them prisoners, and Robert Beckwith replied that he would; that he came for that purpose only, except it was necessary to kill them while taking them. The man called "Dummy" came up, walked in where those parties that asked to be taken were. John Jones, Robert Beckwith, and myself followed. When we got to those parties that asked to be taken, we were fired upon by someone secreted in a small chicken house. Bob Beckwith was killed. McSween and the others made a break to get away. We commenced firing as they ran. McSween was killed."

Another reported that Salazar had run into a room and found only a very old woman. His pursuers were at his heels. She lifted the bread board from her flour barrel, took out the big wooden tray in which she mixed dough for tortillas, and motioned for him to step into the barrel. When the searchers burst into her house they found her calmly mixing dough.

"You knew he was in the barrel, Bill? How?" asked his mother.

"It wasn't the right time of day to be mixing bread. Besides, there was a little dust of flour on the floor."

"And you said nothing?"

"I'd already seen too many killin's."

•   •   •

When the Jones family returned to Seven Rivers, Ma'am, despite the protests of her sons, decided to ride to the Beckwith Ranch.

"But Mrs. Beckwith has never come here to see you. And you came here after she did."

"No. But she's lost a son, her first-born."

When she returned the boys had supper on the table. She removed her bonnet, half-expecting Hart to hang it up for her.

Wallace Olinger had met her, lifted her from her horse, and presented her to Mrs. Beckwith. The visit was brief and formal. Though Mrs. Beckwith summoned a *criada* and served wine, she was aloof. When Mrs. Jones thought fifteen minutes had elapsed, she arose. Her hostess accompanied her to the door but did not invite her to return.

"I shall hope to see you again under happier circumstances," said Barbara Jones.

Mrs. Beckwith burst into tears and drew her guest back into the house. When she could control her sobbing she produced a letter and asked Barbara to read it.

"From my son," she said.

Barbara complied. The boy spoke of sending his love to them and to his sister's baby.

"Captain Johnson's and Camilla's child. They have a fine little boy." Mrs. Beckwith said.

Bill Jones said, "You won't go back, will you, Mother?"

"Why not? The first call was hard, but she urged me to come, and often. And we have few enough neighbors."

Heiskell came with freight. He told the family that he'd sold the Roswell houses to a Captain Lea. It seemed there had been a previous owner, a Mr. Van Smith, for whose father the place was named. He knew of no deed, no bill of sale, but Captain Lea offered to pay him

for a relinquishment of the claim in Turner's name so that entanglements might be avoided. Both agreed to compensate anyone who
might later demand pay.

Ash Upson continued to operate the postoffice and Heiskell to
haul merchandise for the trading post.

There were tense weeks following the burning of the McSween
house. There were investigations and indictments. Rumors from
Lincoln were appalling; but, so far as the Jones family knew, no
arrests were made on the Pecos.

"I'm standing hitched," said John.

"Me, too," agreed Jim. "They know where we are; and if they
want us all they need do is send word. We were on the side of the
law and will stand trial."

"For what?" asked Ma'am.

"Well, John and Turner are indicted for killing McSween. They've
got me on several counts I didn't even know had happened. And we're
not the only ones. I know of no man except Old Ash Upson who's not
indicted for something. Every worthwhile man in the country's on
the list."

●　　●　　●

Mr. Upson went to Seven Rivers for Christmas. He was ill and
despondent. Knowing him to be an alcoholic, Ma'am Jones put him
on an allowance, gradually decreasing the amount of liquor she permitted him to have. She prepared a liquid diet, consisting largely of
milk and beef broth. What she thought he needed was chicken soup.
She'd long wanted chickens, but getting them was difficult.

"Couldn't you bring me an old hen and a setting of eggs from
Vegas, Heiskell?" she asked.

"The eggs wouldn't hatch. Even if they didn't break from all the
jolting, they'd be addled."

"Yes, I suppose they would. How about making a coop and
bringing back some chickens in it?"

"Take a lot of room in the wagon. And chickens have to be fed
and watered; but if you want 'em —"

"It's eggs I want most. It's almost impossible to make a good cake
without them; and they'd be wonderful for cornbread. I'd surely like
to have them for breakfast, too; it's been years since we did."

"I'll make a coop and try to find some chickens in Vegas."

"Wants them for Ol' Ash, I bet," said Sammie. "Got him on spoon
victuals; now she wants to feed him aigs."

"If she wants 'em to throw at the dogs she's goin' to have 'em," said his father, "an' I don't want to hear of you faultin' your mother, no matter what she does. I ain't never frailed you yet, but I'm startin' in with a club when I do. Where'd that eye of yours have been if she hadn't fixed it back?"

"I'm sorry, Pa; I won't do it again."

Barbara planned for her Christmas baking. She'd make cookies and cakes, and fry doughnuts. Christmas was months ahead, but much of the pleasure of celebrating it was in the anticipation. She promised the boys gingerbread and mince pies. Pa Jones could always get apples — dried, of course — and raisins. And they'd have a tree and invite everybody on the Pecos.

Settlers

22

Sunday afternoons the neighbors assembled at the trading post for Sunday School. They sang hymns to the accompaniment of a mouth organ. They listened attentively while Ma'am read the lesson. They entered into discussions, and they enjoyed the services, especially when Mr. Upson, fortified by a few drinks, undertook to preach. Ash was considered gifted in what was then called "the art of augurin'." It seemed to be his way with words rather than his ideas that fascinated his listeners. Even the trail-weary pilgrims were impressed.

When Ash had finished, Ma'am served a big pan of spicy gingerbread covered with a thick mixture of apple butter and cream, with coffee and milk. This brought about a feeling of hospitality and friendship very gratifying to Ma'am. It was remarkable, she thought, what food does to stimulate interest in religion. And if the people wanted to dance awhile before returning to their homes, fine! That, too, might induce them to come back.

These gatherings gave Ma'am an opening for attempting to start a school. Several children lived within riding distance, and it was high time they got some education. It could be given in the store, with mothers taking turns conducting afternoon classes. The older children could help the younger ones. None of the five families could

afford a private tutor, as the Beckwiths did, but in Ma'am's plan there
would be no expense entailed — just the time and work.

They would teach the girls to cook and sew as well as read and
cipher. And the older girls — boys, too — could take turns preparing
the lunch. It would increase the size of Ma'am's grocery bill — fifteen
dollars last month! But there had been many travelers, and nearly all
had paid something for their meals. Fifteen dollars was a lot of money,
but even if it were more, a school was worth it. All the transients,
mostly "reps" from the ranches, strangers looking for claims, peddlers,
people going through with no apparent objective — all had to eat.

The Rustlers, too, must be fed when they came to trade. Bob
Speakes had gone to the Jinglebobs, but his bunch was still on the
Peñasco. Selman and Scarborough were thought to be stealing horses
and cattle, but not, so far, from the Jones family. John and Sammie
stayed with the herd, and the other boys worked for Rufe Segrest and
Tom Gardner. Gardner, whose son Joe later became a great roper,
had made a good cowboy of young Tom Jones. Gardner was a well-
educated man, too, and was teaching Tom things about rocks and
minerals. He said there were people, and not miners, either, who
made their living by studying rocks. He was a good citizen, and Tom
was fortunate to have a job with him.

• • •

There came alarming news of indictments: Marion Turner, Hall,
George Davis, and John, Jim, Bill, and Heiskell, for killing the Feliz
family (spelled "Phalis" by Governor Wallace). The governor evi-
dently did not speak Spanish; few "furriners" did. But none of the
Jones men received a summons. They went calmly about their own
affairs, ready to report if ordered to do so.

Mrs. McSween was appointed to administer the Tunstall estate,
but the Rustlers went from Seven Rivers and not only took the Tunstall
cattle but also compelled the two men left in charge of them to help
with the theft. Some of these cattle were sold to the Jones boys, who
received a bill of sale signed "Sam Collins."

Mrs. McSween sent a detective to Seven Rivers to determine the
location of the cattle. There were about two hundred, valued at
approximately $2500. The detective found them in the possession of
Bob Speakes, who had quit working for Chisum. He was a formidable
figure and Mrs. McSween could not induce the sheriff to attempt to
recover the herd.

She heartily disliked Major Dudley because of his refusal, during the siege, to interfere in the destruction of her home and the killing of her husband, but she swallowed her pride and went to him. Dudley, then a colonel, said that if application were made by the sheriff he would send troops. This was done, and Captain Carroll was ordered to leave Roswell to bring the herd back. He brought it to Roswell, but Mrs. McSween did not recover the cattle. Kimbrell, who succeeded Peppin as sheriff, tried to induce Dudley to turn the cattle over to the justice of the peace, but Dudley refused. Mrs. McSween consented to their being delivered at the Brewer ranch, where Smith took care of them until she could sell, which she did — for one thousand dollars. From this sum expenses were deducted, leaving little money to turn over to Tunstall's parents in England.

Investigations showed that the Slaughter and Jones families had bought some of the cattle; but strangely enough only Bill was charged with obtaining them illegally. He was in Rocky Arroyo with the Jones herd and decided to go to Seven Rivers. To do so he had to cross the arroyo at Dead Man's Gulch. In a dense fog he rode into the midst of a troop of cavalry.

They took the boy to Fort Stanton and chained him to a bed in a cell. He was held seven weeks, during which time he almost died of pneumonia. As soon as John learned of his arrest, he took two fleet Spanish mules and prepared to ride.

"Why not let me go?" asked Jim. "I know the fort — every foot of it. I know the corrals, the roads, and the Indians."

"Know some myself," replied John. "It's Magoosh who makes the medicine up there."

John was right. Magoosh did. John got access to Bill's room but could not induce the boy to leave with him. "Not goin'," said Bill. "Don't even know why they arrested me; haven't done nothin', and I'm goin' to stand trial. I'm not goin' to be on edge the rest of my life for somethin' I didn't do."

"Then you're going to have the best lawyer in New Mexico," said John.

"Who?"

"Don't know his name, but I'll choke it out of Murphy."

Just what occurred at that interview the Jones family never learned, but John took the trail to Santa Fe. He returned with Mr. Thornton, partner of Tom Catron.

Neither John Slaughter nor Bill Jones was tried. During Thornton's stay in Lincoln, John Jones kept him under surveillance. And in spite of the efforts of the McSween faction, no warrant was served on John.

•   •   •

When the Jones boys came back to Seven Rivers they found Billy Bonney at their home. He had returned like a homesick child. How people could believe this boy responsible for the bloody Lincoln County War, Ma'am could not understand, but he was under indictment for killing Sheriff Brady, and might be arrested at any time. He made no explanations, offered no apologies, and the Jones family asked no questions.

For a year Billy came and went, usually for an overnight visit only, but occasionally he stayed several days. He was, he said, frequently with George Coe when he went to the Ruidoso. The Coes were Billy's friends, and the Mexicans also liked him and often hid him. Sometimes, with guards posted, they had dances in which he joined.

The Jones family had their dances minus guards. John always claimed his mother for the first dance and Minnie for the second. Billy followed. Then both began, as Ma'am had taught her sons, with the oldest lady present, and asked every woman and girl for a dance. The men so far outnumbered the women that they were given numbers and danced with men until their numbers were called. Those who took the part of women tied handkerchiefs on their arms. In addition to waltzes and schottisches they danced squares, known as "B flats"; and they loved the vivacious Mexican dances they had learned on the Hondo.

Disturbing reports of cattle-stealing reached them. It had long been the custom that whenever people wanted meat they killed the first fat animal they found; but whole herds — that was different. Cattle were being driven in from Texas and to the Tularosa. Someone was receiving them, and it was openly charged that the Kid's gang did the stealing, and that Pat Coglan was the "fence."

On Billy's next visit he told of an inquiry from Governor Wallace, and of his reply. He had told the governor that both the Beckwith and Jones boys were at home on the Pecos attending to their own affairs until Marion Turner had come to them to stir up trouble. Turner had convinced them that this was their only chance to escape John Chisum's greed for land and that it was now or never for the small men. The governor had offered Billy immunity from arrest provided he would lay down his arms and promise to do no more fighting. But Billy said he would not live five minutes without his guns and that he could not accept the terms.

"Don't you boys get mixed up in this," Billy warned them. "So far you're in the clear. Stay there."

"We're indicted — Turner and I — for the killing of McSween — and all of us older boys and Pa for the Feliz family."

"I didn't know that. Well, stay clear as well as you can, anyway."

•   •   •

Under Ma'am Jones' leadership that summer, with donations of labor and materials, a little adobe building was constructed on the banks of the Pecos and a subscription school started. Those who could, paid, but no child was barred if the parents were unable to pay.

A railroad was built from the east to Pecos, and Heiskell began freighting from the nearer point. Business increased in volume and profit. The Jones cattle did well, and the boys were busy with them, or working for neighboring ranchers. But again Barbara had forebodings. Hadn't prosperity always preceded trouble? She voiced her fears to John.

"You're not like yourself, Ma'am; you're talking like a woman."

"I am a woman."

"But you've never had a woman's failings. You've had more courage than any man I know."

"Your father has a courage you don't understand; it's the courage to keep out of trouble. Before we married he promised he'd never fight."

"I know," said John, "and it's been hard for him to keep his word. People have underestimated him because he's quiet and controls his temper."

"If that's a failing, I wish everybody had it."

John decided that a dance might enable his mother to overcome her somber mood, and he sent the boys out to invite everybody in the country. Sam and Nib took the wagon to collect the girls and women. The big problem in driving the wagon was to keep the oxen moving fast enough to get back before supper. There were no lines with which to drive and no means of stopping the team except by command. The boys started home with a wagonload of women and food. Heel flies attacked the oxen, and they twisted their tails and started for a clump of *bois d'arc* that had been planted for posts. When Sam realized that he could not stop the team, he climbed into the wagon and began handing the girls out to Nib. As the oxen struck the thicket, Sam rescued the last of his cargo. The brush was so thick that the oxen could not penetrate it far. There stood the team until the boys walked to the ranch and returned with another conveyance.

Even Ma'am Jones was astonished at the number of people who attended that dance. The country was settling up fast. Men bringing in herds for syndicates liked the range and returned to it with their families and cattle.

• • •

Rocky Arroyo, which the Jones boys considered their private range, was invaded by herds in spite of the fact that the Apaches used it for raiding the Pecos. Bill built a rock house there; it was just one large room equipped with a fireplace.

On a trip up Rocky with cattle, Bill found an aged Apache under a tree. The Indian was ill. Bill loaded him onto a horse and took him to Seven Rivers. Ma'am looked at him and told the boys to take him to the river and bathe him. He submitted to the indignity without protest.

"Do they turn them out like old worn-out horses to die?" she asked.

"No. He probably knew he couldn't keep up with the rest and asked them to leave him. It was really his only chance to live." Bill explained.

The Indian was delighted to hear his own language and accepted their care gratefully. The boys called him Mose; they didn't know why. They gave him a bedroll, and he slept just outside the door. He refused to enter the house either to eat or sleep. What they would do with him when winter came they could decide later.

"It's bad to die from a bullet, but I think being abandoned by your people is worse," said John to his mother.

"Then you'd better be thinking about getting married," said she. "Age isn't sad if you have your family about you."

"How would you know?" he asked. "You're not old. And you're the prettiest girl in the country, and the best dancer."

Revival on the Pecos

23

"Run along and gather the eggs, Sammie; I want to make a cake. I'm hoping there'll be enough that I can cook some for breakfast. They'll be good with that ham your father just cut."

"Sure hope none of them pesky pilgrims comes," said Sam. "I ain't et at the first table for months."

Toward evening Ma'am heard the sound of wheels. Wagons rumble, but this was a rattle. She arose and looked out the door. Sam came in with a hat full of eggs.

"Funny-lookin' little runt in a hard-boiled hat," said he, "ridin' in a contraption somethin' like a buckboard, only it's got a lid on."

"A lid?"

"Sort of a cover over the top."

They were interrupted by John's arrival.

"What's he doin' now?" Sammie asked.

"Feedin' his horse. Says he's reppin'," John answered.

"Who for?"

"God."

Ma'am stared at him.

"Well, that's what he said. I asked him."

154

The boy had been watching the stranger unceremoniously make himself at home, and was disapproving.

"Then he's a man of God," Barbara told them, "and, of course he's welcome. But most men wait to be invited before feeding their horses. He's coming in now. Behave yourselves."

"Lookin' for a place to hold Divine Service, Ma'am," said the stranger officiously as he entered the store.

"You're welcome to use this room, "Ma'am replied. "It's our store. I've hoped for years that a minister would come along. And we have plenty of sleeping room for you."

"But this here's a saloon."

"Yes. And it's also a Sunday School room. It's our living, dining, and kitchen room, too."

The stranger seated himself by the fireplace and the boys looked at his belligerent back with open contempt. Ma'am set about the cooking of a meal for him, and the boys withdrew to talk among themselves. Fearing that he might overhear, their mother hastened to admonish the group.

"Don't look like no *padre* to me," said Tom.

"He isn't a *padre*. He belongs to some other church," said Ma'am.

"Is there more than one church?"

"Certainly; many."

"How do you know which one's the right one?"

"All of them are right. They all lead to the same place."

"Beats me," said Sam, dubiously.

"He's got his satchel out of the rig," said Ma'am. "Now I want you boys to ride around and get word to the neighbors. We'll have a sermon this evening. I'm hoping everybody on the Pecos joins the church."

"Us, too?"

"Of course. I had the older boys and Minnie baptized when they were babies. There's never been a preacher for you younger ones, but I've put your names in The Book. And I'm going to have you baptized while he's here."

"An' you done that to John and Jim?"

"They were sprinkled, yes; and also Minnie and Bill."

"But we're too big."

"I did the best I could for you."

Ma'am showed the stranger to a bed, one of the large ones usually used by the boys. Luckily he could have the room to himself, unless travelers happened along, for the boys infinitely preferred sleeping on the roof.

"Mother," said John, "as a judge of men and horses, I never saw your beat. If this preacher had come on any other business would you trust him?

Ma'am looked at him without speaking.

"The boys trust you absolutely. You've never lied to them. But you're too smart to have any respect for this man."

"I know nothing about him yet."

"You've seen him and that's enough. He's self-important. He thinks this place isn't good enough for him. He has bad manners, too. How can you expect the boys to trust him?"

"Sort of keep order, John," Ma'am pleaded. "Don't let Sammie talk —"

"Anything else?"

"If anybody comes during the service don't sell them liquor."

"Anything else?"

"We'll go ahead just as usual. Anything else would be hypocritical."

"I'll do what you ask. There's not a man on the Pecos who would intentionally offend you. I'll ride herd on this one, if you say so."

•   •   •

People flocked to the evening service. The boys rolled kegs in and laid boards across them for seats. It was the first sermon her boys, some of them grown, had heard. Ma'am wished fervently that the preacher would not saw the air so violently nor damn his audience so irrevocably as he did. He seemed to get much satisfaction from predicting a horrible eternity for all who did not conform to his orders. He all but took his helpless victims by the scruff of their necks and held them over the fire to sizzle.

When his demand for converts was met with a stony silence, he was obviously puzzled. Ma'am hoped that his urging them to come forward indicated that the meeting was terminated, but it occasioned his launching into another tirade that lasted two hours. She was exhausted before he released them.

The younger boys scampered up the ladder to the roof, but John lingered. She looked pleadingly at him, and he tried to restrain his mirth. "If that's a fair sample," he said, "I don't think we've missed much by having no preachers."

"But it isn't, John. I've never heard anything like this before."

"And he ordered them to come back every night for a week. Reckon anybody's dumb enough to do it?"

"I don't know," Ma'am replied. "But whatever you do, don't let the boys know how you feel about him. They think that whatever you do is perfection. Some day a different sort of preacher may come."

"Talks like he thinks we don't believe in God. I was never so insulted in my life. Are there people who don't believe in God?"

"I've never heard of any."

"I've seen some pretty rough men, but never one who didn't believe in God."

"But I so want the boys to get the right start that I don't know what to do. Tell me."

"You've already given them a good start. You don't need to worry about them."

"But I want them to join the church and be baptized."

"That's something they must decide for themselves, isn't it? This man tries to work people up to some kind of drunken excitement. If the boys ever join a church they ought to be sober and in their right minds when they do it."

Ma'am's distress touched him.

"I can heist him along if you say so."

"No, we couldn't do that. We'll just have to trust in God."

•   •   •

The next morning Ma'am proudly placed a huge platter of ham and eggs on the table. She poured fragrant coffee and took fluffy biscuits from the Dutch oven. The preacher was served first and he scooped off a huge slice of ham and slid five eggs onto his plate.

"Looky there!" said Sam, in an undertone which Ma'am heard distinctly "Time second table's down they won't be a aig left."

"Catch me settin' there all night again with him cussin' us," growled Tom. "I'm not fixin' to take no such talk from no man, not even for Ma'am. Reckon she's lost her mind?"

"Beats me. But you better toe the mark, 'cause she's workin' on John, and you know he'll do anything for her."

"He's startin' in on biscuit and gravy now," said Sam. "Maybe we'll get a aig."

The preacher had taken a handful of biscuits, broken them, and covered his plate with the halves. He poured rich ham gravy over them and set the empty bowl back on the table. Ma'am made gravy by pouring thick cream into the skillet in which she cooked the ham, and letting the mixture simmer till it was thick. They watched hopefully while she refilled the bowl, but the preacher emptied it again over another plate of biscuits.

When he drew each side of his long mustache through his mouth and loudly sucked the gravy from it, they thought surely he had finished. The others at the table declined to take another egg, but he tipped the platter and left it empty.

"Better eat it, too, you old s.o.b.," muttered Sam. "Might as well eat the platter while you're at it."

A warning glance from Ma'am headed off any possible further comment. When the boys were summoned to eat she cooked more eggs. Whether or not she'd foreseen the situation they never knew, but she had reserved an egg for each. Sammie hadn't expected to get one, but he looked up gratefully when she placed it on his plate. There was unmistakably a twinkle in her snappy black eyes.

For several nights the preacher exhorted, but to no avail. Nobody came forward to give his hand to the Lord. "Guess he means hisself," said Tom when they were reprimanded for their hesitancy.

"You're breakin' Ma'am's heart," John told the younger boys. "Somebody's got to join him. Figger it out for yourselves, but one of you's got to do it. She means it for your own good. You know that. Bein' baptized's not goin' to hurt you. You break the ice and go in the Pecos all winter."

"I ain't going to be bullied into it," said Sam. "I don't mind bein' saved if Ma'am wants it, but they ain't nobody goin' to *make* me do it. I'll just take my medicine."

Defiance of John's edicts was a new idea to the younger Jones boys. It was to John, also; but he made no reply. After a long silence he said, "Well, you play poker to decide which. Draw straws, or run a horse race. The loser's it."

"It ain't fair," said Henry. " 'cause they're all bigger'n me."

"I know it, but figger it out. Then maybe he'll leave."

"We can take care of him leavin'!"

"No! I promised Ma'am you'd behave."

The next morning a woman came into the trading post breathless from running and excitement. She carried an egg which she placed on the table for inspection.

"Found it in the nest. Writin' on it. Look!"

There was. Crudely but legibly it bore the words, "Puppair to meat thi goD."

There was a silence. Ma'am put the egg on a saucer and turned it slowly. The preacher pushed his way to the table. "It's a warnin' to this Godless country to join the church," he announced solemnly. Then he left.

Ma'am Jones held a summary court martial. Nobody knew anything about the egg. "Somebody's done it for a joke. It's a poor one. It's irreverent, and it's disgraceful."

"How could anybody do it? The writin's in the shell. It's raised up — rough."

"The words have been written with grease, a candle, likely; and the egg's been soaked in vinegar to eat away the shell. Left the letters standing up."

"Then it ain't a miracle like in The Book?"

"Miracles do happen, but this isn't one. And I want to know right now who did it."

"It wasn't me," said Sammie. "You know I couldn't spell them words."

She turned helplessly to John.

"Who stands to profit by this, Ma'am?" he asked.

"That's unfair," she answered. But her sons were convinced that the preacher was the culprit.

●　　●　　●

That evening the store was crowded. Men squatted on their heels along the walls; women crowded together on the benches. Children sat in the aisles; all listened attentively to the sermon. When the invitation was given, people flocked toward the preacher and knelt at his feet. Ma'am looked imploringly at her sons, but the whole force stood pat.

There was a generous collection. The preacher announced a baptismal service the following afternoon. He intended starting to Roswell Sunday morning, he said. The Jones family felt intense relief.

When the boys went to the roof, John stayed to speak to his mother. The preacher approached him and said, "Don't you think it's about time you made your peace with God?"

"Who? Me? I never had any trouble with Him. He's helped me out of lots of jackpots."

The preacher threw up his hands and went to the bedroom.

"And after all I've done for him!" said John.

"He won't be here but one more night. Don't let anything happen. Please don't."

"What could happen?"

"I don't know, but boys think of things."

John followed the crowd to the Pecos and rode his Spanish mule into the swift water. He uncoiled his rope and sat, ready for a rescue.

Heiskell grasped the preacher's coattails firmly and braced him while he immersed the converts. Then they returned to the store for dry clothing and the farewell message.

The preacher's trip to Roswell may have been a bit rough, but he did not discover the cause until somebody pointed out to him the fact that a front wheel had been exchanged for a rear one — a parting gift from the Jones boys.

Magoosh   *24*

After Hart's death Ma'am felt insecure unless John were at home, and he seldom came. Jim was away and Heiskell was freighting. Though both Sammie and Tom were expert marksmen, they were children. She was often unable to sleep, and she was annoyed with herself because she needed rest. One morning she awoke before her usual time, aware that a noise had disturbed her. She threw a heavy robe about her and thrust her Winchester through the slit that served as a window. A hand grasped the gun and a voice spoke. She recognized that voice.

" 'Migo," it murmured.

"Magoosh!"

"*Ow* [Yes]. Hurt."

"Wait. I'll let you in."

She admitted the Apache, bolted the door, and stirred up the coals in the fireplace. Then she saw that his clothing was wet and that blood was dripping from his arm.

"Tejanos," he said. "Close — be here quick."

She ushered him into her room before wiping blood spots from the earthen floor. Then she pulled a buffalo robe over the damp spot before putting wood on the fire. As she finished putting a tourniquet on his arm and wrapping it in a towel, she heard horses in the door yard. She lifted Bruce from the trundle bed and placed the child in her own. Henry followed. She motioned Magoosh to get into the small bed, and she pushed it under the large one and adjusted the ruffles to conceal it. Then she answered a knock at the door.

"Who's there?"

"Texas Rangers, Ma'am."

She opened the door. "Come in, Captain; you're out early."

"Chasin' a red devil, Ma'am, beggin' your pardon."

"Sit down. I'll fix you some breakfast."

"Ain't seen him, have you?"

"No devils," said Ma'am, firmly.

"Reckon you know what we want, Ma'am," said the leader, apologetically.

"I should. I've fed you often enough that I should. Just sit down, all of you, and I'll have breakfast in a jiffy. I've got to get some beef from the roof — unless one of you would take this butcher knife and cut some steaks? Go through the boys' room and up the ladder."

She set a Ranger to building the fire and began mixing biscuit dough. When the man returned with the meat she put it in the Dutch oven while another man ground coffee. With her hands sticky with dough she stopped and listened.

"Captain, would you mind looking at the baby? If he's awake he may fall out of bed. Right through that door — "

The leader was not a captain, but in Ma'am's experience no man had ever declined a promotion. He arose and went into her bedroom.

"He was mighty clost to the aidge. I rolled him over agin the wall. An' the little lady in the single bed — I took a look at her; she's asleep."

"I surely thank you."

They ate and rode away, but Ma'am did not relax her vigilance. When the boys had eaten she stationed Tom on the roof to report the approach of any horseman. Then she took a pan of hot water to her bedroom and dressed Magoosh's wound. She found a bullet lodged in the muscle of the upper arm. She slit the skin, probed with a knitting needle, and pushed the piece of lead until there was a bulge at the opening through which it had entered. To get it out she had to make an incision. When she had finished Magoosh was weak from loss of blood. She gave him whiskey to drink and used some to cleanse the wound. Then she bandaged the arm and had him return to his hiding place.

"Good woman; *gouyen*," he murmured.

"You're to stay with us till that has healed. Then we'll give you a horse to ride home."

"Turn loose and come back like before," he replied.

"But you must keep hidden."

"*Ow.*"

Ma'am knew that the Rangers might return. There was little probability of their having been deceived. They were trailing a man afoot, one whose only chance lay in hiding.

They might have separated, surrounded the place, and be waiting for Magoosh to attempt to leave. She must keep him there. They might know that he was wounded; and they surely would know that he had made his way up the river — probably in the water. They might expect him to attempt an escape that way.

Many people came for mail and purchases. The neighbors feared the Apaches. Though no one would be apt to report Magoosh's presence, anyone might betray it. Nobody must know he was there, and the safest place for him was in Ma'am's room.

Minnie, Sam, and Tom knew, but the smaller boys did not. During the day they would not miss their bed, but when night came they might. Fortunately Heiskell was away. If he were at home he would approve and help, but if he were questioned —

When the wound had healed, the boys scouted the country for signs, but they found no indications of the presence of the Rangers. They saddled a horse for Magoosh, put a blanket and food on it, and started him home after dark.

• • •

When Heiskell arrived with a load of merchandise he brought news of a battle between the Rangers and some Apaches, supposedly from the Mescalero Reservation. Magoosh, he said, was the chief in command. The Indians had put up a game fight and escaped. The officer in charge had divided his troops and sent small groups in search of the fugitives.

"A bunch came here," Ma'am informed her husband.

"Didn't find Magoosh, I reckon?"

"No. They ate breakfast and rode toward Roswell."

Heiskell might miss the horse Magoosh rode, but since the boys had a big remuda and kept from eight to ten mounts each with them, he might not. So long as he knew nothing he could truthfully answer any questions he might be asked.

"There's strange Indians as Mescalero. Victorio's a big chief, and things ain't so safe as they used to be. Better keep an eye open for fires in the Guadalupes."

"If they meant to attack Seven Rivers they wouldn't warn us ahead of time, would they?"

"No. Of course the Mescaleros ain't going to bother us."

"I'm not afraid, but it will do no harm to watch."

The boys and Minnie listened without a word. When their father had gone Tom asked why she hadn't told him.

"Your Pa's an awfully poor liar," Ma'am replied. Then she explained that it is much easier to tell the truth than to attempt to evade it. "Liars," she said, "have to have good memories. If they don't, they give things away. I'm glad your father can't lie well. I wanted to save him the necessity of doing it."

There were signal fires in the mountains. The neighbors were frightened, and some brought their children and spent their nights at the trading post. One morning Frank's old gray mule was missing. The loss was nothing; he'd been stolen several times but always returned, once with the arrow-brand of the reservation on him. But the fact that somebody had come to the corral was alarming.

The neighbors let their cattle roam but brought their horses into the village at night. There was such general concern that Ma'am thought a dance might relieve the tension. The boys butchered a beef and barbecued the meat. She baked pies and cakes and cooked a huge kettle of frijoles. She baked gingerbread also, and set sponge for sourdough biscuit.

They danced to the music of a mouth organ and violin. For the bass, Tom beat a tub. At midnight there was another meal, and again dancing till breakfast. When the men went out to hitch up their teams and saddle their horses they found that there were only nine in the corral. They had heard nothing during the night, although with the noise of the dance, that was not strange.

Men and boys started out to round up mounts. As Bill left the corral Mose drew him aside and warned him not to follow. Old Sitting Bull, he said, and all his warriors were in the Guadalupes. No White Eye who went up there would return. Bill should stay at home. He returned to tell his mother and ask her to get some food ready for him to take with him. It had been several years since the Custer massacre, and that Mose could have known of it amazed Barbara.

While the men were obtaining horses and stocking ammunition, Ma'am prepared food. There was plenty of meat cooked, and they could live on that awhile. As they rode out Bill called to the men, "If you want to catch an Indian you've got to ride on his tail. Don't wait to fill canteens. We'll be on Rocky all the way."

Jim, Bill, and Sam Jones went; so did Charlie Slaughter, Pete Corn, Bill Nelson, Walter Thayer, and Sam Ashby.

"We oughter catch 'em," said Jim. "We're not like the cavalry; takes them two days to get ready to move. And they carry so much plunder that they wear a horse down in no time. Reckon they don't want to get close to Apaches, anyhow."

At the entrance to Rocky Arroyo, the men were riding so close that they forced the Indians to break camp before time to eat. But they did not overtake the Apaches until they reached a little bald, round-topped mountain twenty miles up the canyon. The Apaches were camped on it, and they were cooking meat. The hide of Pete Corn's pet stallion, a beautiful two-year old, was hanging on a rock. They had driven some cattle before them, and had left them in a little side canyon. The horses were on the slopes. The men stampeded the cattle and headed them down the arroyo, then attempted to cut the hobbles and recover the horses, but a shower of bullets interrupted that effort.

"Whoever said the Apaches ain't got Winchesters was *muy loco,*" said Jim. "They got Winchesters, and they know how to use 'em. They got ammunition, too."

Sam Jones, years later, told this story: "We rode 'round and 'round the mountain, shootin' up at 'em. They had rocks for cover, and they had the advantage of shootin' down. I don't know yet why they didn't kill every one of us. They did kill every hoss we had, right under us. So, if they'd wanted to they could have got us easy. As it was they put us afoot, and done it easy. We'd started a few of the horses they'd stole down the arroyo, but we never did catch up with 'em. All we could do was take our saddles and bridles and hoof it home. When we started, you'd orter heard the Indians laugh. Goin' without food's nothin', not if you have water. But walkin' and carryin' a saddle — God A'mighty!"

When they reached Seven Rivers, men had brought horses; so the party secured food and headed back for the Guadalupes. The Apaches had a two-day start and were never sighted. The men found no bones except at Round Mountain, where they found an Indian burial.

On that trip they stopped at a beautiful waterfall to camp. Because of Mose's story they named it for Sitting Bull, and a narrow pass they called Dark Canyon. When they hit the last living water, Walter Thayer suggested a name — Last Chance Canyon. The names are in use today.

Further pursuit being useless, the men turned back and camped a short distance below Round Mountain for the night.

Bill Jones examined the place carefully. There was excellent range, abundance of water, and canyon walls that would hold cattle without their being herded. By closing two narrow places above and below, a man would have ideal range, sheltered in winter, and ample for hundreds of cattle. There were stones lying about, plenty for building a house and walls for a corral. Bill decided right there to return and establish a ranch at this spot.

"Not a cow camp," he told the men, "but a reg'lar house with a fireplace. The more I see of Rocky the better I like it. The water doesn't flow in a channel. It spreads out wide and seeps down. There's good grass and plenty of water. Brakes for shelter. Good land for farmin', too."

"Who'd ever farm?"

"Don't know; somebody might want to."

"Not any Joneses."

"Anyway, this is my ranch. I'm going to bring my cattle up here right away."

"And risk being run out by the Indians?"

"I'm not afraid of 'em; you saw how they did. They could have killed every one of us."

"Then why didn't they?"

"Magoosh, I expect," said Bill.

Her Warrior

25

"Sammie," said Bill, "you're always talkin'. Can't you get me a girl for the dance tonight?"

"All the folks 'round here bring their daughters their own selves. They don't let no cowboy take 'em."

"There's a pretty little *señorita* down by the Pecos. The family just moved into that old *chosa*. 'Lope down and ask if she'll come with me."

When they reached the house both dismounted. Mother and daughter stepped out the door and Bill nudged Sam.

"I'm Sam Jones and this is Bill. They's a dance at Corn's tonight and we come to see if you'd go."

The girl turned to her mother and spoke so rapidly in Spanish that neither of the boys understood what she said.

"I don't got any shoes," she told them.

"Would you go if you had some?"

"*Sí, Señor,* but I don't got."

"I'll bring you some from the store," said Bill. "I'll measure your foot with my horn string and bring some this evening."

He set off leading a horse with Ma'am's saddle on it. He rapped at the door and the mother answered. He handed her the shoes.

Bill thought the girl was taking a long time primping, and he rapped again.

"Teresita — she gone," the mother demurely informed him.

"But she said if she had some shoes she'd go —"

"But not with you, *Señor*. And not to the dance. She go with her sweetheart; already gone."

Girls were terribly scarce in the region about the time that Jim Campbell of the High Lonesome, near the Texas Line, moved to Seven Rivers. He and his family, including two daughters, stayed at the Jones home until their house was ready for occupancy. Shortly after they were settled in it Bill again went to Sam for help.

"If you want to keep company with Miss Annie, why don't you just spunk up and talk to Jim Campbell?" Sam asked.

"I'd just make a mess of it, and I want this done right. You know what Ma'am thought about Marion Turner for not askin' the girl's father."

"Who's goin' to do my courtin'?" asked Sam.

"You're gabby enough for the whole family. Now, go ahead, Sammie, and I'll give you a heifer."

"Pickin' my own heifers," was the reply.

"I mean a calf. You know what I mean."

"Can't tell from what you say."

By accident Sam met Jim Campbell and turned his horse to ride beside him. They drifted along in silence till Campbell suddenly asked what was on Sam's mind. He'd considered many methods of approach, but blurted, "Bill wants to know if he can keep company with Miss Annie."

"Pretty young, ain't he?"

"He's nineteen; and he's got a range and a herd of his own."

There was no response.

"He's a good shot, and he ain't afraid of the Indians."

Still no answer.

"Ma'am thinks a man orter go to the girl's father."

"So do I."

Another prolonged silence.

"I guess it'll be all right."

Sunday morning Bill set out in the family's new buckboard — the first they'd owned. He drove the Jones' best team and was groomed for the occasion. He ate dinner at the Campbell home and in the afternoon took Miss Annie for a drive. He returned before sundown and told his mother, "I wasn't drivin' awful fast, but a wheel hit a stump. It threw Miss Annie out. I thought I'd killed her, but she wasn't hurt much."

Ma'am laughed. "Queerest sort of courting I ever heard of; do you think Mr. Campbell will let her go again?"

"I told him, and when he seen Miss Annie wasn't hurt he just laughed."

"She's still a little girl, Bill."

"She's fourteen; she's nearly as old as you were when you got married."

"Married! You surely haven't any idea —"

"Next Sunday. Mr. Campbell's willing; so's Miss Annie."

There was a prolonged silence.

"Well, ain't you glad, Mother?"

"It's so sudden. You scarcely know the child."

"I knew the minute I saw her that I'd been waiting for her. She's a lot like you, Mother."

"Where will you live?"

"At my rock house up the arroyo."

"It isn't really yours yet. You can't file on it till you're of age. Then it will be three years to wait."

"It's mine, just the same. I'd like to see anybody try to take it away from me. I'll teach Miss Annie to shoot and to cook. She's already a good rider."

"Who'll perform the ceremony?"

"Ash Upson. I'll go after him tomorrow."

"And you'll take Annie fifty miles from a neighbor; and you'll leave her alone when you're out with the cattle?"

"I'll take her with me. She's not afraid of anything."

Bill was the first of Ma'am's flock to marry. He proudly took his girl-bride to the house on Rocky Arroyo. She began her duties as homemaker and cowhand; and she became proficient in each field. Bill had plans for a bigger and better herd. Ranchers were buying good bulls. He'd do that. And he'd build another room just as fast as he could pick up the rock and do it.

His ambition caused him to consider another investment. He knew there were faster ways of making money than running cattle, though it was a good one. He would build a saloon at Seven Rivers, and sell liquor.

"Who's going to run your place? Annie?" asked Ma'am.

"No. She's going to stay right with me every minute for the rest of her life. I'm hiring a man, name o' Collins."

"I've seen him," said Ma'am, shortly.

"You don't think much of the *cantina*, do you?"

"I'm afraid of it."

"But you sell liquor here. And there's never been any rough stuff."

"That's because Minnie and I live here. There'll be nobody but men at your place, and there's sure to be trouble."

Bill looked doubtful.

"What does Annie think about it?"

"She doesn't say. But it will make money."

"There are things more valuable."

He nodded. She made no further effort to dissuade him. He and Annie stayed on until the venture was launched.

John was frankly amazed at the project. "Bill's not going to be in that business long unless he quits ranching and runs it himself. Why didn't you stop him?"

"Ever know of anyone's talking Bill out of anything?"

"No."

"Besides, I'm counting on Annie. She's young, but did you ever see anybody handle a man like she does Bill? He just eats out of her hand."

"He's gettin' bridle-wise, all right," admitted John.

"I wish you and Jim were as lucky. Annie's a good brake for Bill."

"That little thing! Butter wouldn't melt in her mouth."

"She's got enough grit to live up Rocky Arroyo, and how many men do you know who'd risk it?"

"Nobody. But she's so quiet and ladylike."

"That's how she manages Bill."

That The Rustlers were still in the country, they knew. It was rumored that they'd shifted their habitat from the Peñasco to the lower Rocky terrain. But nobody could be sure till Bill and Annie rode in one evening with a body on their pack horse. They found it at the little gulch below their house. Bill heard shots and rode out to investigate. The man was not dead when Bill found him. He said he'd been gambling with Selman, Speakes, and Scarborough, and had won all their money. There had been a quarrel, and then shooting.

"Who is he?" asked Ma'am.

"Don't know," replied her son.

"And I thought I knew every man in the country. Well, we'll have to bury him."

"We can't stay, for we left the cattle alone. Annie and I must go back tonight."

Ma'am thought a warning in order. "So long as there were no white men up there we weren't worried about Annie; now I don't know. It was so calm and peaceful before the white outlaws came. We seemed very close to God. It's different now; it is because of all this greed —"

"The biggest hog gets it all, just like John Chisum did," said Heiskell. He turned to the task. "Get those boards I split out of that cottonwood log. I made 'em for shelves, but we'll have to use them for a coffin."

They laid the corpse to rest on the banks of the Pecos. This was the first death since Hart's. Eventually the place must be fenced. They marked the grave with a crude cross and piled brush about it.

A month later a bunch of drunken Rustlers rode into the settlement, broke into Bill's bar, and wrecked it. Sam went to Rocky Arroyo and returned with Bill and Annie. They looked over the debris.

"I'm not sorry it happened; never liked the idea in the first place," said Annie.

"Don't mind much, myself," admitted Bill. "And I'll promise you I'll never own another."

Ma'am had little time with them. Before they had gone she said to Annie, "Bill's the only one of the boys who never touches whiskey; but none of them drink when they're at home. What they do when they're away I don't know. I don't like drinking, of course, but forbidding a thing doesn't stop it. I do tell them that if they must drink I'd prefer they do it here so I can look after them."

"I think that's very wise, Mother. Bill tells me I'm like you, and I try hard to be. Do help me to manage right so I'll have the respect and love of my family."

"You will. From the very first I knew that."

She told Heiskell and John, "I've always wanted more girls in the family, and I love Annie very dearly."

"You're not breaking the news that we're to have a baby sister?" asked John.

"No. I wish you were, but there will be no more children unless you boys provide them. You might do as Bill did."

"I'm a confirmed bachelor, Mother. Better talk to Jim."

"You just haven't seen the right girl yet."

"And never will. There aren't any more like you."

•   •   •

"I'm goin' to make a trip to Pecos," said Heiskell. "Cousin Brown's goin' along. We figure on drivin' a few steers down there an' sellin' them."

"You can't drive both cattle and the wagon."

"Brown's goin' to handle the steers."

"Reckon you can risk him? He's far from being a cowhand."

"He's growed up, ain't he? Never learn any younger."

They set out down the river. Mr. Brown had little trouble till they camped at the mouth of Pierce Canyon. The next morning he could not find some of the steers. Heiskell decided they'd pick them up on their return trip. Again they camped in the opening of the canyon. Heiskell left his load of supplies and helped look for the missing animals. They found only one. When they got back to Seven Rivers with it, John smiled and saddled his mule. The next day he returned with all but one. "Pick it up later," he said, "It's branded so there's no hurry."

Ma'am underwent a period of sleeplessness and depression for which she could not account. She was annoyed with herself, because she needed rest in order to keep up her busy routine. Heiskell and the children recognized her distress and did what they could to help. When she put the big kettle to boil they helped with the cleaning. They were amused at the great amount of food she cooked, but they helped with its preparation.

They were at the supper table when a man rode in with tidings: John Beckwith had been killed in Pierce Canyon. There had been a dispute over a steer; the brand looked as though it had been burned. It had been a duel, a fair and open fight.

"John?" asked his mother.

The man nodded.

"Where is he?"

"Don't know, Ma'am. He's not the kind to run. He'll stay in Pierce Canyon, I reckon, till the Beckwiths take it up, if they do."

"I'll go, Mother," said Jim.

"He wouldn't want it," she said, quietly.

She turned to the messenger. "I thank you for coming. Have supper and spend the night with us."

"The name's Ramer, Jim Ramer. I've been knowin' John a long time."

"I thought you'd been here before."

Before the customers Barbara maintained her composure. When she was alone she walked and prayed. How long could she stand this uncertainty? Should she have let Jim go? Would the Beckwiths seek revenge? And how would it end?

She found the solace she could in cleaning and cooking. And she watched the trail for her son. Would he never come?

Four days later Jim Ramer returned. He went to Ma'am and grasped her hands without speaking.

"He's gone."

With tears in his eyes, the man nodded.

"I've come for the wagon."

Heiskell and Jim went with him.

When they returned with her warrior, they took the cottonwood boards that framed the door and made a casket. Ma'am covered it with black cloth, and lined it with white. She took the pillow from her bed and put an embroidered case on it. And they laid his head upon it.

The neighbors came and she showed them where he was to lie, in the little plot beside the Pecos.

"Now, go back, Ma'am. We'll tend to everything."

To the family she said, "I've been wicked. I've loved John more than the rest. I could see no fault in him."

"We all loved him the same way," said Jim. I've always known he was better than me. I know just how you feel; we all feel as you do. Don't blame yourself, Mother."

The neighbors came, read a chapter from The Book, sang hymns, and led Ma'am Jones back to the house. Before putting the Bible away she made a new entry, on a new page.

The Escape

26

Frank Jones took Billy Bonney's horse, and Ma'am greeted him at the door. He put his arms around her and for the first time since John's death she found relief in tears. Billy stayed several days, during which he helped Ma'am prepare meals, wash dishes, sell merchandise, and feed pilgrims. When he announced that he must leave the next morning she asked him to walk to John's grave with her. When she knelt beside it Billy sank beside her.

As they returned to the house he said, "I don't know Ma'am whether you can talk about it or not. I've already asked Pa Jones not to take up the fight and not to let the boys take it up. He's promised, and so has Jim. Pa Jones said he'd given his word to you many years ago that he'd never fight a duel. I've told Jim that I have personal reasons, and I think he'll respect them, because he's given his word. But I haven't seen Bill. Your boys are not mixed up in anything, and I don't want them to be. I know how it feels. Besides, I want to take care of Olinger myself."

"I've always distrusted him," said Ma'am.

"So have I. He's a bully and a coward. He thought it a feather in his cap to get John."

"Billy, don't do it. It won't bring John back and you'll be next on the list."

"I'm already on the list."

Billy waited.

"There's been far too much killing already. I don't want any other mother to suffer as I have."

"You're the only mother I have, Ma'am."

"And I don't want you to live the life of the hunted. I've seen men who hide. When they come for supplies they always face the door. I'm thankful John was spared that. And I don't want you to endure it."

"I know that, Mother. And I'll give you my word that I won't seek a meeting with Olinger. But if it comes to a showdown — "

"No, Billy. You're a good boy. You've been driven to things you wouldn't otherwise have done. Drop this. Go away before it's too late. You're not yet of age. There's time to go elsewhere and make a new start."

"It's too late."

•   •   •

Mechanically but efficiently Ma'am Jones went about her customary tasks. She tended the sick, ministered to the wounded, and prepared the dead for burial. There were many pilgrims. People were flocking into the Pecos country. Many came to trade — good, bad, and strange. She welcomed all and gave them the best she had. When she began leaving her home to nurse the ill, Heiskell protested.

"There's no doctor closer than Fort Stanton. And that's days away. I can't let people die," she replied.

"Somebody else could do some of it. There's other women in the country now."

"Children are dying of measles, and hardly anybody knows how to take care of them. I've got to keep going till the epidemic's over."

Many families lost members, and rows of mounds in the little cemetery mutely recorded the number. When the epidemic passed, it left the community sad. Barbara Jones was sad with them, but she realized that the strong spirit to meet trials ahead must be revived. So she said to Sammie:

"You saddle up and invite everybody to a dance Saturday night. We'll have one, just as we did when John was with us. It's good for folks to forget their troubles, get together, and renew their friendships. Tell them not to bring any food. I'll do the cooking. We'll barbecue a beef and we'll roast sweet potatoes in the ashes. I'll cook a big kettle of frijoles, with garlic and chilis. There's lots of cabbage. We'll make a tubful of slaw with sour cream dressing. And pies — "

"Want me to tell 'em what they're goin' to have to eat?"

"It wouldn't do any harm. Anyway, they know what we've got in the way of food."

When Sammie left she told the boys to kill the first fat yearling they encountered.

A cowboy who stopped for tobacco was riding to McKittrick Spring. He agreed to tell everybody he saw about the dance. The Gordons at the Spring had recently come to the country. They had several girls, and Amanda (who later was to marry Nib Jones) was a wonderful rider and roper — a good dancer, too.

"Tell them to plan to spend the night with us." Ma'am said.

People came on horses and in wagons. Babies were put into Barbara's room. Long tables were set up in the store, and food was heaped upon them. There was much excitement when the Gordons arrived. Ma'am went to the yard to meet them, and the boys took their horses. In spite of Barbara's message, almost everybody brought food. A row of cakes was placed in the middle of each long table. Hams and turkeys were sliced and huge platters of beef cut.

When the dancing began, Nib stood on a bench beside the fiddler and called:

Pass the Ace an' swing the Queen;

High, low, Jick, Jack,

Git in the game!

Do-si out where she come in,

An' down to the center

An' swing 'em agin!

When he was out of breath he called for a waltz. Every other dance was a "B flat," a square dance. Then Ma'am and Jim undertook to teach the Varsoviana, which they had learned on the Hondo, to those who did not know it. It was a graceful dance and the guests loved it. Minnie, in a ruffled, flowered calico with bare shoulders was, Ma'am thought, the prettiest thing she'd ever seen. Heiskell pointed out that she looked very much as Barbara had when she was Minnie's age. Fifteen! Why, Minnie was a young lady and as sweet and modest as a flower. In spite of her being the only daughter she was unspoiled and considering all the attention she received, that was remarkable. But here she was, older than Annie, who had been married a year.

Ma'am poured coffee, surrounded by a group of men clamoring for a dance with her. With males outnumbering the women six to one, there were no wallflowers.

"We've got your pardners wrote down," one explained, "so we won't get beat out of a dance. And I'm next on the list."

MINNIE JONES, *one daughter among the ten Jones offspring, was a delight to her family and a favorite partner at the square dances held by the Jones family for the whole region. In her early teens Minnie became postmistress at Seven Rivers.*

When dust became thick the boys sprinkled the floor with water, heated the big shovel, and smoothed it down. Ma'am took advantage of the intermission to serve supper. And they'd all stay for breakfast, of course.

Ma'am could think and speak of John now, but shrank from details of his going. Men who came to buy were gentle and courteous but refrained from expressing sympathy in words.

Several brought disturbing rumors about Billy Bonney. John Chisum had brought in officers to arrest Billy and his gang. Chisum had votes enough to elect whom he pleased. He pleased to elect a long, lanky man named Garrett. A visitor said, "Ol' Pat, he left a mighty fine wife when he got in trouble over in Texas. Went buffalo hunting till they was 'bout all killed off. Good shot, I reckon, but I don't think he's any match for John Jones. Beg your pardon, Ma'am. It's said that Pat Garrett rustled as many cattle as Billy ever did. Been hangin' 'round Fort Sumner, too broke to buy a meal. Now he's doin' Chisum's dirty work."

"We never knew of Billy's stealing anything. If he's doing it now it's because he's outlawed and can't get work."

"Sure. They's lots worse men runnin' big outfits or wearin' a sheriff's star."

It was useless to question Jim about Billy's activities. If he knew of any wrongdoing he would not admit it. When Billy came in late one night, Ma'am asked no questions but spoke hopefully of his possibilities in some far distant place. He shook his head. Two days later Heiskell started to Fort Sumner and took Sam with him. Billy accompanied the wagon. He tied his horse to the end gate and rode beside Pa Jones. Sammie stood behind the seat and listened to their conversation.

"Ma'am's right, Billy. They got John, and they'll get you. It's just a matter of time. Why don't you make a fresh start some place else? The West's a big place."

"It wouldn't matter where I'd go; they'd get me anywhere. If I can just get Olinger first, I'll not mind. I'm sorry I promised Ma'am not to go after him."

"Do you know how it happened between Olinger and John?" Heiskell asked.

"No."

"I got Charlie Slaughter to talk to Jim Ramer for me. He said John had killed Beckwith in a fair fight. He'd tried to settle some other way, but couldn't refuse to fight when it was forced on him. When he rode up to the Pierce camp, Old Milo was layin' on a cot outside on the porch, facing the door. John got off and started to the house. When he turned to shake hands with Pierce, Milo held on to his hand. Right hand, of course. Olinger come out the door and shot John twice in the back. One bullet went through his body and struck Pierce in the hip. Pierce is lame; always will be. Jim Ramer was there and saw the whole thing. They told him that if he ever told the truth about it he could expect what John got."

"John was shot in the back?"

"Yes; both bullets went through his body. I tried to keep Ma'am from knowing, but she would bathe him herself."

"There's nobody like her," said Billy. "I've seen many mighty brave men, and John was the bravest of all; but Ma'am has more courage than anyone I've ever known."

"Know the new sheriff at Lincoln?"

"Pat Garrett? Everybody knows him. Chisum put him in to get me."

"He's sheriff, Billy, regardless. Whatever he does will have the protection of the law. You haven't a chance."

"I'm outlawed," said Billy, slowly. "And it hasn't been long since I was a law and Old Pat an outlaw. Funny thing, the law."

"Why does Chisum want to own the sheriff?"

"Several things. It's commonly thought that the Murphy-Dolan bunch paid no taxes when they owned the sheriff. Maybe Old John thinks it's his turn now."

"Nobody's ever asked us for taxes."

"They will. All this takes money. Bob Olinger's been deputized by Garrett. That means he's scared. Safest place in the world for a murderer is to get a job as deputy."

"We've always thought well of Wallace Olinger. Ma'am likes him, and where there's a man or a horse involved nobody fools her."

"She's had plenty of chances to study them," said Billy.

"I'd like to know what she'd think of Garrett."

"Ol' Pat can act all right when he wants to."

"Billy, I still wish you'd go somewhere and make a fresh start."

"It's too late, Pa Jones."

As they approached Roswell, Billy mounted his horse, gave a handful of coins to Sam, and rode away.

The next news they had was of Billy's arrest for the killing of Sheriff Brady. Ash Upson gleefully prophesied that he hadn't a chance in the world — not with the judge and district attorney against him. He'd be hanged. Just wait and see. And serve him right.

"Old he-hen!" grumbled Jim. "After all you've done for the old drunk! When he's here he's our friend, and when he's with the Chisum outfit, he's theirs. I can respect an honest enemy, but I detest a treacherous friend. I was tempted to boot him out of the house.

"Anyone we admit to this house is entitled to good treatment and protection as long as he's here. There are no hotels, and we have to take in everybody who comes."

"He's a spy for Chisum — nothing else. We should never have put up with him."

"Perhaps not. But he's old and friendless. Besides, I've seen worse men than Ash."

"Turner, I suppose. I never liked him myself."

"Your father found that Turner had registered John's cattle under his own brand; claimed to have a bill of sale for them, but couldn't produce it. Now he has John's herd, and we can do nothing about it."

"I can." Jim stood and buckled his gun belt around him.

"Just sit down, now. He's not worth going to prison over. Neither are the cattle. Don't get into trouble." Ma'am said.

"If he's in the country I'll find him."

"He isn't. Bill's been looking for him. Turner's gone and he'll probably stay gone. He's treacherous, but no fool."

•   •   •

Billy was tried at Mesilla. He was charged with killing Sheriff Brady, at whom several men had fired simultaneously. He had no money for an attorney and the court appointed one. The judge and the district attorney were inimical to Billy. Both were Catron's men. He was pronounced guilty and sentenced to be hanged. He was taken to Lincoln by Bob Olinger and other deputies. Olinger handcuffed Billy's wrist to his own at night.

"I know what you want," said The Kid, "and I'm not going to attempt to escape."

"I've been hopin' you'd try it," replied Olinger, who towered almost a foot above the boy.

They put him on the second floor of the building that had been the Murphy-Dolan Store. It had been acquired by T. B. Catron through foreclosure and sold by him to the county for use as court-house and jail. The room in which Billy was confined had an east window overlooking the yard and affording a view of the street. Billy's feet were not only shackled but chained to the floor. Olinger flourished a double-barreled shotgun and warned him that it was loaded with buckshot, especially for him. The other guard, J. W. Bell, treated him kindly and permitted the women of the village to bring Billy choice dishes. Godfrey Gauss, who had worked for Tunstall with Billy, was employed at the courthouse as handyman. He tried to make the incarceration pleasant. The children of Lincoln ran errands for "Billicito," whom they loved.

Pat Garrett left for White Oaks to arrange for the construction of a scaffold and warned Olinger to keep close watch over The Kid; said that he was tricky, and would undoubtedly escape if an opportunity came.

Jim Jones went to Lincoln. The guards would not permit him to see the prisoner, but through his friends he got word to Godfrey Gauss that he was there to help with Billy's escape. Gauss replied that Billy had plans, and that Jim was not to spoil them. He was just to wait.

"But I've got to do something. If John were here he's get Billy out pronto."

Always the Mexican people had looked forward to Billy's coming. They would say, "We love Billicito. When he drive cattle through Lincoln a steer run up the hill, and Bang! Billy shoot and we make a fiesta. We help if he say so. And Jeem, it much better that you go away — come back later. We do what Billy say."

There were many men who would gladly have aided escape, as Jim well knew, but if Billy really had something in mind, interference might wreck his plans.

•   •   •

Jim was in Roswell when news came of Billy's escape. It was Olinger's custom to go across the street to the Wortley Hotel for his noon meal. He left Bell on guard. Francisco Salazar and Florencio Chávez told him substantially the same story: Billy asked Bell to conduct him to the outhouse behind the building. Bell, in order to do this, had to release his shackles from the floor. Billy had arranged to have a six-shooter, wrapped in paper, left in the little building. The young boy who placed the gun caused no suspicion, for he often entered the outhouse. A visitor had tipped Billy off when the gun had been placed.

Billy's wrists were small enough that he could slip them from the handcuffs. He did this, and got possession of Bell's pistol, telling Bell that if he obeyed orders he would not be harmed. Bell was to unlock the armory at the left of the head of the stairs. Billy followed the guard as closely as he could shuffle aiong. When Bell reached the stairway, he attempted to bolt down, so Billy fired two shots and Bell fell. The Kid then took Olinger's shotgun from the armory and returned to the window of the room in which he had been confined. As Billy had anticipated, Olinger heard the shots and ran across the street. As he passed under the window, Billy called to him, then fired both barrels, and Olinger fell.

Downstairs Godfrey Gauss tossed Billy a miner's pick through the window at the south end of the hall, and the Kid used it to loosen one of the shackles. Then Gauss and Severa Gallegos, a small boy playing in the street, helped catch a horse from the corral. The clanking of the metal attached to one ankle so frightened the horse that Billy had trouble with him, but he took his time about riding away. No effort was made to detain him.

"Thank God!" was Ma'am's reaction. "These boys have died because they are mere pawns in the game played by rich men too cowardly to use guns. They've been duped by rascals, and they're much better than the men who use them."

"You seem pretty sure, Mrs. Jones," said Ash Upson.

"I am."

"You seldom talk, but you're usually right when you do. Who are the men behind this trouble?"

"The ones Murphy sent John to, when Bill was in trouble — the Santa Fe Ring."

"People are saying the war won't end till Billy is dead," was Ash's comment.

The Beckwith-Olinger Faction 27

The case of the Beckwiths illustrates the eventful and well-nigh incredible histories of some of the families on the Pecos.

Sir Marmaduke Beckwith, of England, and his younger brother came to the States. The latter purchased a plantation in Georgia. He was prosperous until Sherman's army burned the house, took his horses, and ordered his slaves to leave. With a pack of bitch hounds he walked several miles to the cabin of an old Negro couple whom he had freed and given a small piece of land. There, his descendants believe, he remained the rest of his life.

His son, Hugh, went West. In California he met wealthy and influential people of Spanish descent, and through them he met and married the daughter of Nicolas Pino, sheep king of the Estancia Valley of New Mexico.

The date of Hugh Beckwith's arrival on the Pecos is not known, but the site of the Beckwith ranch is marked on some of the earliest maps of the river. It was to an adobe dwelling designed for defense that Beckwith took his bride. With her went furnishings far more luxurious than those in common use. She took also servants from the Pino hacienda. *La Señora* too claimed to be of a titled family.

● ● ●

Despite the protests of Captain Johnson, Beckwith's son-in-law, he and his wife, Camilla, lived in the Beckwith home. Wallace Olinger, on the other hand, quietly took up his abode in the bunkhouse with Hugh Beckwith's cowboys.

Reports of Chisum's hiring only gunmen came to Beckwith, and he decided to augment his forces by sending for Bob Olinger, brother of Wallace, from Oklahoma. When Bob arrived with reddish, shoulder-length hair, Wallace remonstrated with him. The young men along the Pecos had discarded long hair, but Bob was unwilling to do so. Moreover he had elaborate buckskin costumes with abundance of beads and fringes. Though many men wore buckskin trousers, and a few wore jackets, they regarded the ornaments as affected, and they ridiculed Bob Olinger. When the new arrival dubbed himself "Pecos Bob" he aroused active dislike among the neighbors. And he made the mistake of posing as a gunman at a time when real ones tended to conceal their dexterity with a six-shooter.

Bob at first refused to live in the bunkhouse with Wallace, but a sharp rebuke from Beckwith took care of that. He informed his cowhand that he not only would live with the cowboys but would do the work of one. Rather than be discharged, Bob Olinger obeyed. Already unpleasantly impressed, Hugh Beckwith was enraged when he conducted a shooting match and found that both Captain Johnson and Wallace Olinger were far superior in marksmanship to Bob.

After the deaths of his sons, Beckwith — always irritable — became morose and unapproachable. The men, reluctant to incur his displeasure, tactlessly started turning to Johnson for orders. He promptly referred them to his father-in-law.

The atmosphere became tense before Bill, son of Captain Johnson and Camilla, was three years old. One evening at dinner, Johnson carelessly betrayed the fact that his military service had been in the Union Army. Beckwith swore and left the table. Camilla took her small son to the *portal* and sat facing the stable into which her father strode. Wallace Olinger was mending harness near the big open gate. Captain Johnson came out of the house, took his small son on his shoulders, and started to the stable. Camilla called to him to return the child to her, and he did so. Then he walked toward the stable door. As Johnson reached it, Hugh Beckwith stepped out, placed a shotgun against the body of his son-in-law, and pulled the trigger. Then he dropped the weapon and sprang upon a saddled horse and rode out the gate. Wallace Olinger, startled by the shots, fired at Beckwith with a pistol and sheared off the end of his nose.

Beckwith continued riding.

Camilla told her mother that she could no longer live in a home where her father had killed her husband. She wrote to Dr. Johnson, her father-in-law, and asked if she might bring her son to his home. He urged her to do so. She explained that the proceeds from her share of her husband's cattle would take care of her expenses, and that Wallace Olinger would care for her herd, sell her cattle, and send the money to her.

She was a beautiful young woman, and her mother would not permit her to make the trip unattended. An older sister went with her. With an escort of cowboys, including Wallace Olinger, the two young women set out in a hack for the railroad. Milo Pierce, who required surgery on his injured hip, went with them. The cowboys rode beside the vehicle to protect Camilla and Helen. At Fort Stockton the party was delayed two weeks by the birth of a daughter to Camilla. Bill Johnson in later years had vivid memories of seeing the cavalry and telling his mother that when he was a man he intended being a soldier.

The party rode southeast to the railroad where the men flagged a train and put the two young women, the children, and Milo Pierce aboard. Then Wallace Olinger and another cowpoke handed their reins to the others and boarded the train. It was, Wallace said, unsafe for the women and children to go to a city without protection.

While in Marion, Ohio, the two cowboys gravely accepted offers of the local people to show them the cattle — Jersey cows penned in small lots along the alleys. Before they returned to the Pecos, Wallace had arranged with Camilla the details of attending to her cattle. She suspected that he sent more money than her just share, but not until after she married Wallace six years later did he admit having done so.

Hugh Beckwith did not return to his ranch. He went to Fort Stanton for medical care. Occasionally the family heard rumors of his having been seen at various places in Texas, and finally a report of his having been killed in a brawl in a saloon.

Bob Olinger became a deputy sheriff and later a deputy United States Marshal. On the Pecos nobody hesitated to say that he sought the shelter of the law, for even at that time the killing of an officer was a serious offense. The type employed in that capacity had little respect in that area, and it was many years before the citizens were to revise their estimate of the "law."

School Days   *28*

Ma'am Jones felt keenly the need for a school. As best she could, she imparted what she knew not only to her own children but also to those of the eleven families within a ten-mile radius. Only the Beckwiths had not, over the years, sent their children to the trading post for instruction.

There was no disciplinary problem, for Ma'am possessed the supreme quality that is proof of a good teacher. Without realizing that she had any part in their inclination, her pupils wanted to learn. When people sagely remarked that one can lead a horse to water but cannot make him drink, Ma'am silently reflected that it can be done by those who know how.

Though she had little equipment, Ma'am made good use of what was available. There was always The Book, which could be used for teaching reading, and spelling also. The older children copied verses from it to be used as models for writing. And Ma'am took from it "examples" for computing solutions in arithmetic. She also based her problems upon costs of merchandise sold in the store, and looked especially for problems that involved the weighing of commodities.

When Seven Rivers had acquired two stores and five saloons, Ma'am thought it time for the neighbors to band together and build a school. The Mexicans started making and laying adobes. Men went to the mountains to cut logs for beams, and Pa Jones brought glass from Las Vegas for windows. He bought a school bell also. It was not hung until two doors for the entrances — separate ones for boys and girls — had been installed. To make a blackboard, Heiskell spent hours splitting a cottonwood log into wide boards that he fitted together carefully and painted black. He made a desk with a sloping lid for the teacher. Beneath the lid could be stored the books and other teaching equipment, not to mention a good heavy paddle.

Teaching the school was a man-sized job, and securing a competent instructor could have presented difficulties. Fortunately a fine, well-educated man — Captain Shattuck, who had seen service in the Confederate Army — had come to the Pecos with a herd. He had brought with him his family and a young boy whom he had employed as a cowhand. In crossing the swollen river at the Horsehead the boy had been swept from his mount and drowned. Captain Shattuck camped there three days and attempted to recover the body. He was an expert swimmer but could not find it in the swift water. It was very cold and the repeated diving and exposure brought on a muscular illness that made physical exertion difficult for years. Captain Shattuck gave the pupils an excellent start, but as his health improved he left the task to less skilled instructors.

In spite of the wages available to cowboys, Ma'am Jones' sons attended school. Jim, trail boss for Chisum, escaped incarceration, but the younger boys had to attend. There were a few things not debatable in the Jones family, and school attendance headed the list.

Sam was particularly unhappy in captivity. He considered various ways of regaining his freedom, but each seemed inadequate. One particular dereliction brought about a discussion of expulsion — an idea new to Sam. The offense had not been sufficiently serious to warrant the release of the culprit, but it furnished Sam with hope.

One morning when the Pecos was in flood, Sam passed the Boot Hill Cemetery on its banks. The water had washed away the sand from about a grave and a leg was exposed. He cut it off at the knee and planted it in the teacher's desk. When Mr. Collier questioned the pupils, Sam made his confession appear to be forced out of him. He held out till he feared there was danger of convincing the teacher of his innocence. Then he finally managed to blunder an admission that brought about a conviction. When Mr. Collier unrolled a quirt and told Sam to step to the front of the room, he did so with alacrity. What was a licking in comparison with freedom? He took his punishment but as a compromise, slapped the teacher.

"An' that fixed it," he later said, trimuphantly. "That was the day I gra'juated. Didn't get no sheepskin. My diploma was made outta rawhide, braided. But it was wuth it."

"Nib, on the contrary, suddenly developed an amazing liking for school. Moreover, he began washing his ears without being roped and tied. Ma'am was perplexed. He was a little young to be getting interested in girls, wasn't he? Still — Nib was fourteen. Saturday night at the dance, her suspicions were confirmed. He danced only with Miss Nancy Jennings, and little wonder, for she was a pretty child, and refined.

Years later, after he had married Mandy Gordon, and Miss Nancy had become Mrs. Jerry Dunaway, Nib said, "At that time I thought she was the prettiest, sweetest thing in the world. I was so bashful that I don't know how I ever got up the courage to ask her for a dance. At school I ignored her until time to saddle her horse for the trip home. I did that for her, and I'd have liked to ride home with her but didn't have the nerve to ask her permission.

"One day the teacher asked Miss Nancy to step to the board and solve a problem. She stood right in front of me. She wore a pretty calico dress with a very full skirt and a tight basque with a ruffle hanging down from the belt over her skirt. I wanted to attract her attention, and when I noticed a little white string hanging from below the ruffle I gave it a jerk. Miss Nancy paid no attention until she started to her seat. Then a big object, made of wire, hollow, and shaped like a beef kidney, dropped to the floor. Although I didn't know it, it was a bustle. She looked down, gasped, stooped and grabbed it, and ran to her seat. She put her head down and began to cry.

"The whole school roared, but I almost died. The teacher tried to quiet the children; when he saw that he couldn't, he dismissed them for recess. Two big girls stayed with Nancy.

"As soon as I got home I went straight to Ma'am. I told her the whole thing. I thought she'd scold me, but she could hardly keep from laughing. That made me feel better. She assured me that she knew I had no idea of the result of pulling that string and that she thought Nancy's mother would understand. I asked if she'd ride over to the Jennings' house with me so that I could apologize. She reached for her bonnet.

"The worst of it was that the boys accused me of insulting Miss Nancy. I'd have insulted an angel straight from heaven just as soon. I had to lick every boy in school before they quit. I didn't mind that, but to be accused of being rude to Miss Nancy I couldn't take."

• • •

Besides the tears and laughter, the normal high and low spots of school life, there were almost always startling events punctuating the lives of the Jones youngsters and their neighbors on the Pecos. The Jennings family, for example, was going to be given some meat by John Northern, who owned a saloon. One morning John dropped by the school to leave a quarter of beef for the Jennings. He put it on the roof and rode away, with the sound in his ears of the children singing, "There is a fountain filled with blood . . ."

That afternoon, just as school was dismissed, the cowhands from the VVN Ranch, headed by Tom Finnessey, rode in across the Pecos, shooting and yelling. Cowboys did not get to town often, and when they did they took over. They headed for John Northern's saloon, and many of the older schoolboys followed.

Tom Finnessey, a highly respected man, was C. B. Eddy's foreman. Sam Jones was working for him at the time, but had not come into town. John Northern also was a good man, and he and Tom were close friends. Finnessey had had a few drinks before he hit the bar, and Northern quietly told him he had already had too many. Words were exchanged before shots were fired. Northern fell across the wooden box. One of Finnessey's friends helped him onto his horse, headed for the ranch with him, and told Sam Jones that Finnessey was leaving. They then turned the ranch over to Martin Merose, a Polander.

Meanwhile Ma'am Jones was summoned to the saloon, but before she could get there, John Northern had died. Ma'am sent for his wife, and Donie Northern arrived, accompanied by Nancy Jennings. People were distressed for both Northern and Finnessey. The men would never have tangled, had not Tom been drunk. A year or so later Finnessey came back, but he was never arrested.

"Us Joneses didn't fight much unless somebody tried to run over us," Nib explained, "and not many tried it. Come to think of it, Henry would fight the quickest of any of us. He was a tough nut. That boy had arms like a bear. If he ever got holt of you . . . ! He was a cowhand from the time he was seven. And stout! You wouldn't believe how stout he was. Fine a cowman as they was in the family, but had crazy notions about wantin' to farm.

"There was a big boy always pickin' on Henry. He did it mostly because my brother wanted to plow up the ground and plant stuff. Henry took it good natured a long time, but finally he just rared back and said, 'I says, anon you better shut up. That's all!'

"When Henry got mad enough to say 'anon' he meant business. Never did know how he got holt of such language unless from Old Ash Upson. He knew a lot of queer words.

"Well, this kid just kept on — didn't have sense enough to stop crossin' Henry. My brother grabbed him, pulled his jacket over his head, buttoned it and 'Pecosed' him. Should have left him drown. But when Henry saw the kid couldn't swim, he jumped in that cold water and dragged him out."

After school hours Nib worked in Al Rheinboldt's store. He kept Ma'am informed as to occurrences: "That new pilgrim got drunk and had a fuss with a vaquero of the VVN's. He left to get his gun and have it out. Mr. Rheinbolt told the pilgrim, 'He'll kill you just as you step out the door. You're drunk. Go in the back room, get your bedroll, and sleep it off.'

Years after, Nib acknowledged that "Seven Rivers was a fright. Somebody was always gettin' killed." The Jones family helped bury several men on Rocky Arroyo. They found some who were clearing brush on Dead Man's Gulch (the scene of previous killings) when they were shot from ambush. Nobody ever knew who the assailants were. All the dead were recent arrivals in the area, and none carried identification. They were buried under the big cottonwood where they died. Except for Pa Jones' help, the interment was made by children of school age.

● ● ●

It was not until the older boys were out of school that George Curry (later to be governor of New Mexico) came to Seven Rivers. He stayed several days at the trading post. Before he left, Henry Jones saw his father count out and hand over several greenbacks to Mr. Curry.

"What you payin' him for, Pa?"

"Don't know, 'zactly," replied his father, "somethin' he calls taxes."

"What's taxes?"

"Kinda hard to explain — " Heiskell looked at Ma'am, and she came to the rescue.

"You see, somebody has to pay for things the laws do, like arresting people — "

"They don't have to arrest nobody, do they?"

"Sometimes. And we have to put up buildings so we can have school."

"But you and the Corns and the Nelsons — all you folks built the schoolhouse."

"And pay the teacher — "

"Pa gave him a bunch of heifers. So did some of the others. Why do we have to pay for these things to that man?"

"The money isn't Mr. Curry's to keep. He's the sheriff and tax collector. He turns it in at Lincoln to — well, to pay the taxes."

"Seems mighty onnecessary," observed Henry. And he never had occasion to change his mind. But then, even the Jones boys admitted that Henry, most lovable of the brothers, was a bit queer. For one thing, he wanted to farm. What's more, he did it. He irrigated the fields and cultivated an orchard and a garden. There were times when his produce was very acceptable to the entire family. But farming, to the other Jones boys, seemed unworthy of a real man.

Nib told how Henry Jones died. "One evenin' he come up missin'. We couldn't find him nowhere. Hunted till most mornin' with a lantern. Found him in a ditch, drowned. Big strong feller like him — an' drowned in a ditch. Best swimmer in the country, too. Nigh broke Ma'am's heart. She'd always encouraged him to farm if he wanted to. An look what he come to."

Her Ewe Lamb   29

While Bill was away on a trail drive, Mandy Gordon stayed with Annie at the Rocky Arroyo Ranch. Both were capable cowhands, and they took care of the cattle, Bill said, better than any waddy he ever hired. Not until their supply of beef was exhausted did the girls feel that they had a real problem. They tired of venison and considered butchering a steer. Keeping the meat was no problem — out of reach of predators, it kept indefinitely. The two girls could rope, kill, and skin a steer, but hanging it might be difficult. Since they expected Bill back shortly they compromised on a goat. They roped it, tied its hind feet to a mesquite limb, and cut its throat.

Fires in the Guadalupes caused Annie and Mandy no concern except for the horses. There were rumors of strange Indians at Mescalero, and even of a killing attributed to Apaches on the Pecos. Each night they rounded up the remuda and put the horses in a corral close to the house. The Gordons had brought eight hundred horses to the Pecos, some of which were registered racing stock. Mandy's favorite mount was a thoroughbred, and she loved him. At night she put a hackamore on him, pulled the end of the rope through the opening of the door latch, and tied it about her ankle. Annie warned her that if an Apache wanted him he could take the horse without waking her.

192

"Reckon these strange Apaches would bother us?" Mandy asked.

"Never have." Annie wrinkled her nose and giggled. "Bill says they don't like white women and think we're ugly because we're skinny. They might steal horses, but they'd never bother us. No Apache has been known to molest a white woman."

Even though they were not afraid, Mandy did lose her horse. Somebody untied the rope and took him. Indians, Annie said, for nobody else could have prowled about the house without waking them. They saddled up and took the trail up the arroyo toward the reservation. They took no food, and when noon came, decided that it would be useless to go further, for the Indians had too much of a start on them.

When they got back to the rock house the entire remuda was gone. The house had been ransacked, and Bill's Stetson, the first he'd ever owned, was missing. Fortunately he and the men had taken the best saddle horses on the drive; nevertheless, the loss was great.

"We can't ride these horses any further today," said Annie. "In the morning we'll go to Seven Rivers where Bill's folks will have plenty of fresh horses. And we may find Bill there, for it's a week later than he expected to be gone."

Where Rocky Arroyo empties into Seven Rivers they met Bill. He decided to take the trail of the horse thieves immediately.

"But you can't go on without fresh horses."

"I'd have to go back to Seven Rivers and would lose too much time. They've got a big start as it is. I know everybody on the Pecos, and anybody will let me have all the horses I need. I'll just pick up some down the river. Got plenty of friends at Eddy [later Carlsbad], too, and they'll let me have horses."

He told the girls to go back to the ranch and look after the cattle; or better still, go on to Seven Rivers and stay with Ma'am.

"We could go back, round up the cattle, and drive them to Seven Rivers."

"I think that's what you should do."

"Got any money with you?" asked Annie.

"No, but I won't need any," Bill replied. Then he and his men rode down the Pecos.

As the two girls went leisurely from the rock house to the trading post, Mandy asked if Annie thought the horses had been taken by Indians.

"No. They'd have headed for the mountains. It was white thieves who got them. And I'm afraid of them." Annie answered.

"But not of Indians?"

"No. Even white men who come to spend the night won't molest women. If one calls to you or knocks at the door you can know you're safe. It's the ones who sneak around who are bad."

As Bill rode by La Huerta, Eddy's headquarters, Mr. Eddy called to him from the door, "Get down, Bill. I want to pay that two thousand dollars I owe you for the cattle — "

"Can't, Mr. Eddy. Just keep it till I get back; right now I'm chasin' hoss thieves."

At Guadalupe Peak they got another change of horses, turned their tired ones loose to return home, and struck out west, following the trail toward the Rio Grande. They depended upon game for food, but after they struck the flats, little was available. At the Rio Grande they killed a calf; in the Black Range they would find deer. The trail led toward the mountains and indicated that their quarry was not far ahead of them. They ate the last morsel of their beef, but did not risk firing a shot for fear it might be heard by the men they pursued. They made camp, tightened their belts, and went to bed cold and hungry.

Seventy years later Bill Jones said, "At the first sign of color in the east we struck."

"The one with the black hat's mine. That's my Stetson, the first I ever owned, and I don't want it ruined by no bullet."

"Want to get all the rest?"

"Might as well. They're all in on this."

"Whatever you say."

"Well, then, every one if you can."

There were five of the horse thieves. And they could and did get them. Then they gathered the horses, including those of the thieves, and turned toward home. The animals were so exhausted that several dropped out on the way.

Bill resumed his story: "We lit a shuck and was almost starved when we hit La Luz on the west side of the Sacramentos. I went in a store and picked out a sizeable lot of chuck. Laid it on the counter and asked the man how much it come to. He figgered awhile and reckoned it come to twelve, ninety-five.

"I'm Bill Jones, Rocky Arroyo, and didn't bring no money with me. Have to charge it till I get home; then I'll start a man back with the money."

The trader remonstrated, but Bill carried his purchases to the pack horses and rode away. They took the short cut through the Mescalero Reservation and down the Peñasco. They could not travel fast because of the condition of the horses. Many of those stolen from Bill were damaged to the extent that they were worthless.

•　　•　　•

They arrived at Seven Rivers after dark and found several horses tied at the hitching post. Bill recognized them and wondered if Ma'am were having a dance. There were two wagons and a buckboard in the yard. Things were strangely quiet at the house. Ordinarily the younger boys met him and took his horses, but nobody appeared. He was puzzled.

The store was full of people, but he saw none of the family. The door of his mother's room was ajar, and he entered.

The family stood about the big bed while Ma'am bent over Minnie. Bill hesitated until his mother saw him, and he went to her. Minnie was ill, very ill; he could see that. As he bent to kiss her she opened her eyes and lifted her arms to his neck. For a few seconds she clung to him. Then she released him, and he eased her to the pillow. For a short time she lifted her eyes to Ma'am's; then the lids slowly closed. She did not breathe again.

Ma'am carefully removed the pillow and drew the sheet over his sister's face. As Annie came to him, he heard his mother murmur, "My ewe lamb, my one ewe lamb."

They followed Ma'am to the store and tried to persuade her to take the big chair by the fireplace, but she shook her head and began preparations for supper. She refused to rest until everybody present had been fed. Annie helped, as did the boys, and Bill had no opportunity to talk with his wife until they had gone to bed.

It was very sudden, Annie said; less than thirty-six hours had elapsed since Minnie had become ill. Cramp colic, Ma'am said — she had seen several cases before. In fact the doctor at Fort Stanton had explained afterward what causes it. A tiny sac on the intestines becomes inflamed, and there is no cure. He told Ma'am that perhaps in time, doctors would learn to make an incision and remove the sac. He thought then there would be a chance that a patient might recover.

As Bill knew, there was no doctor closer than Stanton; they had sent for him, but he had not had time to get there.

The following morning Bill Jones started a rider to La Luz with money for the food he'd bought.

And he helped dig another grave in the little cemetery by the Pecos. Beside John, they laid Minnie Jones.

Trail Drives 30

"From the time we went to Seven Rivers in 1877 some of us Jones boys was going up the trail," said Nib. "First it was with Segrest's herd, the S Cross. And we went for Gardner, and for Day and Sherwood, who owned McKittrick Spring then. We went for the LFD and the Turkey Tracks. The first bunch of our own we took we joined a pool; but we kept on till we had herds of our own.

"When I was just a button, Sam and me went with a pool herd. Ned and Dolph Shattuck was along. Nigger Dick was the cook. It was a drouth year, and we was short of chuck. Didn't figger on havin' to go so slow, either. The further we went, the drier it got. Some of the cattle was so pore they had to be tailed up. We saw old cows go off and leave their calves, and when a mammy does that she's really thirsty.

"We wasn't makin' more'n five miles a day, and that with dry camps. We run out of every kind of food but dry rice. Didn't have no coffee; didn't have no sugar if we'd a' had coffee. The steers was so pore they wasn't fit to eat; and so many died on us that we was short on what we was supposed to deliver, anyhow. If they'd been eatable, we'd of eat them. They jest wasn't. We went thirty-one days on nothin' but just pure D brown rice without sugar.

196

"When we got close to the railroad west of Clayton, Walter Paddlefoot said, 'Let's go down to the old Mexican shack on the railroad an' see if we can git some aigs.' But they wasn't nobody home, and every aig we could find was addled.

"We was gettin' pretty clost to Clayton when I come in from guard one evenin' and Nigger Dick had a big pot of chicken and rice. We really feasted. It jest seemed to me that nothin' had ever tasted so good in my whole life, and I'd been hungry plenty of times. I kep' wonderin' where he got that chicken, but I wasn't askin' no fool questions. It was my time to git in fuel for mornin'. Behind a clump of mesquite I kicked up a big pile of white fuzz. I took a look at it, and my chicken got right oneasy. I didn't know whether that fuzz was from crows or buzzards, but it shore wasn't no chicken feathers. Well, the rest of the boys was happy for onct, and I saw no reason for spoilin' it.

"Goin' back from Clayton the hosses got locoed. Ever try to move a locoed hoss? Well, then, you don't know nothin' about trouble. We lost a few. A man came 'long and tole me to cut the second bar in a hoss's mouth and bleed him for loco. I tried it, but it didn't work good. I cut four bars on one, an' he died. But in spite of our doctorin' most of 'em got over it.

"On another drive with Segrest's herd, S Cross — (whose earmark was overslope an' underbit the left, and overbit and underslope the right) — it come up a hailstorm and they wasn't a bush nor nothin' for shelter. We jerked off our saddles and held them over us for pertection. The hail was big as marbles and pepperin' thick. We stuck out considerable. It was beatin' my legs off. I doubled the best I could. When the hail got as big as turkey aigs we doubled again. Sam yelled, 'How you makin' it?'

" 'Got plenty room for two more men.' I kep' doublin' till I got my laigs in.

"That hail cut holes in our saddles like you'd took a hammer an' pounded them. It kilt two sheepherders, but of course, they didn't have no saddles.

"On that drive, just outa Clayton, west, we was holdin' the herd while the boss went in to see 'bout sellin'. Long come a man ridin' a wore-out lookin' hoss and leadin' a little gray pack mule, loaded heavy. Said he was goin' to Clayton an' would we let the mule graze there till he come back? We said we would. He went on without unpackin' it. We thought o' doin' it, but it wasn't our mule. Toward evenin' he come back, took the mule, an' left. Later we heard it was one of Black Jack's gang, and that they had just robbed a train. The paper said they got forty thousand dollars. We always wondered if that was what he had on that mule."

• • •

Nib recounted other stories from his trail drives:

"Frank an' me went up the trail with a bunch that wasn't much force as cowhands. Some of 'em didn't even know what a rope was for. They would swing one wild with a big loop an' the steers would jest go crazy. Frank an' me would drop a little loop over their heads, slow an' easy, and take 'em out quiet.

"Baldy Haines, a little bozo, was boss for the outfit, which was the N Bar N — the Neetingham Cattle Company — owned by some furriners. All the English and Scotch was goin' crazy about the cattle business 'bout that time. It was afore the price broke. That partic'lar outfit had made its money making gray granite cookin' pots.

"Them English, I noticed, always had an American for trail boss and general manager. Theirs was Jim Harris — a good man. They had a big ranch at White Deer, Texas. That's right acrost the canyon from Adobe Walls. Frank an' me was workin' for 'em.

"They gathered all the N Bar N cattle and moved them to the White Deer Pasture near a little town outa Amarillo. White Deer Creek was a solid mass of wild grapes, and they'd been makin' wine by the carload and shippin' it to England. We moved them cattle down near the XIT. There's a ranch cornerstone, about eighteen feet high, that marks the corners of New Mexico, the Strip, and Kansas.

"So we crossed the Canadian at Adobe Walls. Cape Willingham was general manager of the Hansford Land and Cattle Company. We met him there.

"We went over to White Deer and put these cattle in the pasture. It didn't have any fences — was jest a pasture. Me an' Frank got our bedrolls an' went to sleep. We hadn't hardly got down before they called us out. Us havin' a reputation of bein' cowboys I reckon they wanted to try us out. We went, an' we let the guards come in.

"It started sleetin' an' snowin'. The wind was terrible. We held the cattle, 'bout 3500, until the storm got bad. Frank come to me an' said, 'Nib, what we goin' to do?'

" 'They're goin' to drift; nothin' on earth can hold 'em. You take the lead, an' I'll bring up the rear. There's nothin' else anybody can do.'

"It was more'n forty hours before we saw any of the outfit. We drifted with them cattle to the banks of the Cold Water. It's something like the Hondo, narrow with deep banks. We put that herd in one of them bends, fifteen feet down, outa the wind. It was a runnin' creek, and the banks was covered with vines full of dried grapes. We were so hungry that we filled up on grapes. An' I got a batch of poison ivy that sure dealt me misery.

"We built a fire and slept awhile. When it got daylight we started the herd back. When we got clost to a little lake, we saw a fellow comin' ridin' like a drunk Indian and runnin' something. It was a buffalo bull, an' it run out a little ways in the lake.

" 'Boys, where you goin'?'

" 'Back to White Deer with these steers. Where'd you git that bull?'

" 'I been tryin' to rope him a long time.'

"Frank rode out an' roped him. I heeled him an' we stretched him out. The fellow stuck him.

" 'Take a hind quarter, boys. I'll go git my wagon.'

" 'No! Keep your bull. We'll make out.'

"He give us a piece of the hump, but I reckon he never knew how bad we needed it.

"Before we got back both my eyes were swole shut. Cape Willingham sent a man with me to Amarillo to a doctor."

Nib continued:

"When I was fifteen I went on a drive with the S Cross. We took some of our own cattle, too. We had nine men, includin' boss, cook, and wrangler. The boss left in the mornin' and went ahead to find water. The cook took the wagon ahead so he could get water and fuel and have a meal ready when the herd got in. There were two shifts. Soon as we got in sight of the wagon in the afternoon, part of us would go to camp and eat; then we'd come back and relieve the rest.

"We got to the Berenda, near Clayton. We threw the herd in that dry wash. They wasn't a drop of water to be seen; but you throw a herd in, they tramp it down, and pretty soon it's a runnin' stream. The water was black because they's coal in it.

"We camped there a day or two, and Tom Ketchum got some liquor. He an' I rode down to a big, old adobe sheep camp some Mexicans had built. In it was an old mother dog and six pups that belonged to the sheep outfit. The pups was 'bout a month old, and cute and fluffy. Tom had been drinkin'. He took those dogs, one at a time, and he cut their throats. It made me sick.

" 'My God, Tom! I don't see how you can do anything like that.'

" 'That's nothin'. Billy Morgan and me killed two women. Tied rocks to 'em and throwed 'em in the Río Grande.'

"I didn't say a word. All I wanted was out. I let Tom walk ahead of me, and we rode off. I sorta lagged behind. When he asked a question I'd try to answer. Mostly we rambled along without talkin'. I'd heard of that killin'. Dick Duncan was hanged for it. He'd lent the women a team, wagon, and driver to go to Del Rio. They had six thousand in cash with them. Nobody heard from 'em, and they was a search. The women showed up in the Río Grande with their feet stickin' up. They had rocks tied to 'em to hold them down. Their heads had been beat in with something 'bout the size of a gun barrel.

"The driver was never found, but Dick Duncan showed up with the wagon 'an team. And there was a gun in the wagon with a bent barrel. He denied the killin' an' said if they'd wait six months the guilty man would be found. Well, they gave him six months, but he didn't find anyone they could prove guilty, so they hanged him.

"Tom Ketchum didn't do that, I'm pretty sure. He was too young. I always thought it was just the whiskey talkin'.

"Then I made an awful mistake. When Billy Morgan came off herd he asked me if Tom had been talkin'. I tole him. He never said a word — just climbed onto the wagon and went for his 44. When Tom came in Billy rode out to meet him, and I never in my whole life heard a man take the abuse that Tom Ketchum did. An' he didn't say a word back, neither.

"That night while I was on second guard, Billy Morgan came to me. 'I'm in Dutch,' he said, 'That big blabbermouth!'

"I didn't say anything. I'd already talked too much.

" 'They'll get us sooner or later.'

"I kept still.

" 'They's a patch of brush this side of the Fort Worth and Denver railroad track, close to where the wagon is camped. I want you to tie a horse, saddled, and with a bedroll on him, in that brush. I'll go down to Clayton, buy a ticket for some place west, and get aboard. When the passenger comes up that long grade it'll have to slow down. That's when I'll step offa that train.'

"I'd seen plenty of killings, too many. So I did just what he told me, horse and all. He wanted Walter Thayer's night horse, a big strong dun with a black stripe down his back. Walter liked dun horses; he called this one Mac. I knew he'd hate to lose him. Billy wanted Walter's new saddle, too; that had cost plenty.

"When Billy Morgan and the horse were missing everybody thought he'd taken off with it. I kept still. But I went for a look-see at that brush. When Billy stepped off that train he stumbled fifty feet before he went down. He'd ridden that dun off east.

"Next night we camped close to the railway station at Clayton.

Before daylight the engineer was out with a lantern oilin' the engine. Tom Ketchum lay in his bedroll with an old nigger-shooter. He always carried one, just like a big old kid. Well, that's what he was then. He was the blamedest man with a nigger-shooter I ever saw. He would fill his pockets with those slugs he got in a blacksmith shop, calks off horses' shoes. He used them. When the engineer found where those shots were coming from he took his six-shooter and ran Tom into the lumber yard. Tom hid in a barrel and the engineer lost him.

"It was a long time after that before Tom went up there again, held up the train, and got shot in the arm. They captured him in Turkey Canyon, and they hanged him.

"I have a picture of him after the hangin' layin' there with his head by him.

"I told you we was shorthanded on that trail drive for the VVN's. Martin Merose was trail boss, and not supposed to work. There was a wrangler, and Willie and Jim Edwards, Hughes Kiles, Tod Barber, a man named Sparks, and me. They were all good hands, and even if I was a kid I was no slouch.

"We were gone nine months. We celebrated my sixteenth birthday at Walsenburg. We went to a saloon and I saw Bob Ford, who claimed he'd killed Jesse James. There was a lot of drinkin' an' he an' Martin Merose matched, but there was plenty of men and they separated them.

"We shipped the twos and threes from Walsenburg to some feed lots in Missouri. That left us with the big steers. When one of the Edwards quit, his brother did, too; and that left nobody but Tod Barber, Hughes Kile, Sparks, and me to herd them. Of course the cook and wrangler didn't herd any cattle, and neither did Martin Merose.

"Tod Barber got a letter from his father tellin' him to go to Ardmore and recover some stolen horses. He was to bring 'em to us because we needed them.

"Mornings we took time about goin' off alone with the steers. We rode ahead to hold them down till they got to grass. It was my time to take the herd out, and there was a blizzard on. It was a reg'lar norther. The steers wouldn't head into it. They went in a meadow and tore down some stacks and some big ricks of hay. I knew we'd have to pay for the damage and that it wouldn't set very well with Martin Merose. I thought as long as we had to pay for the hay, anyway, the steers might as well eat it. They were already doin' it. They were little trouble to handle, and I didn't take 'em back to camp till dark.

"I was hankerin' to get back, for I was nearly froze. When I got clost to the fire I just fell off my horse. They had prized the ties off the abandoned spur of the railroad track and were huddled around the fire with a pile of bedrolls behind them. Hughes Kile called out, 'Here, Nib, take my place. I'll tend to your hoss.'

"Cold as I was I could see that Sparks was mad about something. I wasn't carin' what. As I come to the fire Sparks grabbed a spade used for putting coals on the oven. Hughes Kile reached 'round to his bedroll, got his 44, and shot Sparks. I stretched him out on his bedroll, and the fool quit breathin'!

"They cut a slit in his coat and got out the roll of money. They stepped off ten paces, dug a hole, and buried it. They said they'd been gamblin' and Sparks had won all the money.

"They sent for the undertaker and the doctor, but neither came. Some men brought a two-horse ambulance and loaded Sparks in. Before they started the team they searched the body. I was glad we'd hidden the money.

"I had three dollars and a knife. I was still wonderin' what to do when the justice of the peace came out. He sat on the tongue of the wagon and talked to us. Martin Merose had cleared out. Hughes Kile stood hitched. I told just how it happened. The justice of the peace found a letter that showed he was from Missouri or some such place, and he was going under an assumed name.

"That left me alone in camp. I took the bedrolls and went to sleep. At first the snow covered me and I was comfortable. But the wind began to blow and it drifted off me. I was awakened by Martin Merose's beating me with the double end of a rope. He dragged me toward an old abandoned depot, whippin' me to keep me staggering along. When we reached the building we found some kindling, coal, and an old pot-bellied stove. We built a fire and went to sleep. That night several sheep herders lost their lives, and hundreds of cattle either froze or drifted before the storm until they were beyond reach of their owners.

"When Tod Barber returned, he and Hughes Kile dug up the money and divided it. It was rightfully theirs, for Sparks always cheated at monte."

Rocky Arroyo

31

For many years the Rocky Arroyo area was exclusively Jones range, until the Edwards family settled on a section in the midst of Sam's vast ranch. Trouble was predicted, but Sam Jones made no effort to evict the newcomer. Not until after Bob Edwards' death did his wife file on the land. Two years later she married Walter Thayer.

In 1886 the Shattucks and Wards met at the entrance of Rattlesnake Canyon; in their wagons they traveled up into the Guadalupes where each settled upon a homesite. The families became close friends, as are their descendants.

The Welches and Nelsons — relatives — were very early settlers and established permanent homes.

Morg Livingston became the first millionaire cowman in New Mexico. He established a bank in Carlsbad and for several years financed his friends during a severe drought. He knew that their word was good, and he lent generously to help them keep their cattle and ranches. His faith in them was based upon their integrity. But neither he nor they were prophetic enough to anticipate seven years of drought, so he lost his bank to help his friends.

•   •   •

Marriages on the Pecos occurred without the formality of a license; they were legal provided the officiating minister recorded them in the presence of witnesses.

The Jones boys, with the exception of Sam, married early and established themselves and their cattle upon homesteads. Cattle were so profitable for awhile that Pa Jones induced Ma'am to let him sell the trading post to Frank Rheinbolt, who in turn disposed of it to R. H. Pearce. Ma'am continued to minister to the ill and wounded, although the number of the latter gradually decreased. Still, the Boot Hill Cemetery was filling up with graves, which represented, in many instances, death from violence. Ma'am kept a white silk handkerchief for those who were shot. She probed for bullets with a knitting needle, sterilized by boiling and given an application of whiskey. After swabbing the wound with the liquor, she administered a good stiff dose to the patient. It was remarkable how many responded to the treatment and in a few days were riding.

• • •

Sam did not marry until he was thirty. As long as he remained at Seven Rivers he helped his mother with the work. He had a home on Rocky, but he hired men to take care of the cattle and relieve him from time to time. He was an excellent cook. Ma'am said with pride that he could make better sourdough biscuit than hers, and hers were famous.

When asked for his recipe, Sam said, "Why, they ain't nothin' to makin' biscuit; anybody can do it. Course you got to have salt 'east. Git yoreself 'bout a quart to a half-gallon o' buttermilk, if you got any, and if you ain't, git some sweet milk and let 'er sour. If you ain't got no milk you can use water by maybe throwin' in a chunk o' tater, or two or three if they're little. It's better to throw in a chunk of sourdough if you got it, pretty good size. Let it work two or three days, however long it takes. Then thin 'er down 'bout like buttermilk. Pour out 'nough for yore biscuit, and thin 'er some more. This here's yore starter.

"Git you a cup of that there 'east — not too big a cup. Put in some sody or bakin' powder, whichever you got. You don't need to measure no sugar nor bakin' powder — jest throw 'er in. The sugar is to kill the taste of the sody if you got too much. But maybe you ain't. Put in a little salt and a little grease. Bacon grease if you got it. Can use taller but it ain't so good. Put in 'nough flour to make a soft dough with blisters in. Git it as soft as you can.

THE JONES BOYS *were likened by Ma'am to a bundle of twigs —*
stronger when joined together. John, the eldest, killed in his early
twenties, is the only son not pictured. From left to right (top), they
are Bruce, Henry, Charles (Nib), and Frank; (bottom), Sam, Tom, Bill,
and Jim. In personal interviews, Sam, Frank, Bill and Nib provided
the author with much of the material for the story of Ma'am and her
boys.

"And don't use a spoon; mix it with yore hands.

"It cooks better in a Dutch oven, but if you ain't got one you can use a stove oven. Better git you a Dutch oven 'cause it'll lift the lid offen one. But if you got to use a stove, get the oven plenty hot.

"And shove 'er in!"

•   •   •

"Old Seven Rivers," Nib Jones said, "was a fright. But most of the killin' wasn't done by folks that lived there. Some man would get outlawed somewheres else and come to the Pecos. An' then we'd have him to bury. Onct a man come in and said they was seven men killed down the river and would we help him bring 'em in? Pa took the wagon, and when we got there we had to bury 'em right where they was killed. They'd been playin' poker when somebody shot 'em. Whoever it was took their money. They was three of 'em, for we found their trail.

"Ma'am got tired of it. I guess the first time we realized she wasn't feelin' good was when a man rode up and got down right in a bunch of little chickens. She ran out. He said, 'A man got killed and we want you to come.' Ma'am told him, 'If you step on one of my little chickens there's going to be another dead man.' But, of course, she went."

•   •   •

In a country where both men and women were, of necessity, good riders, Sam was considered one of the best. Judge Shattuck insisted that Sam Jones was the most graceful rider he had ever seen, and he confirmed the tradition that Sam had never been thrown from a horse. He told of a roundup at the CABar — Jim Hinkle's ranch — where there were ten thousand cattle. About a thousand were Mexican steers brought in and turned loose. Everybody had good mounts and plenty of them. But Sam's gave out from being ridden down. Cis Stewart roped a big Mexican steer — a dun — those cattle didn't get heavy, but they were wiry and tough. Sam saddled that steer and rode him.

And he never got hurt. As long as a man can stay on his horse he seldom is hurt. It is those who are thrown who are injured.

Nib said, "Once Sam roped a wild stallion, got it cornered in a bend in a canyon, and roped it. That horse was old enough to be mean and I was afraid it would kill him. Sam fought it out with him and rode him home. But he wasn't much good, anyway not for ridin', for his spirit was broke."

Nib and Frank were considered among the best ropers in the area. They competed in local contests but won so consistently that there was not much satisfaction in being awarded the prizes. In later years Frank entered, just for the fun of it, and he usually beat the younger men. Once he missed his calf. "I saw him lookin' back," said Sam, "and knew what that meant. I'd been takin' 'em off his string all my life, and I wasn't there. Broke his heart, gettin' beat did. And he'd orter won, for he wasn't but seventy-five."

•   •   •

Things were going so smoothly that Ma'am Jones again became apprehensive. Though neither Heiskell nor her sons saw any reason for her moodiness, they did not disregard it. They had witnessed many instances of her intuition. Why not, they suggested, leave Seven Rivers? Why not build a house on Rocky, somewhere near Sam's? They were in a position financially to do anything they wished. And she was not really needed at Seven Rivers now that Carlsbad had a doctor. As long as she stayed there nobody would send for him, and the poor man had to make a living some way.

She admitted that he did, but for the first time within their memory she was indecisive. Pa shook his head and warned Sam that something was going to happen. It did. A man waked the family to get her to help a wounded man — two wounded men. And would she come quick?

Charlie Perry, sheriff from Roswell, and his deputy, had ridden down the Pecos to arrest Jeff Kent. He had fled to Si Hogg's trading post at the mouth of the Peñasco and stopped for food. The officers were trailing him; they also needed a meal. Si Hogg warned them that they would not not take Kent.

Charlie Perry said, "Not if we take your advice. But if I don't arrest him I might as well give up my badge and quit."

They rode into Seven Rivers after dark and hid behind some old adobe walls. Across the street, the doors of Les Dow's saloon and Pearce's store were open also, and in the light they saw Kent walk from one to the other. Men were sitting about the stove whittling and talking. When the officers entered, the group knew nothing until they heard Perry say, "Throw up your hands, Kent; you're under arrest."

"I'll consider myself under arrest, but I won't throw up my hands for any man," was the reply.

Perry ordered the deputy to search Kent. When the officer walked up to him Kent grabbed him by the collar and held him between himself and the sheriff. Shots were fired. The deputy was hit under his left eye. Kent got a bullet in his breast. Though Perry wasn't hit, he fell as though dead. Kent walked over him, out the door, and to the saloon. He asked Les Dow to get a horse for him. It was so dark that when Mr. Dow brought the horse he couldn't see Kent. He located him by his groans. A man helped carry him to Joe Wood's where they laid him on a cot and sent for Ma'am Jones.

An hour later Perry went over and asked if there were any chance that Kent might live. Joe Woods, outside the door, told him that Ma'am thought not. The sheriff demanded to see the dying man.

Kent overheard the conversation and said, "Joe, give me my gun and tell him to come in."

Perry left.

A short time later Ma'am told Mr. Woods that Kent was dead. Then she hurried to the deputy, who had a wound from a 45 under his eye. He lived about an hour.

Neither man did any talking.

To Ma'am's consternation, Tom Jones, not yet sixteen, was accused of shooting the deputy. Though present when the killing occurred, the boy had been unarmed. The Jones family took him to Lincoln for the trial. Several witnesses testified that he had not had a gun, and he was acquitted. On the way back to Seven Rivers the Jones family stopped at Si Hogg's on the Peñasco. Hogg noticed that Ma'am was distrait, and he advised Heiskell to get her away from Seven Rivers to a place where there might be fewer tragedies.

•   •   •

Sam's house on Rocky was not occupied; in fact neither of his two houses were used much of the time. Besides, the family would be close to the little cemetery to which they had moved John's and Minnie's bodies. When the Pecos had begun washing away the graves on its bank, the Jones family had fenced a little plot not far from Sam's house and moved their dead to it. Without consulting his mother, Sam had sent word to Bob Berkshire at Lincoln to come to Rocky and make tombstones for his sister and his brother. Berkshire had made nearly all of those in the cemeteries at Lincoln and at the Fritz Ranch. There was little marble available, and Berkshire used sandstone, which was softer. The monuments were handcarved and beautiful. His work had a certain artistry that made it recognizable at sight. But he had not yet made the trip to the Pecos country. If Sam could get his parents to move to Rocky, Berkshire might come;

and if Ma'am knew there was a possibility of it, she might consent to the move.

So Mr. and Mrs. Jones did move to Sam's ranch. And shortly after they arrived, Berkshire did also. As a matter of custom he moved in with them, and he selected some sandstone and chiselled designs and inscriptions pleasing to them. When he was finished, he continued to live with them. When, Ma'am thought, had they ever been without people in their home? Hadn't they taken Hart in? Hadn't Marion Turner lived with them? And Billy Bonney? And Mose, the aged Apache? What would she do without someone to care for? Even Ash Upson had been welcome in their home.

Then came a rare thing — a letter. It was addressed to Ma'am and was from Marion Turner. In it he asked her advice about returning to the Pecos. He didn't like California and wanted to come back to New Mexico. She asked Heiskell's advice and he told her, a bit shortly, that Bill should be consulted before she replied, whereupon her son requested her to tell Marion that the Pecos country might prove "onhealthy" for him.

And they heard no more from Turner.

Lord Trayner

Except for the Edwards' one section of land, the Jones boys controlled the Rocky Arroyo area. Bill Jones ramrodded the cattle drives, and he ran the wagon when the Jones boys were on the works — the annual roundups.

They were camped on the Pecos when Cape Willingham, manager of the Turkey Tracks, rode in with a new species of pilgrim. Contrary to custom he introduced the stranger — Lord Trayner, recently come from England. Since it was not customary for the manager of a big cow outfit to leave headquarters and act as its rep, the Jones boys were curious. In the days of barbed wire, just coming into use, men did not ask questions, and the pilgrim did not look particularly formidable. Anyway, as Sam said, "Us Joneses stuck together; whoever tied into one of us had the whole kit and caboodle to lick. Generally, nobody bothered us much."

As the men squatted on their heels about the fire at supper, the pilgrim made known his mission: he wanted to learn the cow business.

"That's why I brought him," explained Cape, "seein' as how Bill Jones dug the Pecos and Jim laid the caprock. You Joneses was the first cowmen in the Pecos Valley — "

"Beckwith was here when we come," replied Sam, "an' John Chisum. They was two, three, men with small herds, but no families."

"And you've got lots of cattle," observed Willingham.

"Considerable many," Sam admitted.

There was a silence.

"Well, what does he want to know?"

"How to run a wagon," replied the Englishman. "Mr. Willingham says that's important."

"Stick around and find out," said Bill Jones, shortly.

Sam was more communicative. "You got to do whatever they is to do," he said, "an' you don't know what it is till it comes up. Runnin' a wagon is a lot like runnin' a army. You got to handle the men, the remuda, an' the critters. Cook, too — reckon he's 'bout the most important of all. Long's as you got plenty of chuck cooked good you don't have much trouble with the waddies. Got to keep plenty for your own hands and all the reps that comes along, and feed the saddle tramps—"

His lordship interrupted to ask what they might be.

"Fellers ridin' the chuck line — like you."

He was not discouraged. "What else?" he inquired.

"Answer fool questions, fer one thing, an' keepin' 'nough horses so'st every man's got ten to twelve mounts."

"Do you use mares?"

"God a'mighty! Not on the works."

"How many horses do you keep?"

"To run a wagon, or a ranch?" Without waiting for a reply Sam Jones answered, "Six or seven hundred, I reckon. 'Course they're not all ropin' horses nor cuttin' horses."

When Sam went out to pick up some cow chips for morning, Willingham followed. "Sammie, I've always been a friend to you Jones boys, now haven't I?"

"What you want, Willingham?"

"Take this here dude off my hands a spell, can't you? He wants to learn the cow business. Heard you givin' him a lesson, and you talked right pretty."

"They ain't no better cowman in the Southwest than you, Cape. So — they's a skunk in the bresh, somewheres."

"Well, yes and no. This bozo's been to one of the collidges in England — Cambridge, he calls it. Served a four-year sentence, and got a sheepskin to prove he's eddicated."

"What does he know?"

"Nothin'. Thinks he knows everything, though. Maybe that's why his old man shipped him out here, wanted to get shut of him. I was up to that new range the Tracks bought in the Panhandle to fatten the cattle on, and them old boys wished him off onto me. Take him awhile, Sammie."

Cape waited expectantly and then added, "He's got money, leastways he will have a hunk soon. His old man sends plenty, comes every three months. 'Course it don't last no time, but if he bought a ranch — and he's just hankerin' for one — he might save some of it. Runs through his hands like water now."

Sam shook his head.

"There's that lower Rocky place of yours," Cape continued, "good house, plenty water, and range. An' you got more'n you can 'tend to with the McKittrick Spring Ranch and your headquarters. Why don't you sell him that ranch below headquarters to him?"

Sam considered awhile and then told Cape it was a deal.

"Good!" grunted Willingham. "Trayner's itchin' to learn the business. 'Course, you'll sorta have to keep an eye on him awhile and learn him what to do. This next batch of money will make the down payment. With the cattle market goin' up steady anybody orter make money."

•   •   •

Trayner bought the ranch, a remuda, a wagon, saddles, and other requisite equipment. Sam waited for him to get to the primary essential — a herd — but he apparently overlooked that little detail. When Sam was convinced that he didn't realize he might need cattle, he introduced the subject and sold him a brand. Then he took the Englishman up Rocky Arroyo where the grass was lush and the hills covered with fat steers.

"All these are mine now!" said Lord Trayner, exultantly.

"No, — jest them with yore brand." And Sam showed him how to identify it. Moreover, he suggested that Trayner employ his youngest brother, Bruce Jones, as ranch foreman. So Bruce tallied Trayner's cattle, and he tallied them honestly. At Bruce's request, Sam sold Trayner a gentle horse — the one on which his own children had learned to ride.

When Sam next saw Willingham, the latter inquired about his protégé. "Still don't know nothin'," Sam replied, "an' won't listen to nobody that does. If he was to listen to Bruce he might come out all right. Has no idea what it costs to operate a ranch; don't know what nothin' costs, for that matter. Take that adobe house now — I built them walls thirty inches thick, had the Mexicans do it to save on heatin'. An' put in little windows to keep out the cold. Now he's tearin' them out and puttin' in big ones. An' he's buildin' more rooms with ceilin's twelve foot high. Wants to waste more fuel, I reckon."

"Don't pay no 'tention to what you learn him?"

"Nary a bit."

"Gettin' his eddication too easy," was Willingham's verdict. "These here English, they're a lot like humans; anything comes too cheap they don't want it. Got to figger out some way to make him pay for his eddication. Gettin' it is generally expensive. I don't know of but one thing that comes higher; that's bein' without it."

"You and me, we didn't get none."

"Yes, we did. Not from one of them collidges, though. We got ours the hard way, workin' cattle. But we learnt from our mistakes, and we listened to the older men. Sammie, the only way to learn this bozo anything is to make him pay high. Then he'll appreciate it."

When Sam got up the next morning at four, Trayner's horse was standing by the gate. He turned him in the trap and waited for the Englishman. When Trayner showed up he stood for awhile, looking at his horse.

"Sammie, that horse I bought — he ran away."

"Did?"

"Yes. And I can't ranch without a horse."

"Sell you this one, Trayner."

"Looks a lot like mine."

" 'Course he does; same mare an' stud."

"Gentle?"

"Gentle as a dog, Trayner. Sixty dollars."

"That's more than I paid for the other."

"This here's a better hoss."

A few days later the horse returned again. Sam Jones put a bell on him and turned him loose. When Lord Trayner came, Sam could hear the bell tinkling up the canyon. He took the owner to look at the horse. His lordship squinted and said, "Sammie, it looks like a fairly good animal, but not so good as those others. Ought to be cheaper."

"That's where you're mistook. This here's a bell hoss, and they're wuth more."

"How much more?"

"Twenty-five dollars."

Trayner shook his head but paid it.

He decided to go to San Antonio and take Sam along to rep for him. Rep? Well, he wanted to have some fancy papers made designating him as a company. Sam Jones had never ridden on a train nor had he seen anything even approximating a city. He went.

"What I liked best," he said, "was that Buckhorn Saloon. I'd always wanted to see it. Pair o' horns on a elk head; card sayin' it was kilt by James Jones on the Mescalero Apache Reservation. And it might'a been. My brother did kill lots of 'em up there. Onct he sold a elk head to Pershing, Black Jack. He was a lootenant at Fort Stanton. An' that fool give him a silver watch an' chain for it.

"An' a whoppin' big steer head with horns seven foot, four. Whole head. Them ears, swaller fork and underbit the right and same the left — that's the Terazzas mark. It would've took a thirty-five-foot rope; took more'n half for a loop. Manila rope, too, for that critter would've broke a grass one."

•   •   •

Trayner's idea of a ranch was fancy paper with ribbons on it; Sam Jones' idea was water, grass, and cattle. But so long as Trayner was paying for everything. . . . When Sam sold the outfit, no papers were signed, for at that time thousands of dollars often changed hands without a contract or note. If a man's word were no good, of what value was his paper? Sam reflected that the second payment on the ranch and cattle was due, and had not been paid, but he couldn't ask for it. Still, so long as it went unpaid, who was paying for that trip, he or Trayner?

"He liked Bruce," said Sam, "and except for callin' him Chappie, he treated Bruce good. That name riled Bruce, and he had to lick every man on the Pecos afore they quit callin' him that. Onct a fellow went to Lovington and up to Bruce's room to have a drink. He said, "Thanks, Chappie." Bruce locked the door an' whipped him with the water pitcher. When he got let outa that room the bozo looked like he'd been clawed by a mountain lion.

"Onct when the wagon come in from Corpus Christi, it brought some clothes. Trayner unwrapped them hisself and helt them up. One of them monkey suits! Bruce looked at it an' said, 'You're not goin' to wear that thing, are you?'

" 'Got it for you, Chappie. Going to promote you; goin' to raise your salary, too. No more outside work for you! This is for you to wear when you serve dinner'."

Sam Jones shook his head. "I reckon Trayner never knowed how clost he come to sudden death. An' from that time on he was rollin' his own.

"When the workmen finished the house, Trayner had them build a winery. A winery! That winery caused more talk on the Pecos than any murder ever had. Nobody in that country had ever had enough

wine to last till daylight, much less to fill a house. Trayner sent
wagons to Corpus Christi, and they rolled in full of bottles, laying
down. And he had 'em put 'em on the shelves layin' down, too.
Folks thought he was goin' to start a saloon, but no, it was all for
hisself. Not that he didn't set 'em up when anybody come. He'd ask
'em to eat, too; I'll say that for Trayner.

"Fore long he sent three wagons to Corpus, and they come back
full of furniture. Old wore-out stuff, mostly. Dishes, too. Next time
he went hisself and married a lady from England — a plumb nice girl.
She didn't have no title, and I reckon that was why his folks didn't
want him to marry her. But she was a lady, and friendly. When the
women went she showed them her weddin' gown, all white satin with
lace and pearls sewed on it. Got her dishes out, too. She had plates
that cost twenty-five dollars apiece. Twenty-five dollars! That woulda
bought a cow an' calf.

"For awhile it looked like Trayner was tryin'. He went to the
roundup — 'course it was right there on Rocky. He was up on a bluff
not a mile from his own house, and he was *lost*. I hollered for him
to go to the wagon, and he had to be shown where it was. He hadn't
even learned to *see*. Said he had a cow up there; I tole him to take
it to the wagon and to pick up everything he run acrost on the way.
We got in 'bout sundown with four hundred critters, but no Trayner.
Some thought we orter look for him, but I remembered what Cape
said and told 'em to let him get there the best way he could.

"We was getting in the bedrolls when he showed up with one
cow. *And it wasn't his cow!*

"After Bruce quit him I found another feller to work for Trayner.
An' he really tried to learn him somethin', but it wasn't no use. He got
plumb discouraged and quit. I went to Carlsbad and got the mail for
everybody out our way. They was a letter for Trayner from the Earl
of Somethin' or other — said so on the envelope. His old man, I
reckon. When I give it to him he apologized for readin' it and stuffed
it in his pocket.

" 'Everyone else is making money,' he says to me. 'What's the
matter that I can't?'

" 'Everybody's makin' a little,' I tole him. 'Ain't you?'

"He shook his head. I hated to come right out and say he was
drinkin' the ranch up. 'Course everybody drank but not like he did.
So I sidestepped a little: 'Trayner, if you really want me to tell you —'

" 'I do.'

" 'All right. If a man wants to get things done right he's got to
know how to do 'em. Got to know how hisself.'

" 'But I pay men to do things.'

" 'An' you don't know whether they're done or not. Generally they ain't. Take that wagon now; I bet it ain't been greased since Bruce quit.'

" 'Greased?'

" 'The axles, Trayner. Go git that can in the barn and I'll learn you how."

Sam sat on his horse while Trayner struggled with the wheel. He finally got it off, daubed the axle with grease, and put it back. The task required an hour's work. He looked up at Sam and asked, "Do I have to grease the other wheels?"

"Hell, no. It'll soak through to the rest."

•　•　•

Soon Sam Jones noticed that Trayner's cattle were diminishing in number. Nobody was stealing the cattle.

"Them really was my cattle, you might say, long's he hadn't paid for 'em," Sam said. "An' everybody knowed if they rustled critters from the Joneses they'd pay for 'em, and with mighty high interest. He was sellin' 'em, a few at a time, to furriners, outsiders, for jest anything offered. Horses, too.

"An' one day in Carlsbad I seen some o' them fancy plates in a restaurant. Them twenty-five dollars ones. I bought nine of 'em for five bucks. Don't know what he got fer 'em. Found he'd been sellin' Lady Trayner's jewelry, too. Guess it had been sold out before he began haulin' the furniture to town. Bill Jones paid five dollars for his dish cupboard. He said it was more'n two hundred years old, so I guess Trayner got all it was wuth. But that jewelry! It might'a been old, but it must have been wuth somethin'.

"Folks felt sorry for Lady Trayner. Everybody could see she was worried, but she was too game to say anything. An' the women cooked up stuff and took it to her. One day I went past and the wagon was gone. The whole place looked deserted. You can kinda feel it when a house is empty. I rode 'round fust — nary a critter on the place. Then I went in the house. Just a few chairs and some clothes left. They'd cleared out — to Corpus, I guess. Lasted longer than I expected. They'd been there mighty nigh three years.

"When I got to Seven Rivers I saw a bunch of bozos ride up to the saloon. They was from the Panhandle where there was lots of furriners tryin' to ranch. I knowed the brands. When I stepped inside one of 'em was askin the barkeep where Trayner lived.

"They was wearin' short pants and baseball caps, red ones. The

cowboys was all standin' back listenin'. One of 'em stepped up to
the bar and says, high-pitched, 'My good man, we want whiskey, and
only the best.'

" 'The hell you do!' says the barkeep. 'You'll drink the same
drinkin' whiskey the rest of us does.'

"Everybody else was standin' back polite, waitin' for the invite
to drink with the newcomers, like is customary. But they didn't have
no manners. One of 'em, he says, 'Every son of a titled Englishman is
to have a drink at my expense.'

"Walter Thayer, he bellied up to the bar and says, squeeky-like,
'Every s.o.b. in the house, have one on me!' An' Walter cuts loose
with his six-shooter an' everybody steps — all but the furriners. They
hits for the door and lit a shuck. An' I ain't seen 'em since. Nor Lord
Trayner, neither.

"And it's right lonesome on Rocky with him gone."

Sprees   *33*

In the days when there was little entertainment excepting what people made for themselves most people especially enjoyed dancing. Because the Jones home offered both ample space and ample food, many people partook of both. Ma'am loved dancing and was in demand as a partner. Her sons had fiddles and guitars and not a little natural flair for music. Cowboys brought their instruments, and one sometimes played the harmonica. After the earthen floor had been sprinkled and leveled with a heated shovel, Nib Jones usually called the dances.

The local people were good people. Just why the Seven Rivers men were sometimes called The Rustlers, nobody knew. This could be said for them: they did not steal cattle, anyway not more than was customary at the time. Everybody in need of a beef killed the first fat one he encountered, and that was considered ethical. But some of the newcomers — maybe it was they who were taking more cattle than custom permitted. Still, if they appeared at the dances they were welcomed. There were some who might have been considered rough in other surroundings, but they always conducted themselves with decorum at the Jones home.

At the Christmas parties Ma'am Jones always had a tree strung with popcorn and ornamented with curlicues made from tin cans. She baked cakes and cookies. She provided a toy for every child within a radius of twenty-five miles. It was customary to open the packages at the party so that appreciation could be expressed to the donor. Things went beautifully except that on one occasion a villainous-looking pilgrim tore the paper from his package and found a corset. He was so embarrassed that he rushed from the house and could not be induced to return.

As the country was settled there were fewer killings, but unaccountably, to Ma'am Jones, the moral tone of the population deteriorated. So long as a man bought a bottle of whiskey and went elsewhere to consume its contents, she had no worries. It was when men imbibed at the counter that she had misgivings. But so long as she sold whiskey no man had ever "raised a ruckus" in her place, and for that she was very grateful. Now it seemed that barroom fights were common.

·   ·   ·

A little settlement sprang up at La Huerta, headquarters of the VVN, the Eddy ranch. Another grew up around a bar about two miles down the Pecos. Although the cowboys went to the bars to celebrate their infrequent trips to town, at first there was little objectionable conduct. Later, after Eddy was renamed Carlsbad, things got a bit rough at times. There came rumors also of disreputable occurrences at Phoenix, the little settlement south of town; but nobody was so indiscreet as to mention details in Ma'am's presence. Nevertheless it was reported that when a very respectable judge and his wife drove through the Phoenix section one Sunday afternoon and left their buggy alone for a few minutes, they found it occupied when they returned. Somebody had bribed two drunken cowboys to put a nude woman in the buggy, and she refused to leave it. The judge was unable to dislodge her, and he found it necessary to give the same cowboys who had put her into the vehicle five dollars to remove her.

This happened shortly before the first train ran from Pecos City into Carlsbad. Many people made the trip horseback to Pecos to ride the train back. It was what was called an "accommodation" train, one of combined passenger and freight cars, and the mounts were hauled in the latter. There were a reception, a picnic, and a dance. There was much drinking, but no shooting.

The inevitable carnival finally arrived in town. The cowboys turned out in force. Before her sons returned from Carlsbad, Ma'am had heard a little about their participation in the spree and determined that they should do some explaining. She braced herself for the worst. Sam was spokesman for the family, and he told her: "They had a merry-go-round, fust one I ever seen. Part of the boys paid their nickels and rode the chalk hosses. The rest lined up to watch 'em and rope 'em as they went past. The hosses don't go very fast and the boys had to spur 'em. You orter seen the chalk fly! Then the mounted ones roped the ones on that contraption and dragged them with their ropes. An' we had to pay for them hosses!

"We went ridin' 'round huntin' for somethin' to do. The section hands live in tents, and seein' them give us a idee. We each roped a tent and dragged it 'round some; wasn't nobody in 'em."

A few weeks later the country got more action.

"Somebody comin' through said they was goin' to be a rodeo at Roswell the Fourth of July, and it orter be a pretty good show. We'd never saw a show, and Nib an' I decided to go. Figgered we'd see a lot of folks we knew, too. So we made that long, hot, dusty ride up there, all for nothin'. That rodeo wasn't nothin' but ridin' an' ropin', and not too good at that. We'd never saw nothin' else all our lives, and we was plenty mad.

"The business district was all of a block long with some buildin's on one side of the street. We seen a man comin' long with a basket on his arm, with some paper sacks in it. We'd never seen a paper sack before, and when he yelled he was sellin' peanuts at ten cents a sack, we bit. Never had seen no peanuts, neither. An' would you believe it? Them peanuts wasn't nothin' but goobers! And we'd paid ten cents apiece for them sacks. Ten cents was a sight o' money in them days.

"It was hot an' dry with dust six inches deep in town. It was the style for women to wear full skirts and lots of 'em, draggin' the ground. We was ridin' down the main drag with people crowded up agin the buildin's. A big fat gal, dressed fit to kill, was crossin' the street. She was heistin' up her skirts with both hands, trying to keep 'em outa the dirt, and showin' thin stockin's with white garters. Them garters had red roses on 'em as big as my hand. Nib took a gander at 'em and says, 'Sammie, you rope 'er and I'll take 'em off.'

"An' I did.

"An' he did.

"That was one ropin' deal I'd never figgered to do, and we wouldn't a' minded payin' for it, but we never heard nothin' more about it. This here law stuff is shore queer. But I always felt kinda bad about that.

"It was like the trick we played on that mule. Roped an old mother bear 'long the timber. She come up that rope hand over hand and we had to shoot her. Then her twins come runnin' outa the woods cryin' like babies. We had to shoot them, too. We tied a pack mule to a tree and loaded Ol' Mrs. Bear on him. When we untied him he run away, with us after him. Every time we'd git clost, that mule would look back and bray.

"Onct a real show did come. This time it come to Carlsbad. An opry troupe come and stayed a week. They put on shows and between acts they'd come out in front of the curtain and sing. The cowboys lined up in the front seats, 'bout thirty of us. They was three of us Joneses, Sweet Chile Livingston, some of the Corns, Joe Welch, Bill Ward — a whole bunch. The head man asked us to join in singin' the chorus. We did the best we could; didn't know the words; didn't know the tune, neither. So some of us bawled like calves and the rest bellered like bulls. We come back every night to help with the chorus, and 'most everybody in town come to watch. We kept it up till everybody got to laughin' an' we had to quit.

"They wasn't hardly no killin's at those sprees; they was more private like — the killin's. The sprees was jest fun, nothin' real bad. Killin's was mostly done by somebody followin' some fellow they had a reason for killin' afore he come to the Pecos. And it was done mostly from ambush. But it give Seven Rivers a bad name; Carlsbad, too. Both kep' on gettin' tamer though.

"I 'mind a bunch of us went to Pepe's place at La Huerta. If we didn't make a rough house outa that! Drinkin' for four days an' nights! I never had my clothes off all that time. We wasn't doin' nothin' really bad, just havin' a good time. But somebody notified the sheriff. He was the fust one we ever had an' he took hisself serious. Dave Kemp was his name. He was feelin' important, and undertook to arrest the whole bunch. Orter knowed better. Nobody had no use for lawmen nohow. Could get along better without 'em; but how'd they get along without cowboys?

"We took to our hosses and lit out acrost the Pecos, a whole bunch of us. Hub Brogden and Tom Wiggins was the leaders. Always gittin' a bunch of kids into somethin' and lettin' 'em take the blame. Hub lit out for the TO's — he was workin' fer 'em. Zack Light was the boss. Wiggins faded, too.

"We was shootin' but not at the sheriff nor nobody else. If we had 'a been we'd 'a hit 'em. We was jest shootin'. Ed Hamby shot hisself, accidental, in the leg, and rolled offen his hoss. So the sheriff got him. The rest of us scattered like beads off a broken string, reg'lar Apache way. Main reason a dozen Indians could keep a regiment of cavalry on the jump and nobody even get sighted, much less caught.

"Kemp swore he'd get every one of us if it took him the rest of his life. He caught two of the boys at Fort Sumner; Tom Jones was one of them. And he finagled 'round till he got everybody but me.

"I was workin' for the VVN's then. I was foreman up till that time. Right then I was roostin' on that little bald mountain beyond Bill's rock house where we treed the Apaches when they went up Rocky with our horses. Takin' a nice little vacation for my health — an' my pocketbook. The sheriff was chargin' the boys high. There I was, on that little peak where the Apaches ate Pete Corn's stallion. Could see a long ways every direction.

"Every night I'd go down to Rocky and get me a canteen of water and then to the Bogler place — they'd bought some land offa Bill. Bogler'd give me beef and bread, already cooked because I didn't dast risk a fire up on that roost. One night he told me that Eddy was tryin' to find me; sent word for me to come in an' stand trial. So I sent word where I was. I'd been up there seventeen days an' nights by myself, and it was gettin' plumb monotonous. Eddy sent word he needed me bad, and I went in.

"It cost me three hundred dollars!"

Rest   *34*

The entire Southwest suffered from a prolonged drought, during which the bottom dropped out of the cattle market. Many wealthy ranchers lost everything. Those unable to borrow money on their cattle took their losses the first year, thereby saving their land. Many of those who pledged their ranches to buy feed the second and third years lost everything. And the seven years without rain left the country in dire distress.

West Texas, too, suffered. Money lenders in Kansas City urged cowmen to borrow money to buy calves. So long as there was rain and prices continued to rise, so did financial hopes. But these hopes could not survive the inevitable drought, and the resulting slump came.

About that time one of the younger Jones brothers became ambitious, bought cattle, and lost his herd. His land was unencumbered, but the loss of his cattle was disastrous. When Sam's wife learned of her brother-in-law's predicament she talked to her husband. They were just lucky they hadn't plunged like almost everybody else on the Pecos. Didn't Sam think they could spare three hundred heifers and a few bulls in order to enable his brother to make a new start?

Sam had been thinking along the same lines. Hadn't Ma'am always preached that they must stick together? But would his brother accept the gift? That he would not, Sam was sure — not unless he were permitted to pay for the cattle later. Telling him that they might eventually need a return of the favor might help; but how could that be done if he didn't have cattle? Well, there was one way: Sam would slap his brother's brand on them and drive them to his ranch when he was away.

Nib, though not so heavily involved as the other, found that in order to pay his taxes he had either to get a job or sell cattle he wished to keep for breeding. Mandy could take care of the herd in his absence, and she encouraged him to seek work. Of course, nobody could hire a cowboy, for all found economy imperative. There seemed to be no employment until from an unexpected source an offer came — the job of sheriff's deputy. To Nib the work was repulsive, but the wages, though small, were sure to be paid. With cattle cheap, and taxes to meet, it would suffice. Unpaid taxes in New Mexico meant that within a year's time his land might be sold to the highest bidder. Still, that might be easier to take than breaking the news to Ma'am. Regardless of the opprobrium attached to the job, he could not refuse it. Things were not as they once had been; there was a time when a man afraid to meet his enemies either ran for office as sheriff or got an appointment as deputy. From the time of Garrett and Turner, Bob Olinger and Kemp, who had any respect for law enforcement officers? Still, Nib had known a few who were honorable men. There'd been Les Dow and George Curry; others, too, perhaps, but just then he could think of none.

The Jones family had never looked upon any work as degrading; but not once, since John and Jim had been deputized to go to Lincoln at the time of the burning of McSween's house, had any Jones been a peace officer.

"I wouldn't go so fur as to say that us Joneses never looked down on nobody," said Sam, "but we shore as hell didn't look up to nobody. But a depitty —" He shook his head and offered no advice. He, too, knew that for as little as a hundred dollars men were losing the ranches they'd worked for all their lives. If Nib would jest use a little hoss sense and borrow the money from him or Bill — but Nib shook his head.

When the bad tidings reached Ma'am she took them in her stride as she had everything else. There was a long pause before she pronounced judgment: "Times are changing. I can remember well the first time we paid taxes. George Curry came down from Lincoln in a buckboard and your Pa gave him some money. Things change and people with them. A job is what you make of it, and so long as you are honest there's no actual disgrace in being a deputy."

"I'll be suspicioned," said Nib. "As soon as it gets around that any Jones is a deputy, people will wonder what I've been up to. I know any of you would sell some steers and help me out, but they's no use for you to give your cattle away, and that's about what sellin' them now would mean. We're better off than most people because we have water and grass. Old Rocky has never failed us yet. Just think of the ranchers out on the baldies who have neither. In time the prices will raise and we'll be all right."

"They's a lot of fellers been wantin' to bring their stuff up here to Rocky," said Sam, "so their cattle won't starve plumb out. Been intendin' to ask —"

"Don't you think you should let them?" asked Ma'am.

"I already did," said Sam. "It'll mean a little more work for us, but I couldn't let 'em lose everything they got when they's plenty of grass an' water here to tide 'em over. Besides, they're old friends and woulda done as much for us."

"Nobody can say but that Nib is still a good citizen," said Ma'am, returning to the subject. "It gives me a queer feeling for one of the boys to be an officer, but it doesn't keep him from being a good man. Like the rest of the boys, he's never failed to pay his debts. He's never refused anybody a meal or a bed, and never will. He's still a Jones. And as long as there's a Jones on Rocky there's still a West."

"We never worried any about what other folks thought, long's we knew we was right," said Sam, "so why should we begin now? Everybody's havin' trouble payin' taxes. They're too high, anyway. Too many buzzards roostin' on limbs livin' offen the people. Too bad a few of 'em didn't have to get out and punch cattle eighteen hours a day 'stead of workin' six. It's a come down for the Joneses, but whenever didn't we stick together, no matter what happened?"

"They'll know Nib isn't doing this through choice," agreed Ma'am. "An' I don't know but that this is a good thing for us, in a way. We were getting to where we just took good things for granted, as though we deserved them. A little hardship makes us thankful for what we have, and reminds us of the Giver."

"An' to hold the twigs together to make a strong bundle," added Sam. "Nobody can say but what you've always done it. You have one that nobody can break."

"Ma'am nodded. Then she said, "Sam, you get a fresh horse and ride up Rocky to Bill's. Tell everybody to come to a dance here tomorrow night. Mandy'll give it out on her way home. And everybody'll tell the neighbors. I'll put on some frijoles — have 'em with chili. And we'll bake some hams an' turkeys. Your Pa will cook steaks and make the coffee."

Mandy said she and Maggie — Frank's wife — would make cakes. "And I know Annie will bring some. How many people do you think we'll have, Mother?"

"Oh, not more'n a hundred. We'll manage all right. Sam'll make the sourdough biscuit. And he'll cut cabbage for the slaw, like he does when we make kraut. He dumps the heads in a barrel and chops them up fine with a spade. Don't take long that way. Got lots of sour cream for dressing."

As they mounted their horses, Mandy said, "Mother Jones didn't turn a hair when we told her about Nib. Isn't that just like her?"

"Head up and tail over the dashboard," agreed Sam.

•   •   •

Having her family and friends together was like reliving the good times at Seven Rivers. She must do this oftener. Distressed as she'd been over Sam's losing his wife, she'd neglected the others. Sam had married a Gordon girl, sister of Mandy, who died when the first baby was born. After about two years he married another sister, who also lost her life in giving birth to a baby girl. Taking care of his two little girls had given Ma'am much pleasure and happiness. She hoped Sam would marry again; perhaps some time he would. (Later, in fact, he did marry Elizabeth Fanning.) People had thought that Sam was the one Jones who'd never settle down, but where was there a better rancher? Or a better man? How many people would take in all the derelicts who wandered by? Mr. Berkshire still lived with them, but he was no trouble. And this last one who drifted in to spend the night — he'd spent it, and he'd spent nearly two years since without ever mentioning leaving. Well, it gave her somebody to take care of, and she and Pa both needed that.

The dance was held Saturday night and continued till morning. The daughters-in-law stayed with Ma'am and permitted their children to practice riding and roping while the dishes were washed and the house made tidy. There was plenty of food for lunch — serving it was no trouble.

In the afternoon Annie insisted that Ma'am lie down; she'd been up all night and dancing much of the time. Didn't she need rest?

"In the daytime? In all my life I never stayed in bed in daylight except two days when a baby was little. Think I'm going to begin it now?"

Annie knew it was useless to insist, but she induced Ma'am to sit on the long *portal* and watch the children rope.

"Plucky little devils, ain't they?" remarked their admiring grandfather.

"They do pretty well for their time," admitted their grandmother. "Of course they don't ride or rope like our boys did; but then, it isn't necessary now."

"It's getting so," said Sam, "that all a man needs now to run a ranch is a pickup an' a pocketknife."

"The old days are goin'," said Heiskell, "an' goin' fast. And folks is talkin' like the old-timers was desperadoes and even criminals. Jest don't know nothin' about it. When did anybody ever say 'Let me know if there is anything I can do to help — '. They didn't ask if anybody needed help. They came and did whatever they saw needed doin'. An' maybe you didn't even know it was done till after the sick one got well. Even then you didn't know who done it. But you didn't need to thank nobody 'cause they knew you appreciated it."

"They say the world's getting better, "said Ma'am, "and it may be in a way; but it seems to me people are putting *things* ahead of folks. They are so bent on making money that they don't look after each other as we used to do. I never thought anything of having a hundred or so people for the night. Now you'd think it was something to talk about. Notice how the new people said they'd never had so good a time. Seemed to think it something special."

"Was to them, I reckon," said Heiskell, and he added, "The boys are saddlin' up to go home. Annie's goin' to spend the night. Guess I'll help with the hosses."

When she was ready to leave, Mandy came to the door but saw that Ma'am was nodding in her chair and tiptoed back to report that she was asleep; they decided she shouldn't be disturbed by the departure of the family.

Mandy went quietly about the preparation of the evening meal, pleased that Ma'am was getting some rest. Not until the men had come in and were at the table would she call their mother. What a mother she had been, not only to her own but to all who needed one! And what a mother-in-law! Annie could not recall of Ma'am's ever having interfered with her plans, not even when she'd asked for advice. Advice undoubtedly had been given, but so tactfully that it had not been recognized as such.

It was late before the men were ready for supper. Not until they were seated at the table did Mandy call Ma'am. There was no reply. She hastened through the door. Ma'am was still asleep in her chair. Mandy could not awaken her.

Sources by Episode

Numbers in parentheses following entries refer to the first episode in which that particular source was cited and the episode under which full details are given.

1. THE PECOS

Big Mouth, Mescalero Apache scout. Interviews, 1952.

Big Mouth, Percy, Son of Scout Big Mouth, and interpreter for him.

Clark, Opal Jones, daughter of Sam Jones. Copy of birth, marriage, and death records from Jones family Bible.

Clark, Nita Jones, daughter of Sam Jones. Interviews, 1951-52.

Cremony, Captain John, *Life Among the Apaches.* Tucson: Arizona Silhouettes, 1952.

Fulton, Maurice Garland, noted historian of the Lincoln County War. Interview, 1949, on Ash Upson letters about going to Pecos with the Jones family.

Murphy, L. G., *Report of Conditions of Indian Tribes.* Washington, D. C.: Government Printing Office, 1867. Living conditions at Bosque Redondo in 1865.

Jones, Charles Nebo (Nib), son of Heiskell and Barbara. Interviews at Globe, Arizona, 1953.

Jones, Frank, son of Heiskell and Barbara. Interviews at McKittrick Spring, New Mexico, 1949.

Jones, Sam, son of Heiskell and Barbara. Spokesman for family and principal narrator of story; interviewed over period of several years.

Jones, William (Bill), son of Heiskell and Barbara. Interviews, 1953.

Second, May Peso, daughter of Mescalero chief, Peso. Interviews, 1953, 1956.

Sonnichsen, C. L. *The Mescalero Apaches.* Norman: The University of Oklahoma Press, 1958.

2. THE HONDO

Big Mouth (1)

Big Mouth Percy (1)

Blazer, Paul, grandson of Dr. Joseph Blazer who bought the mill on the Mescalero Reservation in 1868. Interview, 1951.

Gallarito, Carrisso (Crook Neck), Mescalero Apache who lived to be more than 100 years old. Interview with James Kaywaykla interpreting. 1953.

Griffin, Fred. Interview, 1954.

Jones, Bill (1)

Jones, Sam (1)

Magoosh, Willie, son of Chief Magoosh. Interview at Mescalero, 1954, and others.

Peso, Alton, son of Chief Peso. Interview, 1953.

3. CATTLE

Bonnell, Bert. Interview, 1954.
Carabajal, Daniel, aged resident of Lincoln. Interview, 1950.
Crane, Judge, R. G. Letter to author concerning death of Oliver Loving.
Deavenport, Belle, daughter of Lib Rainboldt. Interview, 1951.
Jones, Bill (1)
Jones Family Bible. Birth records.
Magoosh, Willie (2)
Wyckoff, Frank. Interview, Tatum, New Mexico, 1951.

4. ROOTS

Big Rope, Bessie, Mescalero medicine woman. Interview, 1949.
Church, Amelia, daughter of John Bolton. Interview, 1951.
Davidson, sister of Mrs. Church. Interview, 1950.
Gallarito, Carrisso (2)
Gonzales, Angela, Michoacan Indian acquainted with rite used for prevention of hail. Interview, 1956.
Magoosh, Willie (2)
Tunstall, John, son of English merchant who came to seek his fortune in Lincoln County. Letter describing turkey trap. M. G. Fulton Collection.

5. THE ISSUE HOUSE

Big Mouth (1)
Church, Amelia (4)
Coe, George, *Frontier Fighter.* New York: Houghton Mifflin Co., 1935.
Curtis, A. J., Mescalero Apache agent, 1871-73. Letter to Commissioner of Indian Affairs.
Jones, Bill (1)
Jones, Sam (1)
Murphy, L. G., owner of Lincon County mercantile firm. Report to commanding officer in charge of Mescalero Apaches at Bosque Redondo. M. G. Fulton Collection.
Sedillo, Sexto, aged resident of San Patricio. Interview, 1949.
Sombrero, Solon, grandson of Natzili, chief of the "Buffalo" Mescaleros. Interview, 1950.
Weems, Charles. Interview at Ruidoso, 1954.

6. SMALLPOX

Jones, Bill (1)
Jones, Sam (1)
Jones, Ola Casey, daughter of Robert Casey. Telephone interview verifying members of family having died of smallpox after coming to Hondo in 1867.

7. HART

Big Mouth (1)
Jones, Bill, Frank, Nib, and Sam (1). Accounts of Hart's being brought to the Jones family and of his death.
Lincoln County Records. John Jones indicted for killing of the Felix family who murdered Hart.

Weir, William. Interview verifying story of Hart's death and John Jones' vengeance.

8. RUMBLINGS

Jones, Bill, Frank, Nib, and Sam (1)
Magoosh, Willie (2). Interview verifying Jones family's relationship with the Apaches.
Maes, Ramon, native of Lincoln. Interview for information passed to him by his father.

9. COMPLICATIONS

Apache agents. Letters including Godfroy's account of moving the agency to Mescalero.
Blazer, Paul (2). Report of conditions on the Reservation.
Carabajal, Daniel (3)
Jones, Bill, Frank, Nib, and Sam (1). Reports on practices of military and traders at Fort Stanton.
Maes, Ramon (8)
Siringo, Charles, *A Texan Cowboy.* New York: Sloane, 1950.

10. THE HUNT

Church, Amelia (4)
Gallarito, Carrisso (2)
Jones, Bill (1)
Magoosh, Willie (2)
Sombrero, Solon (5)
Titsworth, Anne Coe, daughter of Frank Coe. Interview, 1954.

11. LINCOLN TOWN

Carabajal, Daniel (3)
Church, Amelia (4)
Deavenport, Belle (3)
Jones, Bill, Nib, and Sam (1)
Maes, Ramon (8)

12. CLOUDS

Apache agents (9)
Burns, Walter Noble, *The Saga of Billy the Kid.* New York, Garden City: Doubleday, Page, 1926.
Caudill, Oscar. Account of Jim Highsaw's experiences working for Chisum.
Deavenport, Belle (3)
Johnson, William. Account of Beckwith and Pino families.
Fulton, Maurice Garland (1)
Jones, Sam and Bill (1)
Keleher, William A., *Violence in Lincoln County, 1869-1881.* Albuquerque: University of New Mexico Press, 1957
Magoosh, William (2)
Sombrero, Solon (5)
Wyckoff, Frank (3)

13. LIGHTNING

Coe, George (5)

Jones, Bill, Sam, and Nib (1). Sam witnessed the killing of Riley and his brothers knew of it from their mother and older brothers.

Lincoln County Records (7). Killing of Riley recorded at Lincoln, 1875-76; county seat later changed to Carrizozo.

14. FLIGHT

Blazer, Paul (2). Report from his grandfather, Dr. Joseph Blazer, of the trip to Arizona made by the Joneses.

Jones, Frank, Sam, and William (1). Recollections.

15. SEVEN RIVERS

Jones, Frank, Sam, and William (1). Recollections.

16. NEIGHBORS

Johnson, William (12). Account of his father and the Olingers.

Jones, Bill, Sam, and Nib (1). Reports on early life at Seven Rivers.

Keleher, William A. *The Fabulous Frontier*. Albuquerque: University of New Mexico Press, 1962.

17. BILLY BONNEY

Apache Agents (9). Record of the enrollment of the Warm Springs Apaches at the Mescalero Agency, 1878.

Blazer, Paul (2). Report from his father of raids on the Pecos and rescue of Pat Carillo by the Mescaleros.

Burns, Walter Noble. *The Saga of Billy the Kid*. (12).

Jones, Bill, Frank, Sam, and Nib. Almost identical accounts of arrival of Billy Bonney at Seven Rivers.

18. ASH UPSON

Browning, Clyde. Son of a buffalo hunter, later a rancher. Interviews in May and July, 1946.

Harkey, Dee, former U.S. Marshal at Carlsbad, N. M. Interviews.

Johnson, Bill. Grandson of Hugh Beckwith. Interviews, September, 1947.

Jones, Sam, Nib, Bill, and Frank (1).

McSween, A., attorney who was a major figure in the Lincoln County War. His testimony, courtesy M. G. Fulton.

Stetson, Frank, early settler at Carlsbad. Interviews at Tularosa, July, 1949.

19. RETALIATION

Brown, Porter, cousin of the Jones boys. Interview at Carlsbad, Oct., 1950.

Jones, Sam, Nib, and Frank (1). Interviews on story of Hart.

Weir, Mrs. William, widow of the man who witnessed John Jones' killing of the Feliz men. Interview.

Weir, Bert, son of Billy. Recollections of father's account of the killing.

20. WAR

Blazer, Paul (2). "The Fight at Blazer's Mill." *Arizona and the West*, Vol. VI, No. 3, Autumn, 1964, pp. 203-210.
Bonnell, Mrs. Sydney. Interviews.
Carabajal, Daniel, (3)
Coe, Mrs. Frank. Interviews.
Fulton, Maurice Garland (1)
Deavenport, Belle (3)
Hinkle, James F. *Early Days of a Cowboy on the Pecos.* Stagecoach Press, Santa Fe, 1965.
Jones, Sam, Bill, Nib, and Frank (1)
Slaughter, Mrs. Sallie. Interviews.
Rigsby, Mrs. Edith Coe. Her father's account of the McSween siege.
Upson, Ashmund. Letter written at Roswell, N. M., June 7, 1878.
Woodward, Jimmie. Interviews.

21. BATTLE

Blazer, Almer, father of Paul. His recollections.
Bonnell, Bert (3)
Hogg, Si. Interviews.
Johnson, Bill (18)
Jones, Bill (1)
Lincoln County Records (7). Indictments following the battle.
Nash, Joe. Report at Dudley Court of Inquiry, courtesy of Maurice G. Fulton.
Olinger, Wallace, his account given to Bill Johnson, his stepson.
Raht, Carlysle, *Romance of the Davis Mountains in the Big Bend Country.* El Paso: Rahtbooks, 1919.
Weir, Mrs. William (19). Interview at Monument Spring ranch, 1946.

22. SETTLERS

Bonnell, Bert (3)
Burns, Walter Noble, *The Saga of Billy the Kid.* (12).
Fulton, Maurice Garland (1). Opinions as to causes of Lincoln County War.
Gilbert, R. M. Letter to Governor Wallace. Courtesy R. N. Mullin.
Hogg, Si (21)
Johnson, William (18)
Jones, Bill, Sam, and Nib (1)

23. REVIVAL ON THE PECOS

Jones, Sam, Bill, Frank, and Nib (1)

24. MAGOOSH

Apache Agents (9). Letters to Commissioner of Indian Affairs on arrival of Warm Springs Apaches from Ojo Caliente, 1878.
Brown, Porter (19)
Jones, Sam, Bill, and Frank (1)
Magoosh, Willie (2)
Roberts, Captain Dan. Account of meeting with Magoosh.

25. HER WARRIOR

Brown, Porter (19)
Clark, Mrs. Opal Jones (1)
Johnson, Bill (18)
Jones, Bill, Sam, and Nib (1)
Lucas, Mrs. Fannie. Interviews.
Poe, Sophie, *Buckboard Days*. Caldwell, Idaho: Caxton Printers Ltd., 1936.
Ramer, Jim. His eye-witness report from Bob Olinger as recounted to the
    Jones family.
Welch, Mrs. Joe, Sr. Interviews.
Ward, Bill. Interviews.

26. THE ESCAPE

Johnson, Bill (18)
Jones, Bill and Sam (1)
Poe, Sophie, *Buckboard Days*. (25)
Stones, Mrs. K. D. Account given by her to Maurice G. Fulton.

27. THE BECKWITHS

Johnson, Bill (18)
Jones, Sam, Nib, and Frank (1)
Mullin, Robert N. Letters.
Stoes, Mrs. K. D. (26)

28. SCHOOL DAYS

Dunaway, Mrs. Nancy. Interview.
Jones, Sam, Frank, and Nib (1)
Shattuck, Judge Edward. Interviews.
Slaughter, Mrs. Sallie (2)
Welch, Mrs. Joe, Sr. (25)

29. HER EWE LAMB

Jones, Bill and Sam (1)
Dunaway, Mrs. Nancy (28)
Ward, Bill.

30. TRAIL DRIVES

Jones, Nib (1)
Jones, Sam (1)

31. ROCKY ARROYO

Jones, Sam, Bill, and Frank (1)
Shattuck, Judge Edward (28)
Ward, Bill (29)
Welch, Mrs. Joe, Sr.
Wilburn, W. E., grandson of W. P. E. Wilburn. Interview at Alamogordo,
    1949.

32. LORD TRAYNER

Clark, Barnard. Letter from Surrey, England, with clipping regarding title
    of Trayner family.
Jones, Sam and Bill (1)
McBridle, Willie. Interview.

33. SPREES

Jones, Sam (1)

34. REST

Jones, Sam, Nib, and Bill (1)

Index